Sir Lawrence Peel

A Sketch of the Life and Character of Sir Robert Peel

Sir Lawrence Peel

A Sketch of the Life and Character of Sir Robert Peel

ISBN/EAN: 9783337012267

Printed in Europe, USA, Canada, Australia, Japan

Cover: Foto ©Raphael Reischuk / pixelio.de

More available books at **www.hansebooks.com**

SIR ROBERT PEEL

LONDON
PRINTED BY SPOTTISWOODE AND CO.
NEW-STREET SQUARE

A SKETCH

OF THE

LIFE AND CHARACTER

OF

SIR ROBERT PEEL

BY

SIR LAWRENCE PEEL

LONDON

LONGMAN, GREEN, LONGMAN, AND ROBERTS

1860

PREFACE.

---·---

THIS work violates no confidence. It is not written to please any family, or party, nor to uphold any reputation, unless truth can uphold it.

It is written by one near in blood to the deceased, but not too near, as he trusts, for impartiality. If otherwise unfit for the office which he has assumed, at least he is free from those disturbing causes arising from family and party connection, which too often convert the biography of a statesman into a panegyric and a satire.

CONTENTS.

SKETCH

OF THE

LIFE AND CHARACTER OF SIR ROBERT PEEL.

CHAPTER I.

HIS BIRTH AND PARENTAGE.

" Though from an humble stock, undoubtedly
Was fashioned to much honour.   From his cradle
He was a scholar, and a ripe and good one ;
Exceeding wise, fair spoken, and persuading ;
Lofty and sour to them that loved him not,
But to those men that sought him, sweet as summer."

A PARTICULAR cast of mind and manners, as well as
of form and features, may often be seen in a family.
As some wild plant, by the accident of a better and
a warmer soil, grows in some sheltered nook, through
several varieties, into one that is fruitful, fragrant, or
pleasant to the eye, so a great character may sometimes be traced back through several gradations in

B

his lineage, to some rude germ of his greatness. Lamartine, in "Le Civilisateur," in a short memoir of
Cicero, observes: "Il est rare que le génie soit isolé
dans une famille, il y montre presque toujours des
germes, avant d'y faire éclore un fruit consommé. La
nature élabore toujours longtemps et sourdement
ses chefs-d'œuvre dans l'humanité comme dans les
minéraux et les végétaux. L'homme est un être suc-
cessif qui retrace et contient peut-être dans une seule
âme les vertus des âmes de cent générations."

Genius, in its lofty wheeling flights, may have sight
of things which lie remote from the range of common
vision. It may be also the safe conductor to the
heart of man of many a truth which appals at first
by its wild light. It may descend for a like freight
into the very depths of the sea, into the very bowels
of the earth. But I must be content, instead of hunt-
ing, like a truffle hound, for those finer delicacies
of aroma which elude a vulgar scent, to gather from
the open lap of our benignant mother earth the
growths which she offers to every searcher, and to
ascribe a curious phenomenon to the impressible and
imitative nature of youth. A picture, a relic, a
banner floating before the wondering eyes of childhood, a song, or a saying, may infuse a faith or kindle
heroic aspiration. The tale which the child, holding

by the lap of its mother, eagerly drinks in of some deed which ennobled one of its line, may give that early inclination which seems inborn. A life acted before us speaks even more powerfully than story. Habits of industry, and love of enterprise, and qualities which seem, more than these, the attributes of genius, may pass from sire to son, as the silent influence of example works in us from generation to generation. The common feeling in favour of one who comes of a good stock, may have been the origin of an ancient opinion which, like many of old, hid its head in the clouds, and robed its shoulders in mystery, to which Dryden, in his lofty style, thus alludes, in his ode on the death of Mrs. Anne Killigrew: —

> " If by traduction came thy mind,
> Our wonder is the less to find
> A soul so charming from a stock so good.
> Thy father was transfused into thy blood,
> So wert thou born into a tuneful strain,
> An early rich and unexhausted vein."

Franklin, in a humorous letter addressed to a lady, suggests that medals, ribbons, and the like decorations, should, like Chinese titles of honour, be worn in the ascending line; for the Chinese, says he, who are a wise people, think that a man's parents must have had more to do with his merit than his children.

The late statesman, a man of simple habits, tentative, laborious, cautious, slow in adopting, but steady in the pursuit of a new course, fearful lest the new wine should burst the old bottles; standing on the old ways; proud to be of the people, their friend and never their flatterer; justly sensible of the value of due gradations; a new man, but clinging to prescription and ancient usage; a mixture in his origin and fortunes of two conditions in life, a Tory and a Democrat in one,— no uncommon or unnatural union,— presented in himself an epitome of all the older line of his family, and also an apparent contradiction which his family history may serve to explain, if not to reconcile.

An anecdote which was told me by the late Sir William Peel will be a fit introduction of the earlier Peels.

He told me that his father, when writing to him, a young sailor-boy at sea, constantly urged him to read Southey's "Life of Nelson," and was always holding up Nelson to him as the model for his imitation. Many of Nelson's finer qualities, his enthusiasm, sensibility, passionate longing for fame, and love of his country, were in the mind of Sir William Peel, and flowed there in part, perhaps, by that conduit. He told me that late one autumn evening at Drayton, his father came out from his study after his day's work, and invited a youth, some relative of the family, whom he found near the house, to join him in a walk. They had not proceeded far before they passed a labourer, a young man, who was sweeping up the leaves in the grounds. Sir Robert, directing his companion's attention to the man, and at the same time to a distant farm on the estate, observed that that man might, if he chose, be one day the tenant of that farm; and observing that the remark excited some surprise, he proceeded to explain how, by dint of frugality and self-denial, the rise might be accomplished. When Sir William Peel had ended his story, I said, "Your father had this from your great-grandfather." Turning on me a bright look, with a smile which brought his very father before me as I first saw him when I was a boy, he said, "Tell me something about those old Peels, they must have been fine fellows." This young hero naturally respected industry; he too was a hard worker, and before the short noon of his glorious life was spent, had done a full day's work, crowding into a few years enough of glory for a long life.

" Grandia pollicitus, quanto majora dedisti."

"England, the ancient, and the free, appeared
In him to stand before my swimming eyes,
Unconquerably virtuous, and secure."

A nation's sorrow for a father and son in quick succession is a sad yet a proud escutcheon.

"So fails, so languishes, grows dim, and dies
All that this earth is proud of."

The family to which the late statesman belonged was one of those families of English yeomanry, the members of which have been described as happy in a golden mean, too high for the office of Constable, and too low for that of Sheriff. The Peels have been described as of Saxon race, but there is no evidence by which they can be traced to any one in particular of the many races, the mingled blood of which has produced that fortunate cross, the feeding, ruminating, enduring, large and largely yielding animal, the English Yeoman. About the year 1600, one William Peele came from East Marten, in Craven, in the county of York, and settled near to Blackburn, in the county of Lancaster, in a melancholy site (whence the family may have drawn some of their hypochondriac humour), a low situation, which gave the farm-house that they occupied the title of De Hole or Hoyle House, for it was written both ways. Hoyle signifies hole. Low in situation as in origin, here for many years they resided. A tradition, I know not whence derived, nor how well founded, existed in the family that this migration (for three of his brothers, with their young families, bore him company) was caused by some religious troubles of the times. He came accompanied also (so it is presumed from the entries in the parish register of Blackburn) by an aged father. I cannot say whether this was a return or an original settlement. The Peeles or De Peles, for the name was spelled both ways, though settled in Craven, were seised of lands in Salebury and Wilpshire, two ancient villes in the hundred of Blackburn, as early as the beginning of the fifteenth century. This appears from two deeds dated the fifth year of Henry VI. (A.D. 1426 or 1427), copies of the material portions of which were made by Dr. Kuerden, and may now be found amongst his MSS. in the library of Chetham College, Manchester, in the following words:—"5. H. 6. Sciant, To: de Pele de Craven et W: de Pele de eâdem ded : Rog : de Walmsley cap : et Jo: Walmsley omn: terr : in Salebury et Wilpshire qu : hab : ex dono Rog : de Bolton et Ceciliæ ux : ejus."

The other deed is a letter of attorney to one Wainwright, to give seisin upon the above deed. The above deed contains no words of limitation, and it is

supposed that the alienation was only for life, and
that the lands reverted to the Peles. This rests, however, on mere conjecture. All that is known with
any certainty is, that the descendants of these Peles
long resided in the parish of East Marten, in Craven,
and that the William Peele who migrated to Blackburn, about 1600, was one of their descendants. The
proprietors in those parts, with the exception of the
Abbots of Bolton, the great lords of Skipton, and,
at most, one or two families besides, were small
holders; and these Peles, though they may have
continued to own some lands in Blackburn hundred,
were still not of the gentry of the land, but in the
position and rank of yeomen only. There were Peeles
also at Blackburn at a much earlier date than 1600,
several of whom were living there at the time when
William Peele settled at the Hoyle House. William
Peele rented the Hoyle House and the farm attached
to it, under a lease from the Archbishop of Canterbury,
for a long term, which was subsequently renewed. He
left behind him, in the part of Yorkshire from which
he migrated, several of the same name, and probably
of the same family. Neither the surname which he
bore, which means " the fortified house of a small
proprietor," nor anything in the precedent state of
his family which I have mentioned, is at variance

with the status which I have heard ascribed to his
family by my father, who was somewhat impatient
of the addition of Esquire to his name, which custom
had then made general. I have heard him, when I
was a boy, more than once, something in the style of
Jonathan Oldbuck, pish to himself over this super-
scription of his letters, half playfully and half pee-
vishly muttering to himself, "A pretty Esquire truly!"
He would sometimes add, that he was a yeoman, and
that his family before him were yeomen. One family
of the Lancashire Peeles was of gentle blood, and
had a coat of arms, and I believe that the last Abbot
of Furness, Roger Pyle, was of this family. He fought
a brave fight against Henry VIII. for the possessions
of the abbey. There was another Peele, a Noncon-
formist minister, a man of some considerable repute
in the neighbourhood of Blackburn, who is mentioned
in a curious diary of the time of Charles I., in Whittaker's "History of Whalley," as hàving preached at
one of the "Exercises" which the diarist, a Puritan
gentleman, attended. No connection, however, can
be traced between any of these Lancashire Peeles and
our family, which, as I have always understood and
believe, had its origin in Yorkshire. I do not seek
to drag down any other pedigree, I am only anxious
to avoid any undue exaltation of my own. No in-

ference of a descent from one stock can safely be drawn from the common use of one and the same surname, though descriptive of a dwelling-house, when it carries with it no local nor any necessary limitation to one family. At a time when many yeomen, as farming tenants, foresters, or other out-lying tenants and householders, were forced to fortify their dwellings against borderers, or nearer disturbers, a description of a person as of a fortified house may have been common to many persons of different families. It is otherwise where a family name is that of a manor, lordship, honour, or other similar acquisition, each limited necessarily to one possessor at one time. A Lancashire gentleman, now no more, a man of some antiquarian knowledge, connected our family with one of the Lancashire families of Peele, and ascribed to it, principally from the use of the same name, and a presumed identity of place, an origin something higher than that which I believe it can claim. A letter which he wrote upon this subject was shown to me many years ago, and it was communicated subsequently to the late Sir Robert Peel, who remarked upon the inconclusiveness of this sort of reasoning, and preferred to follow the traditions of his family, — traditions which may safely be trusted when they are at variance with common aspirings.

The grandson of William Peele, Robert Peele, was a manufacturer of woollen cloths at Blackburn; this was about the year 1640. The cloth was stamped with patterns from wooden blocks on which they were cut. Some of these blocks were seen by my father, when a boy, lying neglected in a lumber-room in his grandfather's house. He expressed his regret that they had not been preserved, and described them as curious from their very rudeness. His grandfather was the eldest son of Robert the manufacturer. Robert the woollen manufacturer was the first prosperous man of the family. He was reputed wealthy, and was so for the times; to each of several daughters he left by his will, which was in the registry of the Archdeaconry of Richmond in Yorkshire, the sum of " nine score pounds," a sum which, mean as it would now be considered, was not then an inconsiderable portion for a daughter, in families of the middle class.

This Robert Peele bore the character of an industrious, enterprising man. He lived hospitably, associating with the respectable families around. The fashion of the times was to entertain at what they called "covered tables." Whatever may have been the diet of their "interlinear days," no "frugal hash" appeared at these "covered tables." The fare,

vain resistance, consisted of such *pièces de résistance*
as cold meats, pies, pasties, and corned beef, washed
down with good strong ale.   What was their dress,
and what their conversation?   I wish I could describe them.   The times were no times for light
topics.   Were they Puritans, Nonconformists, or
Churchmen, Monarchy or Commonwealth-men?   Did
the mighty literature of their time enter into
their minds, and tinge their conversation?   If so,
what a treat would those covered tables have afforded!   What a nooning for the gods!   At least
we may suppose that they had not attained that
sublimity of refinement which, if it advance, is likely
to deprive man of his distinctive character amongst
animals,—laughter.   A man of wit, in the reign of
right reason, may be forced to dine, as it were,
with a valve in his throat, to prevent the exit of a
good thing, and one may chance to meet a starveling
good "diner out," his occupation gone, sitting, with
no plate before him, at a street-corner, chalking, with
a cold sigh, a sigh of emptiness, "Impransus" on the
stony pavement.

Robert Peele left two sons, Robert and Nicholas.
Nicholas took holy orders, and was Curate of Blackburn.   Robert, the eldest, purchased, after his father's
death, a small estate in the neighbourhood of Black-

burn, called the Crosse, since and still called Peel
Fold. This estate is still in the family. He settled
it by deed on his son William, who married Ann
Walmsley, of Upper Darwen, and who was the father,
by her, of Robert Peel, the grandfather of the late
minister. In speaking of this Robert Peel and his
descendants, I will not offend his shade by retaining
the final *e*, which he dropped from his name for
no better reason than the utilitarian one which he
assigned, that it was of no use, as it did not add to
the sound. He was born at Peel Fold, to which he
succeeded afterwards by inheritance. His father,
William, was a man of very delicate constitution,
who was prevented by continued ill health from
exerting himself to improve or maintain the condition
of his family. Robert Peel, my grandfather, was
educated, I believe, at Blackburn Grammar School.
He had certainly received a good education. In
1744 he married Elizabeth Haworth, of Lower Darwen. They were married by licence at Blackburn.
Her father, Mr. Edmund Haworth, of Walmsley
Fold, in Darwen, was a descendant, through a junior
branch, of the ancient family of the Haworths of
Haworth. My account of the humbler origin of the
Peeles seems to me to be confirmed by a trifling
circumstance,—that in Beetham's Baronetage, in the

account of the family of the first Sir Robert Peel, drawn up evidently for insertion there, whilst no claim to gentle blood is advanced for the Peels, his mother's father, Mr. Haworth, is described as "gentleman."

Although Elizabeth Haworth came of a better stock than her husband, her condition in life was not superior to his own.   He seems not to have derived from his father any other property than the paternal estate of Peel Fold.   The property which Robert the manufacturer had acquired, had in the interim somewhat diminished.   My father estimated his father's inherited property at about one hundred a year, and an uncle of mine, the late Mr. Jonathan Peel, used to say that there had always been in the family two working bees in succession, and then a drone ; and I suppose the drone had been more successful in devouring than the working bees in making the family honey.   My grandfather, Robert Peel, supported himself and his family at first by farming, and I have read that the family added to their means by the occupation of hand-loom weaving.   Robert Peel, my grandfather, had a natural genius for mechanics.   He had been married several years, and had several children born to him before he began the business of a manufacturer and printer. It is difficult, after the lapse of a century, and in the absence of contemporaneous accounts, to give a correct history of his rise in life, which was coeval and intimately connected with that of the cotton manufacture in Lancashire. A very short time before that of which I am now writing, the use of calico manufactured in England had been prohibited by a statute as opposed to the spirit of the common law of the land as light is to darkness. Mr. M'Culloch, in his "Commercial Dictionary," under the head "Calico," remarks thus on this statute : "To prevent the use of calicoes from interfering with the demand for linen and woollen stuffs, a statute was passed in 1721, imposing a penalty of five pounds upon the weaver, and of twenty pounds upon the seller of a piece of calico! Fifteen years after, this extraordinary statute was so far modified that calicoes manufactured in Great Britain were allowed to be worn, provided the warp thereof was entirely of linen yarn. This was the law with respect to calicoes till after the invention of Sir Richard Arkwright introduced a new era into the history of the cotton manufacture, when its impolicy became obvious to every one. In 1744, a statute was passed allowing printed goods wholly made of cotton to be used." About this time, a manufacture of calicoes, called Blackburn Greys, was carried on at Blackburn. The cloth was sent up to London in the rough, to be printed there. When printed, it was sent back into the country for sale. My maternal grandfather, Mr. Haworth, was reputed in his family, and I believe with truth, to have been the first calico-printer in Lancashire. He had learned the business in London, where he resided several years when a young man. He possessed a general knowledge of business, with extended views of commerce. On his return to Lancashire, he was bent upon introducing the business of a calico-printer into his own neighbourhood. He communicated his design to his brother-in-law, Mr. Robert Peel. They consulted together, and after mature deliberation, resolved upon a trial of the scheme. Mr. Peel raised money for the undertaking by the mortgage of his small paternal property. Mr. Haworth had some money, but their united means did not furnish capital enough, and they, therefore, looked out for a partner with money. Mr. Yates, or his parents, had kept a small inn at Blackburn, called, I believe, the Black Bull. In that line he, or they, had made and saved some money, he was willing to embark it in a scheme which promised well, and the three commenced business together under the name, style,

and firm of Haworth, Peel, and Yates; they manufactured and printed their own cloth, and established
a warehouse in Manchester for its sale. This firm
effected at an early period some considerable improvements in the machinery for spinning cotton.
I wish I could recall all that my father once told
me, when I was a boy, of his father's career, his
inventions, and the struggles of his early life. I
remember that it struck me, even then, as an interesting account of the life of an enterprising man.
My father particularly dwelt upon one part of his
father's life, when he turned his back as it were
upon Lancashire for a time, and went southwards,
after the destruction of his property in a riotous
assemblage of the hand-loom weavers. He spoke
of the energy and determined will of his father,
who would not be beaten, and who used to say that
a man, barring accidents, might be what he chose.
My father, who had a great insight into character,
and could so mark one with a few touches that one
felt it must be a likeness, whose reading by choice
was commonly amongst works of a satirical vein,
was not a setter up of idols, and when he praised,
it was done with a just discrimination and without
excess. I learned to trust much to his characters,
and felt that I could always depend on the fidelity

C

of his descriptions. It was from him principally that I derived my knowledge of those members of our family who had passed over the stage of life before my own entrance upon it. He told me that his father was both a thinker and an inventor, that his genius for mechanics was considerable, and that he was the real inventor of one very important improvement in the machinery for cotton spinning, for which, if he had chosen to claim his own, he might have had a patent. He added that his father was a shy and reserved man, who was averse from putting himself forward.

I am unable to state, and it is not possible now to ascertain, the precise nature or value of the discoveries and improvements which this firm effected, or to assign his due proportion of merit to each of the partners. Whatever their improvements were, they gave offence to the hand-loom weavers of the neighbourhood, and were not looked upon altogether with a friendly eye by some in a superior station. A skilled mechanic, whom the firm employed in working out their inventions in machinery, was kept for a time concealed in the private house of Mr. Haworth, and worked there in secret, as if he were engaged in some mystery of wickedness. In the course of their experiments in printing, they introduced some improvements also in that art, but I know nothing as to their nature or degree of importance. My father did not speak of them to me as he probably would have done, had they been considerable. One story of several which are in print, relating to the first steps which they made, I am able to confirm, as I have heard it from several members of the family; and as, independently of family associations, it possesses a certain interest in itself, I am glad to repeat it. Mr. Peel was in his kitchen making some experiments in printing on handkerchiefs, and other small pieces, when his only daughter, then a girl, afterwards Mrs. Willock, the mother of the postmaster of Manchester, brought him in from their " garden of herbs," a sprig of parsley. It is some proof of taste in so young a girl, that she could discern beauty in a common potherb, since I believe that the common thought even now about parsley, once like the laurel leaf in honour, is that it was created for a garnish or a fry. She pointed out, and praised the beauty—exquisite beauty of the leaf, and looking by habit of imitation, naturally, to the useful side, she said that she thought it would make a very pretty pattern. He took it out of her hand, looked at it attentively, praised it for its beauty, and her for her taste, and said that he would make a trial of it. She, pleased not to be pooh-poohed as discoverers amongst juniors often are, lent her aid with all the alacrity of fourteen. A pewter dinner plate, for such was then the common dinner plate in families of that degree, was taken down from the shelf, and on it was sketched, say rather scratched, a figure of the leaf, and from this impressions were taken. It was called in the family Nancy's pattern, after his daughter. It became a favourite; in the trade it was known as the parsley-leaf pattern; and apt alliteration, lending its artful aid, gave its inventor the nickname of Parsley Peel, which not having the least mixture of ill-nature in it, no barb to make it stick, did not adhere. Cobbett prided himself in his Register on never having giving a nickname which did not stick.

After the violent outbreak to which I have re- ferred, Mr. Peel, fearing to expose his business again to similar interruptions, and his property again to injury, removed to Burton-upon-Trent in Stafford- shire, where he took a lease for three lives from the Earl of Uxbridge, of some land favourable to his purpose, part of which abutted on the Trent. He built three mills there, to supply one of which with water he cut a canal, at the cost, as I have been told, of 9000*l.* All the works which he erected or caused to be made there were of a solid and enduring kind;

the same things would be done now in a better and more economical mode, but they evidence a man who built upon solid foundations, and liked nothing of a flimsy character. His business from this time prospered and underwent no further material change. It proceeded in a course of uninterrupted prosperity, and enriched himself and his family.

He understood thoroughly every branch of the cotton trade. He instructed his sons himself; he had no drones in his hive. He loved to impress on their minds, the great national importance of this rising manufacture. He was a reflecting man who looked ahead; a plain-spoken simple-minded man, not illiterate, nor vulgar either in language, manners, or mind, but possessing no refinement in his tastes, free from affectation, and with no desire to imitate the manners or mode of life of a class above his own. His sons resembled him, and a strong likeness pervaded the whole family; they were, without one exception, hard-working, industrious, plain, frugal, unostentatious men of business, reserved and shy, nourishing a sort of defensive pride and hating all parade, shrinking, perhaps too much, from public service and public notice, and it may be too much devoted to the calm joy of a private station. They were "loyal men," Tories in politics, a party on which

their opponents have since dexterously affixed the
un-English name of "Aristocrats," a kind of moral
retribution certainly, since it was first applied by the
Tories to the heads of the Whig party, a party whose
strength nevertheless has commonly been derived
from the best support of a party, the middle ranks
of the people.   Tories, however, as the Peels generally were, they were at all times fair samples of the
English national spirit of self-reliance, and sturdy
independence.   Sir Edward Bulwer Lytton, in his
"England and the English," alluding to the propensity
of new men to side with power, has treated it as a
mark of a servile mind, and termed them the "lac-
queys of the great."   It is oftener, I think, a sacrifice
of gratitude, the first-fruits which the grateful hand
returns to the shrine of the protector.   To a new
man, whom his own industry has raised, success
appears to afford a practical refutation of many
theories which flow more readily into the ears of the
unprosperous.   I have noticed how a misdirected
patriotism had once proscribed the wear of calicoes.
A strong prejudice long continued to exist against
the new manufacture.   The raw material was "an
exotic."   It was eastern too.   Here was a fine
theme for a deep-mouthed denunciation of luxury!
A Sybarite fabric introduced to displace the homely

serges, with which our grandmothers had been content. The legislature, with a benign protection, had given even the cold corpse the comfort of a warm woollen shroud. I remember a story which my father told me of a learned divine, whom he met occasionally in his early life. Once in a conversation after dinner, which he was apt to lead somewhat in the Johnsonian style, giving his little senate laws, and with no one on the other side, he insisted, in my father's presence, on the un-English character of the new manufacture, contrasting it unfavourably with the woollen manufacture, and concluding with an expression of a pastoral solicitude lest the softness of the vegetable wool, in its delicate handling, enhancing the pleasurable sensation of touch, might introduce wantonness. When my father observed that a similar objection might, with equal reason, be applied to the silk manufacture, he was visited by a grave displeasure, and a penal exclusion from an otherwise general invitation to dinner, which, delivered orally on the spot, marked by its one pointed omission the sin and danger of dissent.

A biography without gossip is commonly a dull affair, more stately than pleasant in its paces. I am not willing to present to my readers a starched blue book, a mere impersonation of diplomacy, a figure made up of shreds from annual registers and parliamentary debates. I like not to have presented to me in a novel some Grandisonian moral and religious hero, of faultless face, form, family, and fortune, who woos and wins a like ideal being, a perfect Utopian woman, but I like to read of real men and women, and to shake hands across the page with real flesh and blood. Doing therefore as I would be done by, I shall serve up an anecdote or two of the olden time. Old Mr. Peel was rather an absent man. When he walked the streets of Burton he used to look downwards, and seemed ever to be calculating some stiff question, and the common folks, shrewd enough commonly in their perception of eccentricities, dubbed him "the Philosopher." They gave him also another nickname, which I have forgotten, which was derived from his habit of looking downwards as he walked. He must have been a philosopher indeed who, walking upon them, could calmly contemplate the then round pebbles of Burton pavement. He stooped a little in his latter days; in his youth he had been remarkably erect. He wore a bushy Johnsonian wig; like that sage, he was dressed in dark clothes of ample cut, he leaned as he walked upon a tall gold-headed cane, and as he was a very handsome man, he looked a figure stately enough for a mediæval Burgomaster. It chanced one day that the Earl of Uxbridge, from whom he rented his mills, called upon him on some business, on the conclusion of which his Lordship was invited by Mr. Peel to his house, an invitation which was courteously accepted. They walked together to the house, which was at no great distance. As they approached it Mr. Peel saw that the front door was closed, and being always impatient of form, and also a valuer of time, he led his honoured guest into the house by the back way on a washing day, and whilst piloting him through a north-west passage, not without its obstructions of tubs, pails, and other household utensils, was observed by the reproachful eyes of his wife, who failed not, with a due observance, however, of time and place, to make continual claim in the name of decorum against an entry scarcely less lawless in her eyes than a disscisin. This dame was quite able to guide the helm herself, as the following anecdote will prove. There was a panic; some great house had fallen. Mr. Peel was from home when the news arrived, which came on a Saturday night. Rumour immediately puffed out her livid cheeks, and began to throw out ugly hints; and she did not spare the Peels, who were at this time connected with a bank on which a run was apprehended. The next morning Mrs. Peel came downstairs to breakfast, dressed in her very best suit, and seeing her daughter less handsomely attired than she in her politic brain judged expedient, she desired her to go up stairs and put on her very best clothes, (for she respected raiment, and did not call it " things "). She counselled her also as to her looks. " Look as blithe as you can," said she, " for depend upon it if the folks see us looking glum to-day, they will be all at the Bank to-morrow." So out they sallied to church, and straight on in their ample garments they sailed slowly, serene, wearing no false colours, saluted, and saluting in return, holding their own, making no tacks, neither porting nor star-boarding their helms, but proceeding as though they could sweep over any ugly looking craft which might cross them. And we may fancy some of their humbler female neighbours mentally pricing their gowns as they passed, with an " Oh bless you, they are as safe as the Church," for people will estimate solvency, rather illogically, by what has been already expended. Who will say that this dame was not fit to be the grandmother of a politic Minister?

Towards the close of their lives, the old people removed to Ardwick Green, then a green suburb of Manchester, where Mr. Peel owned a good house, which he had built. Here the last years of his life were spent. Mrs. Peel was afflicted with asthma, and by the advice of her doctor smoked stramonium for her complaint. She was however somewhat ashamed of her pipe, and used to take this medicine in the kitchen. They had some neighbours named Marsden, of a good and respected family, in whose house also there was much ill health, and in both sickness received its worship of fear, such as even Mr. Woodhouse himself would have rendered. The families did not visit; nevertheless the day passed not over their heads, on which each house did not send to the other, by a messenger of its own, the politest of compliments and inquiries, a ceremony not without a considerable share of kindness on both sides. At this time there was in the house of the Peels, a petted little inmate, a granddaughter, who had noticed grandmamma's sensitiveness on the score of her pipe, and in her own mind, with a child's sportive malice, she hatched a little plot. It chanced that Mr. Marsden, who was sometimes the bearer, in his own person, of the Marsden inquiry for the Peel bulletin, was observed at the door by this little girl, who contrived so cleverly that an apparition of their neighbour appeared to Mrs. Peel, detected in the kitchen with her pipe in her mouth. The politest of inquiries remained unanswered by her in her vexation, as she eagerly explained to her visitor what

and why she smoked, whilst an upheld minatory
finger enhanced the delight of . the little urchin
something between a pleasure and a plague.

But now the day approached which no calumets
of health can avert, when the politest of inquiries
must mingle condolence with hope. Mr. Peel died
first. He died in September 1795, aged 72. His
widow survived him about nine months, dying in the
March of the ensuing year, aged 73. She had wished
to survive him. One evening near the close of their
lives, as they were seated by their fireside, sur-
rounded by some of their descendants, conversing
with the calmness of age upon death, the old lady
said to her husband, " Robert, I hope that I may
live a few months after thee." A wish, so opposite
to that which wives in story are made to express,
surprised her hearers, but not her husband, who
calmly asked her, " Why ? " as if guessing her
thought. " Robert," she replied, " thou hast been
always a kind, good husband to me, thou hast been
a man well thought of, and I should like to stay by
thee to the last, and keep thee all right." A speech
which, if it literally convey an undue sense of her
own importance as a prop, was probably free from the
leaven of self-conceit, and conceived in the true
spirit of a woman's tender heart. She died at Great

Harwood, in the house of the Rev. Borlase Willock, the husband of her only daughter, and was buried by the side of her husband in a vault which he had caused to be built in St. John's churchyard at Manchester.   The burying place of the family was at Blackburn, in the middle aisle of the old parish church, where many of the family lay buried.   When this old building was pulled down, about sixty years ago, these tombs becoming unhoused were covered by a monument erected over them by two members of the family at their joint expense, a work of reverent piety, in harmony with the characters of those who rendered it, viz., Mr. Jonathan Peel of Accrington House, an uncle of the late minister, and Mrs. William Peel, a lady the sorrows of whose life, in the early deaths of her husband and of her only child, a son, distinguished at Oxford, destined for the church, and promising a life of good, left unappropriated a never-failing spring of love, which flowed thenceforward for the use of those who mourn.   She was called often to the house of mourning, wherein her sweet patience, the gift of God, and the herald of peace, shone like the soft light of morning on a shadowed dwelling.   Robert Peel left to his family of numerous descendants something more valuable than the wealth they inherited, his motto, " Industry," and his life a good comment on it, — a life of labour and successful enterprise, of homely wisdom and undistracted piety.

The old people were present at the christening of their son Robert's sixth child. Their grandson Robert, the late minister, used, when a child, to visit them at Ardwick; he spoke of them always with respect and affection, and used to describe his grandfather as a venerable, fine-looking old man. The gold-headed cane, of which I have spoken, was cherished as a relic by one of the old man's sons, Mr. Jonathan Peel of Accrington House. It had the very leathern string, well worn, which used to encircle the wrist of its first owner. After the death of Mr. Jonathan Peel, who lived to a very advanced age, the relic was presented to the late Sir Robert Peel, as the most worthy of the old man's descendants, and by him it was received in the spirit in which it was offered to him, and prized as a relic of one who still lived in his affectionate remembrance.

CHAP. II.

HIS EARLY LIFE.

" The boy is father of the man."

" The liberal soul shall be made fat, and he that watereth shall be watered also himself." — *Prov.*

" The hand of the diligent shall bear rule." — *Prov.*

SIR ROBERT PEEL, the first baronet, the father of the minister, was the third son of Robert Peel of Peelfold. He is said to have had very early in life, whilst yet a child, a notion that he was to acquire great wealth, and be one day the founder of a family. This is perhaps an antedated thought. If such a vision first presented itself when he was entering upon the active business of life, at the close of his childhood, it would have been little more than a first sight of the new land from the mast head. It is said, however, that his mind had been occupied by such a thought at an earlier age, and that by the discovery of it, he drew upon himself the ridicule of his elder brothers, the sheaves of the elder born being then, as now, and as of old, indisposed to do obeisance to the sheaf of a younger brother. If so, since we may not ascribe true presentiments to mammon, what were such thoughts, what are they in any mind, more than the day dreams of boyhood, the airy structures of young castle-builders, gay bubbles from the mouth of young vanity? It is the nature, however, of such hopes, to realize themselves. Of the many who fancy that they foresee their own greatness, some must escape the mockery of the mirage, and success then lifts the chance suggestions of a swelling mind into an early consciousness of native power. He certainly evinced at an early age sagacity and forethought, and a desire to depend upon himself alone. When he was eighteen he told his father that he thought they were "too thick upon the ground;" these were his words, and he offered to go elsewhere, if his father would give him 500*l.* to begin life with, a proposal which was not then conceded. It is not my intention to write the life of the first Sir Robert Peel, for which indeed I have not full materials, but I shall say something concerning him, as the character of his son Robert much resembled his own in some of its best parts, and was in a considerable degree formed by him:—in horticultural language, an improved variety. What many great men have owed to their mothers, the late minister owed to his father—the inspiration of an early faith, a bent, a purpose, and an aim. It has happened to the instructor, as it often happens when a son eclipses his father, that the abilities, strength of character, and virtues of the sire have been overlooked or dwarfed by disadvantageous comparison. Had he come one generation later, to receive, with the same advantages of position, an equally good education, with a similar direction, he might have been that which his son became, who had little of which the germ at least did not exist in the mind of the father.

In his business, the first Sir Robert Peel was an originator and a reformer. He joined his maternal uncle, Mr. Haworth, and his future father-in-law, Mr. Yates. He was a very young man at the time. He left his father with the full concurrence of that thoughtful parent, who conceived that it would be for his son's advantage to accept the invitation which Mr. Haworth gave him, who selected him from amongst the sons of his brother-in-law for a partner. Eventually, Mr. Haworth left the firm, and Mr. Yates became its senior partner. He, however, deferred a great deal to his junior partner. To every remonstrance which the innovations of young Robert Peel excited amongst the older hands, Mr. Yates, his Goulburn, and an excellent second, used

D

to give invariably this one answer, "the will of our Robert is law here."

He was a man of untiring energy. For many a day his life was one of hard, incessant labour. He would rise at night from his bed, when there was a likelihood of bad weather, to visit the bleaching grounds; and one night in each week he used to sit up all night, attended by his pattern drawer, to receive any new patterns which the London coach, arriving at midnight, might bring down, for at first they were followers and imitators of the London work. But they soon aspired to lead their masters, and it was soon apparent to the Londoners themselves that their trade would desert them, and flow into these new channels. These were the days of thrift, on which Mr. Carlyle tells us the foundations even of empires are laid. On this foundation the first Sir Robert Peel built. He had had an example in his father, whose frugal life was at first a necessity, and then a habit. None of the elder Peels ever departed from this habit, or indulged in any expensive tastes. Although they did not live meanly, their expense was in general very moderate when contrasted with their means. The first Sir Robert Peel, for many years before his marriage, boarded in the house of his partner Mr. Yates, paying a very moderate sum

for his board.   He was rapidly increasing his fortune
at this time, but his expenditure kept no pace with
the increase of his means.   He used to state, in
after life, that at this time, the greatest difficulty
which he had to surmount was the want of capital to
keep pace with his schemes of extension.   The pro-
fits of the business were exceedingly great, and it
admitted of great extension, but for some time the
firm were hampered by the limited amount of their
capital and credit, and he used to contrast the advantages of the extended credit of a later time, with
the disadvantages under which he had laboured in the
beginning of his career.   There was a sufficient
reason, therefore, for keeping his own personal ex-
penses very low.   At the age of thirty-six he married.
He was even at that time a wealthy man.   Mr. Yates
had a daughter Ellen, a young girl of sweet disposition, sense beyond her years, pleasing manners, and
with a handsome person.   On her, whilst she was
yet a school girl, Mr. Peel fixed his thoughts and
resolved to win her; with his father's maxim, no
doubt, in his mind, he willed to become and became
her husband, though he was a grave man of business,
thirty-six years of age, and she a handsome lively girl
of eighteen, with a large dowry.   She was an excellent wife, affectionate, and sweet tempered, possessed

of a good understanding and a sound judgment; she
conformed in all things to her husband's tastes and
views, and though naturally inclining to a gayer life,
she reconciled herself at once to those quiet domestic
habits, which were in a manner indigenous amongst
the Peels.

He was an ambitious man. He loved money, but
he loved it principally as an instrument of power.
He was the very reverse of a selfish man. He possessed a genial, generous nature ; he loved young
people, and loved to see all about him happy.
He was eager to diffuse happiness. He was
at all times bountiful, and often munificent in his
gifts. As his possessions were great, it was his
duty to give largely ; but still, even so viewed, his
was a bountiful hand. He dealt with money as one
who, if he knew its value, with how much toil and
anxiety it had been won by him, felt also that God
has impressed wealth with a trust, and that the
trustee must pass his accounts. He gave much, and
by preference he gave in secret. He gave also with
delicacy of manner, and the nice feelings of a gentleman. His was no narrow nor one-sided benefi-
cence. He knew no distinction of politics or creed
when a man needed help. He was grave in exterior,
yet a humorous man, with a quiet relish of fun. He
had small respect for a man of idle life, for any one

in short who was not useful, and neither fashion nor rank without good service of some sort won any allegiance from him. He was the true child of commerce. The productive industry of England, its value, and its power, these were his abiding themes, and he was the greatest of ministers who most advanced these interests. He was a moral and a religious man. I am aware that some, who attach a literal meaning to figurative expressions, will doubt the religious mind of a millionaire. But when will men of religious earnestness learn the truth, that true religion has many sides and many coverings. The temptations of riches are so truly and constantly insisted upon in Holy Writ, that we are apt to forget the scriptural instances of men rewarded with riches for their trust in God, and to overlook the abundant metaphors founded on the blessings of fatness. If these writings be read as a whole they present no arguments for the preference of an ascetic life, whilst they afford abundant and excellent warning against the abuse of any good gift.

Indeed, if men would but reflect to what state a general following of any ascetic precept would conduct the world, to what state of poverty, increased sin, misery, depletion, depopulation it would inevitably lead, they would perhaps perceive that such

precepts must be limited in their application by a
rational interpretation founded on reason and experience. I cannot, therefore, conscientiously treat
the mere accumulation of even great wealth by
a continuous course of honest industry as in itself
a worldly stain upon the white robes. The absorbing
pursuit and the abuse of wealth merit a very different judgment. We may best learn the evils of the
common cravings of our nature by observing their
common direction and end. No country was ever
ruined by industry or saving, but many have been
ruined by indolence. "No state," says Dr. Johnson,
"was ever ruined by luxury:" very few persons can
ever possess more than a sufficiency of the neces-
saries of life. Luxury can be but the disease and
corruption of a few at the head, and if a state be
founded, as it should be, on broad foundations, the
worthlessness of these few triflers at its summit will
never ruin it. If luxury in such a state becomes
more general than is commonly seen, it cannot be
so diffused without a vast concurrent increase of industry and healthful labour, the children and parents
of virtue. The child of industry, whose rise is also
the rise of others, which he designs; whose wealth
diffuses itself, and creates industry the parent of
many virtues; who works for others as well as for

himself, for their good as for his own, — in the case
of such an one, the creator and dispenser of so much
good, I am disposed to fortify myself with the authority of the great moralist, who moving along with a
dignified pace in the wealthy printer's depressed
coach (the well-tried springs of which nevertheless
could bear up the lexicographer), and complacently
chuckling over the triumph of letters which a printer's coach afforded, weightily opined " that there are
few ways in which life is more innocently spent than
in making money."

A knowledge of the powers of mind of the first
Sir Robert Peel is not to be gathered from his public
performances; he shared some of the errors of his
time, and on some questions relating to the trade,
revenue, and currency of the country, he advanced
opinions which experience has refuted; but on the
whole he was somewhat in advance of the times
on commercial questions, and upon the subject of
the corn bill, his arguments in opposition to its
enactment, though pushed somewhat to excess, were
sound in their foundations and clearly expressed.
He was a man of a sound and vigorous understanding, what is commonly called " a long-headed
man." My father, who, though he loved his brother,
was not blinded or biassed by natural affection,

always spoke with great respect of his brother's understanding, and allowed him the palm for sagacity and ability as a man of business. I remember asking my father, I hope in no spirit of impertinent curiosity, why it was that the "Bury house," of which my uncle was the head, had so far surpassed in success that in which my father and his other brothers were partners; he said, after a short pause, "I think they had more brains." As my father had a very good head of his own, and possessed much originality and freedom of thought, I may be excused for doubting whether he did not too much exalt his brother over himself; but his opinion of his brother's capacity is fully borne out by the testimony of all who knew him intimately, whether in the relations of business, or those of private life. What was less observed and known was the enthusiasm which lay latent in his mind, and which occasionally found expression in some few deep and forcible words of piety or reverence. His son Robert was his third child, his first child and his second were girls. When the glad tidings reached him that he was the father of a son, he fell on his knees in his closet and returned thanks to the Almighty, and in the same moment he vowed that he "would give his child to his country," an offering which, however lightly it may have been treated by those who knew not the deep earnestness of the man's nature, was as piously formed in hope, and as gratefully in spirit, as was ever, in times of old, a solemn dedication made of a child of hope to the service of God.

As the child grew, its father set to work seriously on the manufacture of another Pitt. He worked at this in the same trust, and with the same earnestness of purpose with which he had laboured to make money. It was a difficult, but still a practicable, work. Industry had accomplished harder things. He would not work by deputy, or trust all to an overseer in this labour of love. Let it not be thought that ambition alone moved him. The love of his country mingled largely with less pure motives. He knew to how hard a life he was destining his son. Labour, perhaps, he accounted, and wisely accounted, a gain; but he knew the trials, the sufferings, the anguish which such a life involves — the thorns which are plaited with the laurel leaf. The following extract from Sir Robert Peel's speech in the House of Commons, on a motion which was made by Mr. Nicholl, during the administration of Mr. Addington, for a vote of censure on Mr. Pitt, will show what sort of a model Sir Robert set before his son. Sir Robert Peel said: "No minister ever understood so well the commercial interests of the country. He knew that the true sources of its greatness lay in its productive industry. The late minister had been the benefactor of his country, and had neglected no interest but his own." He chose a great model, and to him and not to men of a lower nature did he direct the eyes of his pupil. I may observe here that my own father entertained a similar opinion of Mr. Pitt, though he entertained no high one of that minister's colleagues or successors. His own political opinions were those of Mr. Pitt in the first years of the administration of that statesman, before the French revolution had made the times unpropitious for political change, and put all the machinery out of gear. He once described Mr. Pitt to me as the fairest minister he had ever known. He said that he was often struck when he attended that minister on deputations from the city, with the great fairness with which he treated adverse opinions, receiving and placing in their best light opinions at variance with his own. My father added that if it chanced, as it sometimes happened, that they had but a poor spokesman, Mr. Pitt would put their arguments for them in the best light which they could receive; "he would

state our own case for us," he said, "better than
we could have stated it for ourselves, and then he
would give his own answer, he never hid himself,
but would say, ' Gentlemen, I have stated your case
for you, now I will state my own.' " I observed
that though he praised the dexterity and ability
of the minister highly, my father praised his openness and candour more. This praise made the more
impression on me because it came from one who
by no means approved of the whole policy of Mr.
Pitt, and remained throughout his life the firm
supporter of parliamentary reform.

It has been said that by an accidental circumstance, his father's house being under repair, the
hero of my story was born under an humble roof.
This fiction, for such it appears to be, sprang from
no bad root — had not a conscious parent. It seems
to have sprung from the love of congruity, true
or false. "Who rules o'er freemen should himself
be free." He who was to take the tax from the
poor man's food, was to be born under a poor man's
roof. An apothegm, the sport, perhaps, of a grateful fancy.

When he was a very little fellow his father would
sometimes playfully lift him on to a little round
table which stood by the breakfast-table, and would

hear from that "tribune" the recitation of some
juvenile lesson. No sounds pleased the father so well
from his boy's lips, as those which showed that the
work was going on.   Hence has sprung up a myth,
that his father trained the boy, even from his cradle,
for parliamentary speaking, and chose that polished
platform, the dining-table, "by footmen rubbed who
burnish and blaspheme," as the training-ground of
the future orator. From this rostrum he is said to
have delivered each Sunday after dinner, as soon as
the cloth was withdrawn, the vicar's improving discourse of the day. This picture of the life of an
English house on a Sunday comes from abroad. It
could not have had its origin in a mind thoroughly
penetrated with a knowledge of the sobriety, the
latent puritanism of the English mind. Had the
grave paterfamilias really set his son upon the table
after dinner upon a Sunday, amidst the wine and
walnuts, to repeat with due emphasis and discretion
the sermon of the day, such an indecorum would
have scandalised the whole parish of Bury, and
would have merited for its author, in the opinion
even of the least severe old ladies, an investment
of that Protestant *san benito*, a white sheet. Nevertheless, this myth, like many others, is a mixture of
things false with things true. At a maturer age, at

about twelve years, the boy was accustomed to repeat each Sunday to his father, commonly in the study, all that he could remember of the sermon, and occasionally a guest at the dinner-table, some member of the family, or intimate friend was permitted to hear that which was more generally repeated to his father alone. He was taught not merely to repeat the discourse, but to give the substance of it in his own words, was encouraged to ask questions, and to obtain a solution of any difficulties which the subject might have presented. This was somewhat the plan of teaching of an old and famous divine amongst the Puritans, Mr. Joseph Meade, whose teaching, if I may judge from the following extract, had in some things that wisdom which comes from above. " I cannot believe," said he, " that truth can be prejudiced by the discovery of truth, but I fear that the maintenance thereof by fallacy or falsehood, may not end with a blessing." Words worthy to be written in the Holy Book. It was the custom of this divine to require the attendance of his pupils in the evening, and to examine them in the studies of the day. " The first question then which he proposed to every one in his order was ' Quid dubitas ? ' What doubts have you met with in your studies to-day? For he supposed that to doubt nothing, and to understand nothing, were nearly the same thing." (Neale's " History of the Puritans," vol. ii. p. 311.) I observed in my limited intercourse with the late statesman, that he was rather a conjugator of this verb. He was always looking at a subject from his opponent's point of view. Of all vicious modes of instruction, none is more common and more injurious than that of roughly checking the questions and doubts of a young and inquiring mind. It is generally the refuge of the ignorant teacher. A rude tutor makes a foolish scholar. To laugh at ignorance is to confirm it. The early mortifications of our self-love make more fools than nature. Ask no questions, is a pestilent nursery commandment. A quiver full of fools is worse in a house than " un enfant terrible."

And what were the natural gifts of this child, the object of such unceasing cultivation? He is described by some authors as one but moderately endowed by nature; but let us not, in our desire to advance industry, exaggerate its products. It is a mighty power, and can produce some of the fruits of genius; but it cannot do all things for all men. I am unable to ascribe to industry alone all that the late Sir Robert Peel became. The raw material was more than commonly good; it was excellent.

He was a quick, clever boy, and also a thinking boy,
naturally observant and reflecting. He was no
prodigy certainly. His parts and his promise were
such as many boys have and give. My father used
to say that he thought his second nephew, William
Yates Peel, had naturally the quicker parts. Nothing, however, is more deceptive than the early
promise of a child. A girl commonly beats all her
brothers in their early lessons, and I have seen no
young people so quick of apprehension as the young
Hindoo; but the after progress is not proportionate
to the early excellence. Byron seems to have given
a correct account of his schoolfellow. He nowhere
speaks of Peel as a genius, neither does he describe
him as a boy of moderate capacity, and superior only
by dint of fagging. Lest I should be thought to
attribute too much to his severe training, I shall
endeavour to show in what it benefitted and in what
it injured him. He received an early aim, one great
advantage. He was stimulated to exertion by the
thought that great things were expected from him;
he was disciplined, and was soon able to go from
the force of habit in that direction to which duty
pointed; then to transfer his allegiance from custom
to a higher motive, and a higher discipline. Hence
it came that, even when not overlooked, he was

"never in scrapes," and "always knew his lesson."
On the other hand, the discipline acted on his mind
like an overtight ligature on a plant; it checked and
dwarfed the plant. His originality and the freedom
of his mind, though not destroyed, were impaired
by it. He grew up graver than becomes a boy.
His thoughts, as his manners, were cast too much
in an artificial mould, and were tinged by a certain
formality. A tendency to follow where he should
have led, was long observed in him. A tendency
to rely too much on authority, to quote too much
the opinions and decisions of other men; as we
should say in the law, of one who cited cases over
much, that he was a case lawyer; he became too
much of a case statesman. These were, in my
opinion, the results of two things, his overtraining
during boyhood and youth, and his too early in-
duction into office; for, in estimating his political
character, it should ever be kept in mind that he
never breathed the bracing air of opposition until
he had had twenty years of parliamentary life. The
consequences of that healthy change are apparent,
to me, in the improved tone and power of the productions of his later age. As a boy, he was always
under a strict discipline, a good boy of gentle manners, by choice rather seeking older than younger.

companions, shrinking from all rudeness or coarseness, praised by the old, and therefore not over popular with the young. He was quick in feeling, very sensitive, impatient of opposition from his young companions, and dreading ridicule overmuch. He would walk a mile round rather than encounter the rude jests of the Bury lads, which his young companions bore with more philosophy. This was not altogether a healthy state, and resembles the tenderness of a forced plant. I have said that the elder Peels were shy and reserved men; he had his full share, naturally, of this defect, and shrank from strange approach.

Lord Macaulay, in his admirable picture of William III., contrasts the coldness of the English monarch to the English people with the warmth and geniality of the same man in Holland amongst his countrymen and friends, the companions of his early years. The true heart blossoms in its native soil, and blooms more abundantly for having been kept back. This reserve cannot conquer the heart, or crush or deaden the affections, but it limits their expansion and the field of their display. Old Sir Robert Peel, to do him justice, was too sensible and too observant a man to make intentionally any grafts of old heads on young shoulders, tempting and

E

meriting decapitation (to steal a thought from
Dickens, who can well afford the pillage.) He
would not consciously have suppressed nature, yet
something of this engraftment and of this suppression had taken place. The fire was so kept down
in Peel, that the world for a time failed to discern
it, and imputed excess of coldness to a man of the
greatest sensibility, whose face glowed with admiration of anything truly great and noble; whilst wits
imputed " the sublime of mediocrity " to a man who
was never so great as when he was most self-reliant;
who under the trier, adversity, proved true metal
and rung true; whose bark, under his own pilotage,
surmounted, unaided, storms which would have shat-
tered any mere polished and painted galley. A
great general is greatest under defeat. To build up
that which is cast down, to give a new life to an old
faith, to rally to victory defeated and despairing
followers, to be always equal to the occasion, and
to rise with and over dangers and difficulties — these
are not the properties of " the sublime of mediocrity."

The account which Lord Byron has given of his
schoolfellow Peel, though often quoted, will bear
to be repeated. " Peel, the orator and statesman
that was, or is, or is to be, was my form-fellow, and

we were both at the top of our remove. We were
on good terms, but his brother was my intimate
friend; there were always great hopes of Peel
amongst us all, masters and scholars, and he has
not disappointed them. As a scholar, he was greatly
my superior; as a declaimer and actor, I was
reckoned at least his equal; as a schoolboy out of
school I was always in scrapes, and he never; and
in school he always knew his lesson, and I rarely;
but when I knew it, I knew it nearly as well; and
in general information, history, &c., I think I was
his superior, as well as of most boys of my standing."
This passage has a pleasant heartiness, and smacks
of the good feeling of a public school. It is manly,
cordial, and generous. There is no damning with
faint praise, no hinting a fault, no depreciation of
a "Tory," no sneer at mediocrity. It is Byron in
his best mood; and if his preference of himself, as
one of higher genius, be but thinly veiled, who
shall wonder at or condemn the judgment? "He
always knew his lesson." Yes, and he owed that to
the cause to which I have ascribed it, not to any
natural proneness to be "the good boy," for he had
his wild nature too. "I was always in scrapes, and
he never." This is also a significant sentence, and
one fraught with painful meaning. "Wild natures

need wise curbs." Byron had not been wisely
curbed. Byron's school course was his life course;
lofty powers debased, and the inspiration of the poet
unheeded. His child's home wanted one whom he
could reverence. The Byron colt had not had a
Rarey.

Robert Peel, and his brother William Yates Peel,
of whom Byron speaks in the passage which I have
just quoted, were reading with a clergyman, of whom
their father one day asked whether William would
be a William Pitt (" still harping on my daughter ").
The reply was, "I hope so, but Robert will be Robert
Peel." This was merely the language of compli-
ment, and many a speech as light has been turned
by time into a prophecy.

From Harrow to Oxford was Peel's next stage.
Admitted as a gentleman commoner of Christ Church,
the young man seemed not entirely devoted to absorbing study. The hen was a good deal off the
nest. He was a boater and a cricketer; his dress,
too, was fashionable. A reading man with boots by
Hoby, and a well tied cravat! He affects the Admirable Crichton! This is a common criticism to
which variety is subject. If a lawyer could write
an essay, criticism, poem, tragedy, or even an elegant
copy of verses, notwithstanding the numerous, even

judicial, precedents in favour of a flirtation with the Muses, and the authority of Lord Coke to boot, he was sure, in my younger days, to be proscribed as no lawyer. Woe betide him if he sang or danced well, or excelled in any one of those graces which of old were thought to sit as well on the lawyer as on the courtier or the gentleman. Dull envy shook her head; you are an admirable singer, but you will never be Lord Chancellor; you dance like Sir Christopher Hutton, but you will never win the seals. So dulness speaks, and so I suppose she will speak to the end of the chapter, for it is a consoling, a comforting doctrine to those who utter it, full of comfort as the tenets of a narrow school are and always will be to the contracted mind. There was not, however, any affectation in his case, nor is there in it anything to be wondered at. Peel had no need of cramming; he had been well fed with learning from the cradle. He brought to college with him more than the ordinary school learning. He was always a diligent and a regular student, he had no fits and starts of application, and required no midnight hours of study. A portion of his time sufficed amply for the studies of the place. A portion of his time might then be devoted safely to the ordinary business of the little world around him. The result proved the wisdom of his course. In a remarkably good year, in which were found the names of Gilbert, Hampden, Whately, he took a double first class. He was the first man so distinguished. At the preceding examinations under the then new system, no one had gained the first class in mathematics.

I have now described fully his early life, and have brought him on to the time when it most concerned the public that he should do well. So far he has done his duty, and his life has been hitherto one success. And what thought was uppermost in that hour of triumph at Oxford? He had a pure, a delightful reward in the pleasure which his success gave his father, who could not for a long time speak of his son's degree without shedding tears. Happy, indeed, is the child who opens sweet fountains in a father's eyes! I suppose no child ever gave a parent more unalloyed satisfaction. I have read that the late Sir Robert Peel remained unforgiven by his father for his conduct on the Catholic question! It was not, however, in the father's heart to doubt his son. The relation of father and son grew in a manner to be reversed — the father reverenced where he had at first only loved. He retained his own opinions on this solemn question; and he gave to his son the credit of purity and disinterestedness of motives. Implacability was not in the father's nature, and he died at peace with all mankind. He had nothing to forgive in his son, and extended no forgiveness where there had been no offence. The following anecdote, relating to the father of the late minister, has been supplied me by his nephew, Mr. Willock, who was present on the occasion which it records. A few days before his death, the first Sir Robert Peel, feeling himself more than usually alert, invited three of his nephews to dine with him. At dinner he asked if the champagne was good, and being told that it was, he drank a glass of it. The wine raised his spirits, and he conversed with much animation about past times. After dinner they played at whist; and after a rubber or two, Mr. Willock, perceiving that his uncle's hand shook a little as he dealt the cards, offered to deal for him. "No, no, Robert," he said; "if I cannot deal my own cards, it is time to give up the game;" and with this characteristic speech he broke up the rubber. He survived but a few days.

He did not live to see his son prime minister, but he lived long enough for the gratification of a not immoderate ambition. His son had gradually risen, had failed in no office, had done his work well, and

had advanced in the world's esteem, performing as
the chief minister of the Crown in the House of Commons, in a time of unexampled bitterness, a painful
task, with full command over himself, and with
great ability. He had risen, but not yet had he
risen to the height of his full stature — the greatest
was yet behind. If he could have looked into the
womb of time, the old man would have seen amongst
his descendants, new honours, crowning new dessert.
I cannot call to mind any instance in any one prosperous family, of an industrious career longer pursued.
Three of his sons rose to be privy councillors, of whom
one was prime minister and declined a peerage, another was a cabinet minister, and a third under secretary of state; in the next generation one grandson has
been under secretary of state and is a privy
councillor, and another earned honour, rank, and an
undying fame in the naval service of his country;
so that, counting from Sir William Peel to his great
grandfather, both inclusive, there have been in this
one family four generations of hard-working men,
each of whom had his appointed aim, worked hard
to reach, and reached it—thus verifying old Robert
Peel's saw, that a man may be, barring accidents,
that which he is bent upon being. We must understand his maxim as he meant it to be understood;

success commonly attends industry, when it aims at some rational end, and pursues its object earnestly by rational means. It is certainly a great triumph of industry; and I hope the memory of it will inspirit the young to the like exertion.

CHAP. III.

EARLY POLITICAL FEELINGS.

"I will not conceal his parts, nor his power, nor his comely
proportion."—*Job.*

> "Self-reverence, self-knowledge, self-control,
> These three alone lead life to sovereign power:
> Yet not for power (power of herself
> Would come uncall'd for), but to live by Law,
> Acting the law we live by without fear:
> And because right is right, to follow right
> Were wisdom, in the scorn of consequence."

BEFORE I begin my account of the public life of
the late statesman, I will describe his person, manners, and character, at the time when he entered
upon that career. I write in part from personal
observation, and in part from the information of
persons on whose knowledge, judgment, and truth
I can place a firm reliance. In person he was tall
and well formed. His figure, slender rather than
robust, made at that time no approach to corpu-
lency. He was active, given to athletic sports; a
good walker; fond of shooting, and a good shot.
I can narrate, from one who partook of the feast,

the first triumph of his gun. The victims were pigeons, not partridges. They were served at an early dinner at Drayton, on a day when the family were starting for Bury, a journey which then occupied, in their mode of performing it in the heavy drag, the family coach, two entire days, and a portion of a third. These birds were placed upon the board, and due honour was done to the young sportsman's first spoil; and though truth compels me to say that the meat proved tough, yet in the same spirit in which the family of Tiny Tim scorned to think their Christmas pudding a small one, the birds received due honour, and their toughness was a hidden truth to be revealed only after long time to a succeeding generation. He was at this time about fourteen years of age.

During their journey, his younger brothers, William and Edmund, rather scandalised their elder companions by the frequency and daring of their practical jokes, which excited much the merriment of the waiters, but were gravely rebuked by their father, who probably, enjoying the while their mischief in his secret mind, bade them take their example from Robert. He, throughout the journey, sustained the character of the "good boy," and very likely suppressed, with some trouble to himself, his natural

love of fun.   At twenty-one he was attentive to his
dress, and dressed well and fashionably, though not
to the full of the outré style which then prevailed.
It was still the fashion to wear powder in the hair at
a dinner or evening party; and this fashion, which
concealed the sandy colour of his hair, and suited
his complexion, became him well.   With good
features, a sweet smile, a well formed head, high and
ample forehead, not too grand a portico, and a
countenance which, when animated, was not wanting
in expression or fire, he was generally thought a very
good-looking young man, though the comeliness
of his next brother, William Yates Peel, a very tall
and then a very handsome young man, threw his
elder brother a little, in this respect, into the
shade.   His appearance and manners were those of
a gentleman.   In any society where he was intimate
he was an amusing, intelligent, and instructive companion.   He had much humour, was a keen observer,
with a sharp eye to detect the ridiculous, and a propensity to expose it, which he di   slily, with a quiet
relish of absurdity.   Still this was a propensity which
he kept in check, and feared to indulge.   He conversed well, and when any subject interested him,
his face lighted up, and you saw by the animation of
his manner, and the glow of his countenance, his

enthusiastic admiration of genius, nobleness, or any
greatness.   I remember that in the year 1814, at my·
father's house, he uttered a glowing eulogium upon
the genius of Napoleon, at a time when that name
was rarely mentioned but to be execrated.   Mr. Peel
spoke with scorn of the folly of those who denied
courage to Napoleon, declared that he had courage of
the highest order, far superior to that of mere animal
instinct, and that as a ruler who understood thoroughly,
and could animate the mind of the people whom he
ruled, his civil genius would stand as high with
posterity as his military genius then stood.   He drew
a just distinction, at the same time, between the high
intellectual and the low moral nature of Napoleon.
Wherever custom or prejudice had not laid a weight
upon him, he spoke from the promptings of a free
and liberal mind ; and in this sense it is true that
Peel had always a leaning to the Liberal side.   But
that he had no Whig leaning at this, or at an earlier
time, and that he had never been suspected of it in
his family, may be gathered from what passed on this
very occasion ; for I recollect very well that when he
had taken his leave, my father, after paying a just
tribute of praise to the liberality of mind which he
had evinced when speaking of Napoleon, and to the
point and truth of his observations, concluded with a

gentle sigh, and a wish that "Robert were as liberal
in his home as in his foreign politics." I have not,
as yet, remarked in describing his manners upon the
coldness and formality which I have often heard ascribed to them. I never observed this manner myself. In my intercourse with him, which was, however,
neither frequent nor close, he was always frank, unreserved, and even kind. Although it is irksome to me
to speak of myself, I think it due to him to say a few
words in explanation of the infrequency of these
interviews. I have heard him charged with neglect
of his relations, and I have heard myself mentioned
as one whom he might without impropriety have
advanced, and did not befriend. It is not my opinion
that he overlooked any fair claim upon his patronage
of any member of his family, taking the term in its
widest sense. So far from considering myself an
object of his neglect, I can recal no instance in which
he did not act towards me as a true friend. When I
was a very young man, living alone in the Temple,
and nearly unknown, he sought me out. He inquired
into my prospects of success at the Bar, and asked
me if there was any mode in which he could be of
service to me in my profession. With proper acknowledgment of his kindness, I assured him that there
was not. I was restrained by some feelings natural

and not discreditable from telling him why I thought that it was best to leave me to myself.

I believe, however, that Mr. Peel penetrated my motives, for long afterwards, when I had received the appointment of Advocate-General at Bengal, and waited on him to take leave on the eve of my departure for India, he, with a freshness of memory which would have surprised me had I not known that he rarely forgot, adverted to what had passed between us sixteen years before, and said with particular emphasis, " Remember, you owe nothing whatever to me, and all to yourself;" an observation which he afterwards repeated to me, in substance, by letter, when I obtained a higher appointment in India. He added on the former of these occasions, in our last interview, that it had been his intention to offer me, had I remained in England, in case he should be restored to office, a high appointment, and his sincerity was never for an instant doubted by me who knew his truthfulness. When I lived in London, previously to my departure for India, I lived very much the life of a student, shut up in my chambers, and devoted almost entirely to the study of my profession. My position was much inferior to his own, and my political opinions long differed on some important questions from his. I desired no political connection with any party, nor any intercourse with the great world; and that my intercourse with him was not more frequent, proceeded not from his neglect of me, but was owing entirely to the causes to which I have ascribed it, and to a sense, I think, on his part, that it was the kindest course to leave me to myself, as indeed it was.

Lord Macaulay, after remarking that Lord Somers had been charged by Swift with formality of manners, contrasts that charge with the very different opinion which others had expressed who knew Lord Somers intimately. Macaulay observes that Lord Somers may have appeared formal to Swift from the defect of Swift's own manners. A reserved nature does not open to many, and never to those who distrust it, nor to those who, by their advances, would force it to expand. It never courts a confidence.

> "He is retired as noon-tide dew,
> Or fountain in a noon-day grove,
> And you must love him, ere to you
> He will seem worthy of your love."

The life of a public man is before the public, his manners are open to the public scrutiny; but all this exposure, instead of operating on the reserved man to make him more diffusive of himself, makes him wrap his cloak the tighter around him. In his hatred of simulation such an one, instead of acting and becoming more generally the good fellow, grows, from a dread of acting, more and more reserved, and opens fully only under the smiles of those whom he knows to regard him with a disinterested affection. The late Lord Hardinge, who knew Peel intimately, and loved him with a warm and lasting affection, once lamented to me in India, "Peel's unexpansiveness" (for those were his words) as the head of the Conservative party. He said that Croker had complained "il ne se déboutonne pas," adding to that remark, "that his reserve impaired his usefulness, and was injurious to the interests of the party." "If he would," said Lord Hardinge, "but show himself as he is."

Lord Hardinge had not known Sir Robert Peel in his very early life, and was unacquainted with his early history. I replied, that much as it was to be desired, this communication of his true self to many others was impossible to a man naturally reserved, and that he would certainly fail if he attempted to play the good fellow to the public. I added that it was a family failing, and that I believed Sir Robert Peel was entirely unconscious that he had the chilling manner which was objected to him. A reserved man hates all seeming; he is generally unconscious that people desire attentions from him, for they are exactly the marks of kindness which he himself finds most oppressive and distasteful ; he loathes them like a gorging hospitality.   Such an one does not, therefore, proffer to others those distinguishing attentions with which he himself would gladly dispense.   An icicle would not offer a seat by the fire.   His manner was certainly not assumed, nor acquired in office.   I never recollect it different.   He certainly did not, like Mrs. Montague, try for a manner.   He had always that same smooth outside, and softness of speech, which have been quizzed as a "bland suavity." Under this smooth, and to strangers, too cold outside, beat, however, a warm English heart, which prosperity never chilled nor hardened; a truth known always to his friends, and revealed to the world in a touching passage of the diary of an unfortunate child of genius.   Who would have said of this prudent and reserved man, outwardly so little moved that he was a man of much enthusiasm, nervous in the extreme, and of almost feminine sensibility?   His tastes were refined.   He loved reading, and his reading was at all times various and extensive.   Far from limiting his reading to the works on the side which he advocated, he seemed to read as much, or more, of those which most ably impugned his own opinions.   To this practice, allied to that of questioning himself as to the grounds of his opinions, may be attributed his great readiness in anticipating and encountering objections. He was well versed in the light literature of the day, with which his conversation showed his familiarity. This appears also in his speeches; but the quotations in them are generally from an earlier school. He quoted more largely from Dryden than from any other English poet.

In politics he was a Tory. Monsieur Guizot says, "Il naquit Tory." A taint, I suppose, of original sin. The meaning, however, of the author is clear — that the politics of his father's house were Tory. At that time the majority of the middle ranks were Tories. The genius of Pitt had won over to that side a body of men naturally inclining at all times, but with moderation, to Whig principles. The horror inspired by the excesses of the French revolution had effected for a time a great change, and an unnatural heat in the mind of the middle rank of the English people; but it was a state in its nature transient, and likely to lead to a reactionary movement as violent, as unnatural, and as little permanent. Moderation is the settled habit of mind of that class. The leaning of the great body of the English people to the popular or democratic side of

our constitution, is a natural and laudable inclination.   Democracy has received an ill character which
it does not deserve.   It has been confounded with
mob rule.   The English are not naturally envious
levellers, and it will require a great deal of false
teaching to make them so; instead of seeking to
reduce all men to one unnatural bad dead level, they
have striven by their own individual efforts, each
man to reach a higher footing, and thus the whole
body is always mounting; a habit of self-reliance
and independent action, which cannot be too highly
prized, or too much encouraged.   Hence the wise
jealousy of centralisation.   I retain the old party
nick names, Whig and Tory, not because they fully
describe now all the men who have ranged themselves
under these distinctive banners, but because they do
not, like our modern Gallicisms, Liberal and Conservative, convey by implication general and unjust
reflections.   The terms Tory and Whig have sometimes been used by foreign writers in treating of our
party divisions to describe the monarchical and republican principles respectively.   Mr. Hallam, with
somewhat too much of the colouring of a Whig,
represents the Whig principle as that of amelioration,
and the Tory principle as that of conservation.   But
the Tory does not mean to preserve a bad thing.

They differ sometimes in their estimates of things. The main difference between the parties (I speak not of individual members) lies in their greater or less adhesiveness to things as they are; in the greater or less attractability of change to them. Every man must recognise in himself, if he looks into himself at all, two struggling principles, the desire and the fear of change. The parties which represent these principles, by whatsoever name they may call themselves or be known, must necessarily endure, because the principles themselves are enduring and indestructible. Since the Whig has most of that spirit which prompts, and the Tory most of that which deters from change, the latter of these parties is more disposed than the former to rest on authority and prescription, to take institutions, like men, as we find them, with their faults and imperfections clinging to them, to look less in societies for speedy conversions and political regeneration, and to put the proposer of change, at all times, to a strict proof of its necessity, a proof more strict perhaps at times, than reason demands, or the convenience of mankind can endure. This feeling, however respectable in itself, is apt to be pushed to an extreme, and then its excess becomes dangerous to the moral growth and good order of society. It provokes then a craving appetite for change. The Whig is not an under-valuer of stability and order; it would be more correct to say that by a rational progress, and a course of gradual amelioration, he seeks to confirm order; he is naturally less averse than the Tory from change, and he is naturally also less prone to, and less full of reverence, and when his desire for change is whetted by an obstinate opposition, it grows so as to exceed the limits of moderation, puts every institution to a test which none can bear, of an examination with theoretical excellence, and often pulls down where it would do best to repair. A free people, possessed with this spirit, may break out into excesses endangering freedom, and so prepare the way for the despotism which it abhors. Thus the extremes of each party lead to the same evil by the violence which they stimulate or provoke. Between the extremes are the moderates of each party, who seem to grow by fine gradations into each other. Neither party has ever yet had the folly to limit itself by articles of political faith. Amidst the folly of party spirit at its highest, it has never adopted inflexible and unalterable rules of policy, nor have parties asserted that their principles are not pliant and plastic. Unless they were both, they would be inapplicable to the shifting conditions of human affairs, and would not represent truly the feelings in which they have their origin. According to my view of this subject, it is not in the power of any truthful man to be perfectly consistent in the course of a political life, if by consistency is meant impermeability to change. We are our true selves under endless vicissitude, which we make as well as endure. A man may call himself what he choses, he may try to put upon himself any fetters which his perverseness may forge, but to be truly a Whig or a Tory is not determinable by the will of man. It is not in the power of man without putting on himself an improper force, and thwarting his own nature, to be of his own will simply either a Whig or a Tory. What he is destined to be, his natural constitution of mind and body, acting on each other, his education, the circumstances in which he is placed, the times in which he lives, the spirit and the degree in which his own principles are worked out by others, the thousand and one things which go to the formation of character, will determine for him.

It was not easy for Mr. Peel to be different, at his entrance into public life from that which he was "Il naquit Tory." His father's house, however, was the house of a new man, and showed the Toryism of the

counting-house, the factory, the mart, and the city,
rather than the Toryism of the manor house or of the
cloister.   Lord Macaulay, with a sedentary man's
disesteem of field sports, calls the Tory squire a Tory
fox-hunter, but foxhunting was the delight also of the
Whig gentleman, and is surely not the characteristic
pursuit of men who are accused of loving to stand
still on the old ways.   The chase of Reynard through
his dodges, might it not remind a Whig senator of
1694, how a Trevor, or a Leeds had doubled or run to
earth, with no pleasant odour of fame, before a full
pack of staunch patriots?   The late minister, though
he hunted occasionally, was never a keen sportsman
in that line ; and he certainly did not pick up his
Toryism by the coverside, or in the saddle, neither in
the cloisters; but it came to him from his father, who
was the Tory such as he is found in the haunts of
commerce, and in the busy hum of men.   His own
constitution and habit of mind led him also naturally
to that side, and naturally also his feelings on that
side were strongest at the age when the feelings have
most sway.   It will be perceived that I do not adopt
certain views which have been put forward concerning
him, nor count it a misfortune that he was born a
Tory.   It is vain to speculate upon possibilities, to
bemoan the accidents of fortune, and to measure the

degree of a man's possible merit or use, had he been
something quite different from that which he was.   It
is an inquiry of much the same nature as one of the
speculations propounded in Martinus Scriblerus,
whether God loves a possible angel better than an
actually existing fly.   What Peel the Whig, or Peel
the Radical, might have been, I cannot even conjecture.   Leaving such a speculation to those bold sur-
veyors who would undertake to map out infinite space
itself, I shall content myself with the mere measure-
ment of one actual man.   This I may say, that Sir
Robert Peel owed that which he grew to be, in some
part at least, to his struggles, and that he might have
been a more ordinary man, had he sailed all along
with the tide.   Monsieur Guizot has given in his
memoirs of Sir Robert Peel, which, inaccurate in
some small particulars, convey nevertheless a just and
striking picture of the man, one anecdote upon some
authority which is not disclosed, which, if it were true,
would show that the mind of the young man inclined
from the first to the Whig side.   I have already stated
enough to show that my impressions of his early years
force on me an opposite conclusion.   Monsieur Guizot states that old Sir Robert Peel saw early, in his
son's mind, something which excited a fear that,
unless he were early inducted into office with the

Tories, he might be found fighting in the ranks of
the Whigs.

This very story involves an anachronism, for would
the Tories in 1809 have cared to suppress the budding
liberalism of a young man as yet undistinguished,
save as a schoolboy and a student? It supposes all
the world, and the minister of the day to have had
the gift of prophecy, or to have thought of him with
his father's mind. The closing years of the statesman have suggested this fiction to one of those minds
which love to reduce everything to an unnatural congruity, and will leave nothing to the accidents and
sports of fortune. It brings into the study of man
the Horatian precept for composition,

> " Servetur ad imum
> Qualis ab incepto procceserit, et sibi constet ; "

and to make the boy the father of the man, it ignores
the real child, and adopts a changeling. According
to this myth the watchful and far-seeing mind of the
provident father, fearing all things, but not believing
all things of his son, saw a danger menacing the
unconscious youth from the witcheries of the Whigs.
Like the young prince of a fairy tale, he was immured in a fortress in order to save him from the
enchanter. The youth thus imperilled, was shut up
with the most tender cruelty in the Downing Street

Keep, where it was hoped the Whig enchanter would
never penetrate.   There the doomed youth sate in
the almost inaccessible depths of a dark chamber, at
the end of a long, hideous passage, scarcely lighted
by one dim feeble lamp, fed with bad public oil, where
the damp-stained walls were lined with maps un-
traceable from accumulated dust, but upon which
when legible no human eye ever cared to gaze.   Indeed they always delineated places where no one ever
desired to go.   In these pleasant fictions, however,
nature or destiny always prevails.   The father's care
never averts the danger.   The old king is always cir-
cumvented, and the malignant Whig fairy triumphant.
Nature will out.   The bride will chase the mouse,
the hand must be pierced by the distaff, the prince
will break bounds and travel, the imprisoned genius
is fished up, and emerges like a ministerial explanation in smoke, and the yawning oak discharges the
tortured fairy.   And so, in the natural sequence of
such suppressions of truth, his suppressed liberalism
is supposed to have broken out at last with gathered
force, and like a shell thrown amidst a serried host to
have scattered the Tory forces.

The real history of his life, however, presents no
such harmony with fable.   He was never suppressed.
His father would not, if he could, have suppressed

his son's opinions, for he was too sagacious a man to
suppose that a mind runs the better for being weighted.
The changes which he underwent were gradual,
such as every man perceives in the growth of natural
things. If any candid man unconscious of change
will yet compare his own matured opinions, with those
which he entertained at some former stage of their
development, he will perceive that they are at once
the same, and not the same, the same in their direction, but not in their elevation ; the same in their form,
but not in their breadth ;—broader leaves on a loftier
tree.   His was a constant growth, he did not so much
change as expand, he was always learning, always
applying to himself the question " Quid dubitas? "
for he had an inquiring mind, and he had also an
honest truthful nature.

The growth of such a mind may be not inaptly
compared with that of the Indian tree, first a feeble
shoot, a parasite, rising from the forked stem of a
decaying tree, it clings to, spreads, and feeds upon a
growth of the earth.   Slowly a root descends to
earth, and penetrates below the surface.   By little
and little the slender sapling grows into a tree.   Soon,
unsupported, it stands alone, and absorbs into itself
its former nurse.   It shoots upwards, spreads its long
arms on every side, and as it grows it sends out at

every joint, its feelers, which, descending, cling together, unite, strike for new strength into the earth
again, and swell into the beauteous columns of the
temple tree.   Thus the mind feeds and draws its
life at first from the sayings of old time.   Timidly it
feeds itself in the dawn of youth.   Soon it sends out
exploring thoughts, takes up its old opinions, uses
what they have of life and truth, and sending still its
new births forward, it spreads on every side, and
finds at last, in its own conclusions, its best support.

" The country," he once said, " had outgrown its institutions."   In like manner he outgrew and cast off
a few of his early opinions, principally, however, on
questions economic rather than political ;— questions
which in themselves have no greater affinity to one
party than to another.   It is customary to hear this
or that question treated as a Whig, or as a Tory
question, by those who consider it only in reference
to its bearing on the actual contests of parties.   But
these parties, like Hamlet and Laertes in their
fence, have assaulted each other with interchanged
weapons.   Indeed, it is not too much to say that
whilst the principles of the parties have remained
substantially unchanged, allowing of course for their
expansion and modification under the growth of
time, and in altered circumstances, the questions, the

badges by which they distinguish themselves from
time to time, have been almost entirely interchanged.
So much indeed has this been the case, that even
George III., in conversation with George Rose, declared himself an old Whig.   This is not at all marvellous, nor does it present any ground for imputing
want of principle or of consistency.

A national debt, the funded system, a state bank,
exclusive trading corporations, a standing army,
foreign wars, and foreign intervention, Protestant
ascendency, and Catholic exclusion, restrictive laws
on foreign products, and protective laws for things of
home growth, the longer duration of parliaments,
and the excise; some of these grew up, and all were
confirmed during the long period of Whig ascendency, from the revolution of 1688 to the accession
of George III.   There was, probably, not one of
these measures which was not either a necessity of
the times, or one so accounted on plausible grounds
at least, and those, which a more enlightened experience has discredited, had for the most part their
origin in an unenlightened and misdirected patriotism, and were not adopted from a desire to sacrifice
the many to the few.   In course of time, the Whig
ascendency ceased, and the Tory party had as long
an innings.   They, principally by the favour of

George III., but partly also by the force of that
weariness in bystanders, which long possession of
office by one party inspires, and from the natural
desire for new things, obtained an ascendency, which
for a time the genius of William Pitt, and the outbreak of the French revolution secured. Then the
old hatred of new courses, and the old adherence to
things established, made the Tories of a century and
a half later the zealous supporters of many things
which had been once the object of that party's in-
veterate hate. The banner of free trade was reared
by Pitt, a disciple of Adam Smith, and there is nothing in the principles of free trade at variance with
the political creed of any party in the state; — they
are principles economical rather than political. A
change upon one or more of such questions as currency, commerce, navigation, corn laws, and the incidence and pressure of particular taxes, or of a
system of taxation, &c. might reasonably be looked
for. Most of these questions had been imperfectly
studied, and were commonly ill understood. They,
more than questions purely political, are apt to be
varied by shifting conditions, and their solution,
especially, is dependent on the unforeseen results of
accumulated experience. States cannot be cramped
by articles, and they fit parties no better. A good .

government, by the improvement of the people, prepares the ground for further changes. On subjects properly political, the mind of the late Sir Robert Peel underwent little change. His views expanded as the prospect opened, slowly and gradually. The questions, his changes on which have been most strenuously insisted on as proofs of at least an unstable mind, are, the currency question, the Catholic question, and the corn-law question. The currency and the corn-law questions are properly, in their own nature, apart from the policy of non-disturbance, economic questions. The last, it is true, involves a political question of a serious character, the question of the security of a state which depends in part on a foreign supply of the food necessary to the support of its people. This remoter part was not, however, left out of the account. His change on the currency question resulted simply from more examination, closer study, and a more full discussion of a complex and ill understood subject. Whether his views in the first instance, or his later views were the most correct is not here the question; but simply whether his change indicated an unstatesmanlike vacillation of mind. It must be remembered that the restriction on cash payments was meant to be temporary, and expected to be short; that an inconvertible paper currency was no part of Mr. Pitt's policy, and that in his time the currency was not depreciated. The question of the depreciation was mooted in an extraordinary and abnormous condition of things. A young man at twenty-three years of age, usually voting with ministers, thinks and votes with them, that the currency is not depreciated; a few years afterwards, after more inquiry and with more knowledge, he changes his opinion, expresses and acts upon the change. What is there in this to arraign or approve? Surely little to censure and as little to approve, save candour in acknowledging an error. On the catholic question he changed no opinion, he simply yielded to an augmented danger. In his treatment of this question, it resolved itself into one of expediency. Did the danger of resistance exceed that of concession? Whilst the first was more remote, and seemed contingent, it seemed also the minor evil. When it bore the dimensions which actual presence gives a danger, it dwarfed the more distant peril. A statesmanlike view of a subject this certainly is not, but it indicates neither dishonesty nor infirmity of purpose. On the last question of the three, he changed in common with men of all parties. It was a question long so ill understood, so connected in the minds

G

of many with the very maintenance of our artificial
system, any change in which engendered vague and
alarming apprehensions, that a cautious and prudent minister, with whom " quieta non movere " is
commonly a maxim, might be pardoned if he left the
question alone, so long as it gave rise to no serious
agitation, or occasioned in his view of it no serious
evil.

Accordingly we find all ministers in succession,
Whig or Tory, long supporting protection of this
branch of industry in some form or other. The
change in Sir Robert Peel's opinions on this subject
may be pardoned by those who pardon, nay, applaud
a similar change in the minds and policy of some of
the Whig statesmen of his time. The formation and
proceedings of the Corn-Law League made inaction
impossible. The question in the new light in which
it was presented to the many,— became one of stirring
interest. Capable of being used at all times as a
terrible lever to stir the people up to mutiny, it
menaced then the very foundations of the state. It
could not be left as it was; some change was inevitable. The country was menaced with famine and
new perils. The Queen was to be counselled, not in
the interest of a party, but under the grave obligation
of the duty of a minister. Under new difficulties,

menacing signs, and new obligation, he yielded, but not before his own mind was conquered,—yielding not to fear, but to arguments which had worked conviction.

This change of opinion so long struggled against, so slowly made, seems to me to show a mind the very reverse of one weak and vacillating.

It is a necessity of the position of a statesman who is at once the leader of a party and a minister of a limited sovereign in our representative system, that he must feel his way, and follow rather than lead the public mind. We must not look in such an office for the forecastings of a sole self-sufficing mind, and the stern will of an inflexible ruler. Our chief minister must ever be necessarily something of a conformer, and a bit-by-bit reformer; for the popular mind is impatient of a minister who goes before it, and the popular is not commonly a forecasting mind. The mind of Sir Robert Peel was pre-eminently that of an English statesman, cautious,—nay, more than ordinarily cautious. Sir Robert Walpole's maxim, "quieta non movere," was his; and in their general policy and powers these two ministers were much alike.

The late statesman's famous Tamworth address shows a mind so like that of his father, and indeed that of my own father, that it seems to me, with relation to greater things, to denote the very spirit which, in lesser things, animated his forefathers. His father particularly seems to me to rise up in every line of that address. The first Sir Robert Peel was a new man, as little disposed as any man to stand still, either on new or ancient ways. Ways out of repair would certainly never have recommended themselves to him, merely by reason of their antiquity. The utility of a thing was with him its chief recommendation. His father again could not even tolerate an useless letter in his name, neither would have joined in Dr. Whittaker's lament over country seats, which were passing from ruined families,— ruined by their lack of thrift, into the possession of new men, the manufacturers of the exotic vegetable-wool. They would have seen in this the natural and appointed course of things. They were of the people, and naturally inclined to the people. Sir Robert Peel might train a Tory, but not an enemy to progress. In the language of party strife the words are accounted synonymes. The corruptions of things, however, are not the things themselves; extremes are not the mean, and party caricatures are not likenesses. The late minister never took one step in advance till he was quite sure of his footing, and had ascertained where the way would lead him; everything was submitted to proof, and every step in his career of improvement is closely analogous to the mode in which his father had conducted his business: a man ever cautious, feeling his way, doing nothing until he saw his way clearly, looking at every side of the thing which he was meditating, resolving on it slowly, proceeding with it boldly, and doing it thoroughly.

The late Sir Robert Peel bore indeed a strong resemblance to his father, it has been more than once remarked upon to me by the late General Yates, who knew both intimately, as a likeness pervading the whole man, extending even to trivial things, and to some habits of domestic life.

CHAP. IV.

BEGINS OFFICIAL LIFE.

"Old writers pushed the happy season back —
    The more fools they — we forward — dreamers both;
    You most that, in an age when every hour
    Must sweat her sixty minutes to the death,
    Live on, God love us, as if the seedsman, rapt
    Upon the teeming harvest, should not dip
    His hand into the bag; but well I know
    That unto him who works, and feels he works,
    This same grand year is ever at the doors."

As soon as he was of age Mr. Peel was returned to
Parliament for an Irish borough, under the influence
of the Treasury; a seat which had been procured for
him by his father upon the ordinary conditions of
such a connection. It was well known for what his
father destined him; and the ambitious hopes of the
prosperous trader were more often the theme of
ridicule than of sympathy. They were pleasantly
quizzed at the time; and it is now pleasant to think
how a smart saying, which found its success at first
in the levelling propensities of our nature, raises now

a different sort of pleasure in the more genial feeling which is inspired by its failure, as we sympathise with the fulfilment of a prophetic hope, which had its root in a father's heart. In a *jeu d'esprit* of those days, a sort of political testament, the testator gave his patience to Mr. Robert Peel until he should be prime minister, a legacy which was to be divested on that contingency (supposed by the testator to be on the very verge of over remoteness), and to go over then to his country, "which would stand much in need of it." Now Mr. Robert Peel certainly enjoyed the legacy of patience long; twenty-five years elapsed before he became prime minister, and then the country disclaimed altogether; it rejected alike the virtue and the man. It took the man afterwards without the condition. A prophetic epigram may end in being turned against its own author. Wits and prophets can never coalesce, for they represent immiscible properties.

During his first year in Parliament, Mr. Peel was wisely silent. Silence, "the silent year" should be the self-imposed condition of every parliamentary infant. He was regular and close in his attendance; an attentive listener, and a studier of other men, very different from some young parliamentarians, whom one has known so eager to hear their own voices, so swelling for combat, such rufflers of their necks, that they resemble some cock chicken piercing the ear of the ruddy morn, and with an unsustained raucous crow, challenging the contemptuous cock of the walk. His was not the stuff out of which such bores are cut. As the wit and humour of one time or company are often unendurable in another, so that which is eloquence to one is often mere balderdash to a different audience. A speech, good in itself, may still fail, by being pitched too high or too low for its audience. A study, therefore, of his audience, as well as of the subject of his speech, seems to be necessary to the success of a speaker. He had heard the great orators, Fox and Pitt, who had lately passed away. In his boyhood his father loved to take him to the House of Commons, when some great debate was expected, when he may have listened to the un-rivalled power of Pitt in an opening speech, and to the fervid, impetuous, sometimes turbid, eloquence of Fox in a reply.

It seems to me that little can be gained, and that something may be lost by the early practice which he underwent. I concede that it accelerates, but I fear the dangers of a forcing system. An earlier habit of fixed attention, a stronger memory, with an earlier power of arranging facts, and condensing

meaning, will probably be gained by it; but memory
is often strengthened at the expense of the imagina-
tive and reasoning faculties, a level poverty of
language is the consequence often of early fluency,
and originality of thought is put in some peril.   The
French proverb says: "all old fools have good memories."   Men may be losing the habit of thinking,
whilst they are remembering too much.   Nor does
there seem to be any need of this early training.
For it must be remembered that practice soon gives
to every Nisi Prius advocate and to every debater,
supposing them to have the stuff in them, the power,
magic as it appears to the rare observer, of instantly
apprehending, retaining, stating, assenting to, refuting, and discriminating; so that this early proficiency
seems to amount to little more than this,— the child
walks at ten months instead of at twelve or fifteen:—
sooner, not better, as the nurses tell us.   What
training can effect, it effected for him, and perhaps
at an earlier age; but it induced a formality of manner, a dangerous fluency and level style, with a certain
coldness of colouring, which caused his early style to
be censured as "an elegant mannerism."   There are
things which lie beyond training, which it can neither
mar nor make altogether, and if Lamartine be right
in his assertion, as I think he is, that a great orator

is a poet, then mere training, though it may restrain wild riot, can never create a great orator.

I feel that I am treading on dangerous ground. I may be thought to oppose my own crude opinion to the weight of Lord Brougham's authority. The advantage of a study by a genius of the best models, which is all that the noble lord enforced in his celebrated letter to Mr. Zachary Macaulay, is not, however, questioned by me, I merely stand up for the wisdom of retarded and moderate culture not indiscriminately applied. I would be as a gardener to the mind. The root-pruning and disbudding which, in order to bring the tree into a bearing condition, are applied to one unfruitful through excess of vigour, would never succeed with a cactus, or any other vegetable tortoise. God has willed minds to be multiform, and their growths and products various. They cannot be ranged in ranks, dressed in one uniform, and directed upon one system. It is best to drink the natural wine of the country. A wise cultivator examines the nature of the soil, studies the climate and the natural products of the land before he determines what seed to sow, and upon what system of culture to proceed. A wise tutor, in like manner, studies his pupil, and if he find in him even one spark of originality, he will blow it with a gentle breath, and fan it to a flame. It is the very soul of the understanding.

An ordinary advocate could no more become a Brougham by study of the Durham philippic, than an ordinary corporal could grow into a Wellington by imitating the cut of his surtout. Yet both are improvable by methods suited to their powers. Nothing can be made of men in general but by the careful improvement of the various stuff which nature has put into them. A daw in the plumage of Demosthenes would be most unmercifully plucked. About a century ago there lived in one of our midland counties, which shall be nameless, a baronet of ancient family, but reduced fortune. He was a remarkably handsome man, not without some good qualities, but eccentric in his habits and wayward in his temper. Without any adequate cause, he chose, for a time, to seclude himself within his grounds, so that a sight of him became as rare as that of a blackcock on the surrounding hills. He had been used to walk on Sundays on a terrace walk, which skirted his domain. A tailor in a neighbouring town bore some resemblance to him in height and size. This man made for himself a suit of clothes exactly resembling one in which he had seen the baronet pacing in state, his terrace; and one fine day in summer a figure was seen at a distance walking slowly on the terrace with an awkward imitation of stateliness. The lookers-on wondered, but one neighbour more sharp-sighted than the rest, detected the counterfeit, and going up to him, exclaimed: "What in the name of common sense man, are you about?" "Hush, hush," said the tailor "they take me for Sir ——."

Sir Joshua Reynolds charged awkwardness to the lessons of the dancing-master, into whose "positions" nature never by any chance led one pupil of her own. The taught positions of the mind have always been equally unattractive to me. I have always found, in its effect upon myself as a hearer, that a studied manner, a mannerism, a frigid elegance, a voice not natural in its intonation, and gestures not prompted by the passion or feeling of the instant, produce the same unpleasant feeling as that which is created on a serious subject by want of earnestness. If indeed the artist can conceal his art, if he be an artist of that high order, then " de non apparentibus et de non existentibus eadem est ratio." But an artist of that kind is rare, and is never found, except in a genius of so high an order that a resort to art at all seems in him a descent. No one can speak well from another man's mind; from an empty mind; or from a fettered mind. I have witnessed forensic débuts only; but I have learned from them to distrust a fluent maiden speech. Diffidence may destroy a man, but it is not a worse enemy than confidence. At the bar there is not a more unpromising debutant than he who is unabashed by the first sound of his own voice in court, who, not having much worked the mine of his brain, more full of himself than of his subject, sails in ballast on his first voyage, on a flowing tide of words.

At the commencement of the session of Parliament in the year 1810, Mr. Peel made his maiden speech in the House of Commons. He was selected to second the address. Of this speech, and some that followed it, Monsieur Guizot says: "Il avait débuté avec un talent et un succès un peu froids." His maiden speech reads coldly, now that the interest of the subject has subsided; but what maiden speech would not appear "un discours un peu froid" to a Guizot? It is in danger too of being contrasted with the speaker's matured productions. At the time, however, when it was delivered, it was not considered a cold performance. It was more than commonly successful. Spoken with animation and well delivered, it satisfied even the highly-raised expectations of his friends.

On a perusal of it now, I find in it little to admire. Its principal fault must, however, in fairness, be attributed to the minister from whom he received his instructions. To invite assent to an address on the ground of its emptiness, is not a very high line at any time for a minister to choose or suggest. But what should be thought of a minister, who, on a momentous occasion, when an inquiry is demanded whether the precious strength of a struggling and almost exhausted nation has not been wasted foolishly and shamefully, instead of eagerly courting instant inquiry, stoops to put forth a mere vote-catching insignificant address? Something of the mind of a minister without a line may be discerned in the following expression : " England desired neither peace nor war,"—a strange state of quietism for any people, and a state not natural to John Bull. What one remarkable man, a Tory of those times, thought of this ministry, may be learned from the following letter of Sir Walter Scott : —

To George Ellis, Esq.

" DEAR ELLIS,   " Ashestiel, Sept. 26, 1809.

" Your letter gave me great pleasure, especially the outside; for Canning's frank assured me that his wound was at least not materially serious. So, for once, the envelope of your letter was even more welcome than the contents. That harebrained Irishman's letter carries absurdity upon the face of it; for surely he would have had much more reason for personal animosity, had Canning made the matter public against the wishes of his uncle and every other person concerned, than for his consenting at their request that it should remain a secret, and leaving it to them to make such communication to Lord C. as they should think proper.

"I am ill situated here for the explanations I would wish to give, but I have forwarded copies of the letters to Lord Dalkeith, a high-spirited and independent young nobleman, in whose opinion Mr. Canning would, I think, wish to stand well. I have also taken some measures to prevent the good folks of Edinburgh from running after any straw that may be thrown into the wind. I wrote a very hurried note to Mr. C. Ellis the instant I saw the accident in the papers, not knowing exactly where you might be, and trusting he would excuse my extreme anxiety and solicitude upon the occasion.

"I see, amongst other reports, that my friend Robert Dundas is mentioned as Secretary at War. I confess I shall be both vexed and disappointed if he, of whose talents and opinions I think very highly, should be prevailed on to embark in so patched and crazy a vessel as can now be lashed together, and that upon a sea which promises to be sufficiently boisterous. My own hopes of every kind are as low as the heels of my boots; and methinks I would say to any friend of mine, as Tybalt says to Benvolio, " What, art thou drawn among these heartless hinds?" I suppose the doctor will be move the first, and then the Whigs will come in like a land flood, and lay the country at the feet of Buonaparte for peace. This, if his devil does not fail, he will readily patch up, and send a few hundred thousands among our coach-driving *noblesse*, and perhaps among our princes of the blood. With the influence acquired by such *gages d'amitié*, and by ostentatious hospitality at his court to all those idiots who will forget the rat-trap of his *détenus* and crowd there for novelty, there will be, in the course of five or six years, what we have never yet seen, a real French party in this country. To this you are to add all the Burdettites, men who rather than want combustibles will fetch brimstone from hell. It is not those whom I fear, however,—it is the vile and degrading spirit of egotism, so prevalent among the higher ranks, especially amongst the highest. God forgive me if I do them injustice; but I think champagne, duty free, would go a great way to seduce some of them; and is it not a strong symptom when people, knowing and feeling their own weakness, will, from mere selfishness and pride, suffer the vessel to drive on the shelves, rather than she should be saved by the only pilot capable of the task.   I will be much obliged to you to let me know what is likely to be done, whether any fight can yet be made, or if all is over.   Lord Melville has been furious for some time against this administration. I think *he* will hardly lend a hand to clear the wreck. I should think if Marquis Wellesley returns, he might form a steady administration; but, God wot, he must condemn most of the present rotten planks before he can lay down the new vessel.   Above all, let me know how Canning's recovery goes on.   We must think what is to be done about the Review.

" Ever yours truly,

"̧ W. S."

We may learn from this splenetic epistle, that a Tory may be no worshipper of the " aristocracy," and also how little some written compositions merit the character which a writing bears in the law of being a deliberate act.   A letter written to a familiar friend reflects often the mere cloud upon the mind, the mood of the time when the spirit does not stir, and the weed is upon the pool.   Who would be judged by the idle words which he himself has spoken or written; and if we would not have them ranked as testimony against ourselves, may we thus measure others? Historians especially should be cautious how they trust to the correspondence and the diaries which it has become so much the fashion to publish. It concerns the character of history that it should not draw from impure fountains; or from narrow and prejudiced sources. However much men may profess to pour out all themselves "as plain as downright Shippen, or as old Montaigne," they rarely do decant themselves finely, but instead of the pure liquor they give us often the mere feculent admixtures which have been held in suspension in their minds with just enough of the wine to float them. It is pleasant to observe, however, in this letter, how one genius discovers another; how Scott observes Canning, and detects in him a star of the first magnitude. Canning was long thought a mere rocket. The solution of this curious depreciation of a great man must be sought in that propensity of the mind, which I have before observed upon, to refuse its homage to Proteus. It distrusts variety of excellence. It overlooks thought, if it be not dressed in a sober livery. The dull eyes of mediocrity are offended by, and must be shaded from, the sparkle of the flashes of wit; but even such a man as Horner could not at first discern in Canning more than the gay and glancing surface of his mind. The river that has its shallows has also its depths.

Notwithstanding the deductions which must be made from a letter written under the influence of excited feelings, it represents correctly enough in the main the feelings of many Tories, the followers of Pitt, who saw in Mr. Percival rather the mind and policy of George III., than the lofty mind and liberal inclinations of the deceased minister, amongst whose colleagues Canning alone possessed in any degree that gift which the two Pitts enjoyed, the mysterious power defying all previous calculation and full discovery of its sources, the power of affecting and moving "all that mighty heart," the collective heart of the English people.

Mr. Peel began his official life under a discredited ministry, I mean not one discredited by its own demerits, but by misfortunes or faults which had preceded its actual formation. The party had lost in Pitt, its great leader, and would not acknowledge in Canning his fittest follower. The ministry of 1807 had the disadvantage of a nominal head, a disadvantage always, since men look naturally for a leader in the council, as in the field. By secession

on secession, including some of its best men, there
remained of the Duke of Portland's ministry but the
remnant of a remnant. The glory of a great name
did not linger by it; for Canning, who had seceded
from the ministry, was regarded by many as the
political successor of Pitt. It had not even the
reputation of stability. When the late Duke of
Wellington returned to England from India in the
year 1805, he wrote thus of political affairs, to his
brother, the Governor-General of India:—"Lord
Grenville has been out of town ever since I arrived in
England, but I went to Stowe in my way to Chel-
tenham, where I underwent a bore for two days.
Bucky is very anxious that you should join the
opposition. He urged that to join the opposition was
the best political game of the day, and his notion was
founded upon the difference of the age of the King
and the Prince of Wales!"

The Tory party were subject also at that time to
a disadvantageous comparison with men who had
lately asserted and lost office in the assertion of a
constitutional principle. Whether Lords Grey and
Grenville had acted wisely "in building up a wall to
run their heads against"—whether more forbearance
at that time would not have marked a higher political
wisdom, considering the nature and force of the

scruples which beset an already clouded mind, may
still be a subject of dispute; but few, I think, will
now dispute that these ministers pursued at once a
high-minded and a constitutional course in refusing
to take a pledge which the King, with too much of
self-indulgence, and some of the querulousness of age,
demanded from them.   He who pleaded so earnestly
for the rights of his own conscience should have
respected more the consciences of his own advisers;
for how could his ministers conscientiously pledge
themselves that, under no circumstances, would
they advise any relaxation of a restrictive law, the
maintenance of which might endanger public
tranquillity?

Mr. Peel's first connection with office was as private
secretary to Lord Liverpool.   With that minister,
rather than with Mr. Percival, was Mr. Peel's original
official connection.   He filled this office for a short
time only, but he filled it long enough to increase
the good opinion which that nobleman, who observed
in him from the first a remarkable love of and aptitude
for business, had formed of him.   It happened that
whilst he held this office, a letter written by him on
some public, but domestic, occurrence of the time,
was laid before the old King, who was interested in
the subject of it.   The King was pleased with and

praised the letter; called it a "good business-like
letter," and then passing on, in his quick manner,
from a commendation of the son's letter to the
character of the father, he spoke warmly in praise
of the latter, concluding with an emphatic declaration
that he was a " very honest man," the culmination
of his praise. Sir Herbert Taylor, who was present
on the occasion, wrote, with much good nature, an
account of the matter to old Sir Robert Peel, confer-
ring thereby all the pleasure which he expected to
flow from this communication.

After a short service in this office, Mr. Peel was
promoted to that of Under Secretary of State for the
Colonial Office, where Lord Liverpool then presided.
On the death of Mr. Percival, Lord Liverpool became prime minister, a fruit which in a manner fell
into his lap. Lord Liverpool, in that high office,
gradually won the esteem of a great portion of the
middle and commercial ranks of the people. We
read in the lately published memoirs of the Right
Honourable George Rose, that George III. spoke
slightingly of Lord Liverpool, then Lord Hawkesbury,
complained of his ignorance of foreign affairs, and
unbusiness-like habits; and we also read there that
Mr. Addington, when prime minister, complained of
needless interruptions, and of many unprofitable con-

sultations, proceeding from the same quarter. George III. was at no time prone to praise his ministers; he was a self-reliant man, a good man of business, and in the habit of directing; on foreign affairs he was generally better instructed and better informed than his ministers, and he especially loved decision. Now a want of decision was the infirmity of the mind of Lord Liverpool. Mr. Addington's criticism, if it were really uttered, was one of those *obiter dicta* of a public man, which it is scarcely fair to report, and which, when reported, is entitled to little respect. Mr. Addington's criticism has a counterpoise in Lord Sidmouth's adhesion and subsequent approbation. The letters which Lord Liverpool wrote, the speeches which he made, the acts which he did, the life which he led, and the schisms which he kept from enlarging, are the best evidence that he was at first somewhat underrated in his public character. His private character was excellent, and was never impeached. In the Londonderry correspondence are some letters written by Lord Liverpool in 1814 to Lord Castlereagh in Paris, which undoubtedly exhibit no very profound views as a statesman, and no very generous spirit towards a prostrate enemy. Lord Castlereagh appears to advantage, in contrast with the lingering hostility of the Prince Regent, and his chief minister. In the life of Lord Eldon, and in the published letters of Mr. C. W. Wynne, are to be found proofs that Lord Liverpool had impressed neither with any high respect for his chief. Yet on the other hand his success in keeping together in some tolerable co-operation and union the discordant materials of the cabinet over which he presided shows that, though not possessed of a resolute will, he had some talent for government. The constitutional sobriety of his mind, his moderation, his quickness to perceive the change which the public mind was undergoing, his knowledge of character, his desire to strengthen his government by the infusion of a more popular element, his freedom from jealousy of more brilliant parts, his selection of moderate men, sound divines, and able scholars for the highest posts in the Church, as well as of good officers in all departments of the state, entitle him to be looked upon, though not as a great, yet still as a safe and prudent minister, as to whom, reversing the old saying of Tacitus, we may declare that he would have been accounted unworthy to lead unless he had actually governed.

In a life of Sir Robert Peel, by Dr. Taylor, which I have had the advantage of perusing, it is supposed that the example of Mr. Percival swayed him in his choice of a side on the Catholic question.   I have observed already that Mr. Peel was more closely connected with Lord Liverpool, who also was an opponent of the Catholic claims, than with Mr. Percival; but neither of these ministers influenced his mind on this question.   His opinion was of an earlier and a home growth.   In his father's mind, and in his father's house, this was almost a religious faith. It is true that the late minister in his posthumous memoirs, supposes, as he would naturally suppose, his opinions on the subject to have been the result of reflection and calm conviction.   Men are rarely good, and never the best, analysers of their own minds, and can seldom give a true history of the growth of their own opinions.

We no more see the inward than we see the outward resemblances which we bear, and the growth of our minds is as much hidden from us as that of our bodies.   In the sense in which Guizot says: "Il naquit Tory;" so it might be said, "Il naquit anti-Catholique."   Equally far from the truth is it, that his choice of a side on this question was the result of a cold calculation of chances.   It rarely happens that a public man starts upon his political career, and takes his line of country upon a calculation, such as that which was suggested at Stowe.   Let us,

in our estimate of public men, look a little more to
probabilities, and place some little trust in human
nature.   The morality of the public men of that day
was less perhaps than that of the present age, for public
opinion is more direct and constant now in its opera-
tion, but still, even then, that sort of cold calculation
was rare.   It would have been not a little remarkable, if this young man, at twenty-five years of age,
with all his reverence for authority, and allegiance to
custom, had separated himself from the cherished
convictions, I may say almost from the religion of
his father's house, in order to espouse the side of
change, against his University and his Church.   In
all matters into which party spirit does not enter, a
grave charge is not lightly credited.   In his posthumous memoirs, the late minister has alluded to this
charge, and observed, not happily upon it.   These
memoirs, the offspring of a sensitive and deeply-
wounded mind, the publication of which some
of his friends regret, contain more than one needless vindication.   A man who is his own advocate always labours under some disadvantage; that
liberrima indignatio, which would inspire an eloquent
advocate to urge in glowing words, the inconsistency
of a charge with a whole life of honour and of truth,
is frozen on the lips of one who is his own apologist.

These memoirs made therefore but a feeble impression.

In allusion to his motives, Sir Robert Peel writes thus:—" To that removal (the removal of the Roman Catholic disabilities) I had offered, from my entrance into Parliament, an unvarying and decided opposition, which certainly did not originate in any views of personal political advantage. When, in the year 1812, I voted against the resolution in favour of concession, moved by Mr. Canning after the death of Mr. Percival, and carried by a majority of 205 to 106, I could not expect that by that vote I was contributing to my political advancement. The grounds on which my opposition was rested are fully developed in a speech delivered by me in the year 1817." The defence does not quite meet the charge, which was that he took this side to gain early the lead on an important question, as there was no opening for the lead on the side which advocated concession. That he had really this bad motive, is not an opinion likely to be entertained by any unprejudiced man who, without reference to the subsequent career of the individual, considers merely the probabilities which his connections, education, and character afford of his sincerity. Such an imputation should not have been lightly cast upon one, who,

upon two important occasions, rose above all considerations of self, and sacrificed himself in a cause
which he esteemed that of his country. A close,
like his, of a life which is not in its nature a purifier,
does not follow on a youthful beginning, conceived,
according to this theory, in a sordid spirit of self-
seeking.

I have said that he took office under a then discredited ministry. It was also a gloomy time. In
1805 Sir Arthur Wellesley wrote thus to his brother:
"But you have the additional consolation that by
your promptness and decision you have not only
saved, but enlarged and secured the invaluable empire entrusted to your government, at a time when
everything else was a wreck, and the existence even
of Great Britain was problematical." With one
great and glorious exception, the conduct of the
British navy, things had from 1805 until 1809, gone
on from bad to worse, apparently, but not really, for
though Napoleon seemed to be at his highest, and
we at our lowest point, his decline had already
commenced. Pitt, Fox, and Nelson were no more,
Austerlitz was lost, the treaty of Tilsit existed, England was alone, she had a weak ministry, and that
divided against itself. The country had endured to
see two cabinet ministers fighting a duel over the

loss of a mighty armament. One lesson this sad time
may give us: we may learn as a nation the wisdom
of courage and of trust in ourselves. Though, at a
particular time of peril, no great man be at hand,
God will send a deliverer, if not by special miracle
and interposition, by the equally mighty power and
merciful workings of his general laws. If a nation
in that hour of peril be but true to its God by being
true unto itself, that people of strong will, resolutely
bent upon not being enslaved, finds in its holy cause
and excited energies its appointed, yet self-earned
deliverance. The resolute will of the people, then,
acts on its rulers, who take, by imitation and the
moral influence of high example, that steady and
resolved mind, which, more than a subtle intellect,
and more even than an informed understanding, is
the first requisite of a ruler.

The people felt instinctively at that time, that
there was but one course,—to fight it out. They saw
also, far better than their leaders, who was the man
to direct the fight. They were the first to appreciate
Wellington. Soon as his star arose, its light lighted
the ministers groping their way; he dissipated their
hallucinations and their ignorance, and his firmness
stayed the vacillation of their feebler minds. It is
a pleasant reflection that Mr. Peel was one of the

very first to recognise a great power in Wellington. The first really eloquent speech which Mr. Peel spoke in the House of Commons, was in praise of Wellington. His theme inspired him, he wanted a a hero, he warmed to a hero, he was full of his subject, and he spoke from his heart. Mr. Whitbread, who borrowed a quotation from Mr. Peel's speech, paid him for it by a warm and eloquent tribute of praise, which made the very ears of old Sir Robert tingle, who reported "how handsomely Whitbread had spoken of Robert's speech." Several years after this, one day when the people were assembled in the park to watch for the Emperor of Russia, Mr. Peel, who was on horseback, rode up to a carriage in which some ladies, nearly related to him, were, one of whom alone survives. Hearing from one of them that a crowd was assembled before the house of the Duke of Wellington, expecting him to come forth, he exclaimed with eagerness: "I never saw him in my life," and rode off instantly to take his chance amidst the crowd, of a sight of the man with whom of all statesmen he was destined to be afterwards most intimately connected.

I pass over Mr. Peel's services as Under Secretary of State, which call for no particular mention. On the accession of Lord Liverpool to the office of prime

minister, he marked his sense of the services and
merit of Mr. Peel, by appointing him to the important office of Secretary of State for Ireland.

Mr. O'Connell, who generally contrived to fasten
his talons on a vulnerable part, did not lose the opportunity of censuring the appointment of so young
a man. He treated it as an indignity to Ireland.
" They have sent," said he, "a raw youth, squeezed
out of the workings of I know not what factory, and
not past the foppery of perfumed handkerchiefs and
thin shoes to govern us." In the present day a
sneer at plebeian extraction would be a dangerous
topic anywhere. The prudence and administrative
skill of Mr. Peel, when recognised, abated the force
of an objection well founded, so far as it related to
his youth. He entered on this office at a time of
great exasperation and difficulty. The Catholics had
been trifled with. The declarations of Lord Grey
and Mr. Ponsonby prove beyond doubt that the
Duke of Bedford had been authorised by the Prince ·
of Wales, to hold out hopes, that on his accession to
the government of the country, the Catholic disabilities should cease. Such a pledge is neither prudent
nor constitutional. No Prince of Wales, nor any
other heir to the throne can, with propriety, give
these political post-obits. They are at best unad-

vised expressions, spoken without a really responsible
author.   The heir to the crown cannot pledge himself, still less can he promise that concurrent and
independent legislative bodies will agree with him in
his kingly exercise of legislative functions.   Yet
party spirit has often applauded these imprudent and
unconstitutional anticipations, of which Frederick,
Prince of Wales, George, Prince of Wales, and lastly,
let us hope finally, Frederick, Duke of York, have
furnished some mischievous examples.   Such promises
had been lightly and inconsiderately made, but not
lightly had they been accepted.   The Irish Catholics
treated them as distinct pledges of future conduct.

At the time when Mr. Peel entered upon his
duties as Irish Secretary, the Irish Government did
not include one member favourable to the Catholic
claims.   The ministry was formed on the principle
of resistance to further concessions to the Catholics.
The Irish Catholic mind was disappointed and exasperated.   The moderation of his own mind ill-fitted
Mr. Peel to be the champion of a religious political
party.   That office indeed he never undertook.   The
Protestant ascendency, or Orange party of Ireland,
placed but little dependence on him.   He stood in a
manner alone.   His manners were thought cold,
formal, and too English.   Ireland showed at that

time rather a roystering court, the style of which was
not much to his taste.   Lady Morgan quizzed him in
one of her novels, and she wrote as many thought of
him.   He laboured, therefore, under every disadvantage which could attend a minister at the commencement of his career; yet he carried away from that
office a high reputation, which no succeeding Irish
Secretary has surpassed.   How was this?   He came
to initiate no new era.   He was not commissioned to
introduce any change of policy.   He had no mission
of conciliation; he was not in the cabinet.   He was
simply a subordinate, though a high officer under the
ministry, entitled certainly to advise and entrusted to
execute their policy.   He was in immediate correspondence with Lord Sidmouth, the then Secretary of
State.   He owed his reputation entirely to his own
personal qualities.   The good which he effected in
Ireland, and the confidence which he ultimately inspired in the minds of many of the more moderate
Catholics, flowed from these personal qualities only.
His very youth supplied him with an increased
sense of the necessity of circumspection.   He became
more cautious than his seniors.   He was prudent,
moderate, just, true, industrious, and able; his great
application to business was daily improving his
administrative skill, and this enabled him to im-

I

prove, by the effect of example, the habits of official
men in the offices with which he was connected.
His administrative skill led to many administrative
reforms.   The changes which he effected in this way
were principally of that kind of which history keeps
no record.   The one most generally noticed, is the
reform which he introduced in the police force of
Ireland, a reform in which he had been anticipated
by Sir Arthur Wellesley, who established in Dublin
an improved force of a similar character.   The policy
which he was sent to support, the old policy, though
from its very nature vexatious to the Catholics, was
not always so in the same degree.   A man who has
no talent for government, exasperates, if he be
employed to conduct such a system, all its evils.
"Retaliation of injuries," says Lord Macaulay,
" marks the furious and foolish partisan ; forgetfulness
of injuries and conciliation mark the statesman."
The zealous champion of a narrow rule, thinks its
very narrowness its merit ; the wise enforcement of
an unpopular law, in stripping oppression of its
insolence, strips it of half its cruelty. Mr. Peel never
dashed his Protestantism rudely in the face of the
Catholic population. He said nothing to rouse, and
did much to calm the passions of a dominant, and
those of a subject race galled by its subjection.   He

never railed at the religions of other men, or assumed whilst disclaiming infallibility. He kept a prudent guard over himself, and endeavoured by the civil force provided by the law to enforce its due observance. He applied himself with success to diminish the employment of a military force in the civil government of the country, to suppress jobbing, and to introduce industry and order in every department of the state. All was done quietly and prudently, without unnecessary disturbance, without disparagement, or any rude shock to feelings; and when he left Ireland, after serving for nearly seven years in that office, he left it with the general acknowledgment that a more honest and able administrator had not previously been known in that department of the state. In the public policy of the country he attempted to introduce no change. Throughout his time the exclusive system prevailed, though the defects of its administration were a little mitigated by his mild exercise of authority. To the credit of introducing a more liberal system into the general government of Ireland no just claim can be made for Mr. Peel. At a later period, after the union of the Grenville party with that of which Lord Liverpool was the head, Mr. C. W. Wynne roused the spirit of Mr. Peel, his colleague, by an observation in the

House of Commons, which implied that the then Irish
Government gave him, Mr. Wynne, a guarantee, by
its very constitution, that the Irish people would be
governed with justice. This awkward observation,
most irritating in the mouth of a colleague, conveyed
what it was not intended to convey, a disadvantageous
comparison of Mr. Peel's Irish administration with
that which had been praised at its expense. It implied that a sort of golden age had commenced, with
which justice had come in. Mr. Peel replied with
some warmth. Whilst vindicating his own Irish
administration, he defied any one to name any act of
his which was fairly open to the censure of injustice.
The challenge was not accepted; nor can such chal-
lenges ever be accepted when the fault lies in a
system and not in an individual officer. An amelioration of such a system is evidenced, not so much by
single acts as by the general tone and temper which
prevail. We see the change in the spirit of the times,
not in single instances but in the whole life of a
people. The improvement in the Irish Government
was best discernible in this mode, and that improvement he himself had had some indirect share in
effecting. It resulted, however, principally from the
improved public morality of the times, from the increased publicity given to all public transactions,

from the general growth of knowledge and true liberality of mind. The very attempt to prevent the dressing of the statue of William III. speaks the growth of liberal sentiments.

Unless we are prepared to say that Lord Wellesley, with Lord Plunkett, differed not in the temper of their government from the Duke of Richmond with Mr. Saurin, we must concede that Mr. Wynne had some reason for an assertion more remarkable, certainly, for its truth than for regard to the feelings of a colleague.

As I am not writing a history of the times, I shall pass rapidly over those days when Mr. Peel pursued rather than originated a policy. Whilst he was Secretary for Ireland, he spoke frequently in the House of Commons, as well on the business of his own particular department, as on the questions generally which came under the consideration of the House. His reputation, as a speaker, gradually advanced. All his progress was gradual. He continually gained ground, without gaining any great victory, or earning any remarkable triumph. Those were the days of the triumphs of Canning, whose genius as an orator then darted its most fertilising and brightest rays and dimmed all lesser lights.

Peel was not a great orator, though he was a great

debater. His style was diffuse, and his diction, disfigured occasionally by official vagueness, had also too much of the smooth regularity which early culti- vation of the powers of expression is apt to give. He rarely gave his imagination her head; and a speech of his, though often admirable as a whole, is still difficult to quote, for the reason that it has no pointed and condensed thought, no bursts of impassioned eloquence; yet even these are not wanting, though they do not constitute the character of his speeches. As an orator, he remained inferior always to some great ones who lived in his time, of whom a few still survive. As a debater, however, understanding truly the temper and modes of thought of his audience, and skilfully accommodating himself to his hearers, as an argumentative speaker full of matter, earnest and persuasive, explaining his views with clearness, anticipating and answering objections, even as an eloquent declaimer he had by this time attained a high reputation in a house which boasted still a Canning, a Brougham, and a Plunkett. He grew afterwards to a somewhat higher stature, the cause of which rise is to be found, I think, in the struggles which he had subsequently to pass through and the stimulants which the new time applied. His conduct of the Catholic Bill in 1829, and his brave struggle of 1835-6, displayed powers which, but for the causes that brought them forth might have lain dormant, buried under the ice crust of caution.

When the elevation of Mr. Abbott to the peerage created a vacancy in the representation of the University of Oxford, Lord Eldon and Lord Stowell lost no time in recommending Mr. Peel to their friends amongst the electors. This recommendation was favourably received by the electors, a majority of whom were eager to choose as their member the champion in the House of Commons of that cause which the clergy, with few exceptions, thought their own.

Lords Eldon and Stowell, in taking this step, had in a manner opposed themselves to Mr. Canning; and as his feelings knew not always control, some sign of irritation might naturally have been looked for. But though the prize which he coveted (and how dearly he coveted it may be learned best from his own eloquent words) was won by another, a younger and a less eminent man, Mr. Canning betrayed no animosity, and generously spoke of his successful rival in the following graceful language : "The representation of the University of Oxford has fallen into worthier hands. I rejoice with my right honourable friend near me, in the high honour which he has obtained.   Long may he enjoy the distinction, and long may it prove a source of reciprocal pride to our parent University and to himself."

It was an honour to Mr. Peel to gain this seat, it was a greater honour to Canning to lose it in the cause for which he lost it.   In the year 1817 Mr Peel made that memorable speech on the Catholic question, greatly and justly applauded at the time, to which he has referred in his posthumous memoirs, in that extract from them which I have already given.   The excellence of this speech is noted in the diary of Mr. Wilberforce, who took the other side.   He says: "Canning was poor, Peel excellent, Castlereagh very good."   Sir James Mackintosh, however, in his diary, speaks less favourably of this speech, and attributes its success to what he terms the material powers of oratory, voice, manner and delivery.   He speaks, also, of Peel as the champion of the bigots, unconscious apparently of the beam in his own eye,—a harsh judgment, and as events proved, a rash one,—for the mind of Peel was not of that order, and had more of the conformer than of the bigot in its leanings.   This speech, ranking certainly above all his former pro- ductions, nevertheless does not equal his best in later years, wherein we may observe a warmth, and an im- passioned earnestness, which that more laboured and colder performance wants. It was not the most learned, but it was the most telling speech on that side of the question; four years afterwards it was admirably replied to by Plunkett, in a speech which electrified the House, and is still read with admiration.

On the resignation of his office of Secretary for Ireland, Mr. Peel reposed for a time from official labours. He was succeeded in that office by Mr. Charles Grant, now Lord Glenelg, one of the most eloquent advocates of the Catholic claims. In 1819 Mr. Peel was appointed chairman of a committee, chosen, on the motion of Mr. Vansittart, the Chancellor of the Exchequer, to inquire into the state of the Bank of England, with reference to the expediency of the resumption of cash payments. As chairman of that committee, he introduced into the House of Commons, and supported the bill, commonly called " Peel's Bill," the fruit of the inquiries, deliberation, and judgment of the committee. This measure, having in its favour an unusual concurrence of opinions of men of all parties, was supported by a very large majority. The two principal parties in the state were united and zealous in its support. Although Mr. Peel disclaimed the authorship of the measure, and with a just and graceful tribute of respectful praise, ascribed it to the late Mr. Horner, yet has this bill, more than any of his own, been coupled with the name of Mr. Peel. A year or two later, during the prevalence of great agricultural distress, much hostility was directed against this enactment. Mr. Peel then stood forward, not as its author, but as its champion, and vindicated the measure, in the general opinion, with ability and success.

The measure itself, which became afterwards a subject of party strife, has had, perhaps, more attributed to it, both of good and evil consequence, than in any view of the subject can belong to it. It was but the fulfilment of a promise, say rather of a solemn pledge, that the former common measure of value should be restored. The Bank Restriction Act was meant to be a temporary measure, and originally it was thought likely to be but of short duration. A depreciated currency was no necessary consequence of the measure. For several years, whilst the restriction seemed likely to be of short duration, the paper currency was not depreciated. That it was not depreciated during this, its first stage, was asserted by Lord Grenville in the year 1811, in a debate in the House of Lords upon Lord Stanhope's Bill. His opinion upon this point is supported by the authority of Mr. M'Culloch. The mere substitution of a more

cheap and more convenient medium of exchange
could not, of itself, have caused a depreciation of the
currency. The Bank was perfectly solvent, and the
credit of the Government unimpaired. Lord Grenville, in this debate, attributed the over-issue of paper,
which, as he alleged, had taken place, to the reckless
war expenditure, and to want of financial ability in
the administrations which succeeded his own. Thus
party crimination mixed itself with, and party spirit
embroiled, a question which would not have been
seen very clearly even had these mists not been inter-
posed. Mr. Peel was a very young man. He had
not previously made this subject his particular study.
His father, whose opinion especially on such a subject
would naturally influence his own, at least at that
time of his life, denied the alleged depreciation of
the bank note. Nor did he stand alone in that denial.
In this, as it often happens in other disputes, the
disputing parties used the same terms in different
senses.

It was one thing to assert that a guinea was then
worth in the market and would actually exchange
for one pound note and one shilling, and another
thing to assert that the bank note, by reason of the
over-issue of bank notes as currency, had fallen, as
to commodities generally, much below its nominal

value. The superabundance of the currency, as the
medium of exchange, or common measure of value,
was to be tested, it was said, by comparison, with the
necessities for which in that character it was fabricated and supplied. Did it, or did it not, bear the
same proportion to the transactions of life and operations of commerce, in which such a measure is
wanted, as the currency, before the time of the Bank
Restriction Act, bore to the similar transactions and
operations of that time? Old Sir Robert Peel af-
firmed that it did, or that if there was any difference,
it was in favour of the value of the bank note. Those
who supported that side of the question ascribed the
high price of gold to its scarcity, and not to the over-
issue of the paper money. That scarcity they ascribed to the very special circumstances of the times,
in which, they said, the ordinary effects of interchange
of trade between state and state, and trader and
trader, were temporarily and violently disturbed, the
closure of the continent counting amongst the causes
of disturbance. If we may judge from his reported
speech on Lord Stanhope's Bill, Lord Liverpool appears to have taken a similar view. He declared that
a merchant of great eminence in the City, one not
favourably inclined to his government, had said to
him that if he wanted ten thousand guineas for any

purpose, he did not know where he could look to purchase them. Again, it was urged on the same side, if the bank note be depreciated absolutely, by reason of its over-issue and mere abundance, then, since it is practically our principal money, all commodities will have advanced in price, but that is not found to be the case, some are high, and some low in price, and the state of market prices generally does not bear out the assertion. It is obvious that a question of this nature might easily be misunderstood, and though the vote of the House of Commons, on the amendment proposed upon Mr. Horner's resolutions, has commonly been relied on in party conflicts, and by party writers, as a pregnant proof of the want of independence of that House at that time, it has always seemed to me one of the weakest proofs, amongst the too numerous instances which their votes supply, of the tendency of a senate to vote unscrupulously in support of its predominant party.

Beyond the ability which Mr. Peel displayed as the advocate and defender of this measure, at various times, and his candour in admitting an error of opinion, the measure itself contributes but little to his especial fame; nor can his error of opinion at an earlier age be fairly viewed as detracting from his reputation.

It does not fall within the scope of this work to

inquire into the causes of that general, deep, and long prevailing distress, which immediately followed the close of the war. Peace did not bring with her that smiling train by which she is commonly said to be attended. The country, from the overstrain upon its powers, sank; after the effort ceased, into a state of collapse, from which the prophets of evil predicted that it would never recover. The distress pressed upon all classes, but the destitution of the lowest was extreme. A full meal was scarcely known in a poor man's house. " Venter non habet aures,"— "le ventre affamé n'a point d'oreilles:" but the proverb might have said also, the hungry belly has ears for mischief, and as long as the devil has a hand in human affairs, pedlars will be ready to present their enticing trumpets to those ears which are deaf to better counsels. Dame Eleanor Spearing's own ears could not have had poured into them a greater torrent of evil, than that which streamed into the ears of a half-fed population. Is it any wonder then that many, forgetting for a while their habitual patience and respect for the law, should have been led to join the habitually turbulent, and to believe that their condition could be improved by violence, and a government founded on crime?

The mournful history of the disaster which oc-

curred at Manchester in dispersing an illegal meeting
need not be repeated here. Mr. Peel took part in
the debates to which this unfortunate occurrence
gave rise. He appears to have been less guarded
than usual in his expressions, since his speech occasioned a misapprehension of his meaning, and he is
said to have offended the manufacturers of Lancashire by remarks from which they inferred that he
considered the factory system as dangerous to the
public peace. This meaning was attributed to him in
the debate, and disclaimed by him at the time. It
was true, however, that vast congregations of men
had been formed without any due attention to some
salutary things, which, in times termed barbarous,
would not have been neglected. Old modes of security had fallen into disuse, and those whose duty it
was to look to the public safety, had provided no
permanent and efficient guards for the maintainance
of order. It was a thought likely to be present in
the mind of one, who had established a valuable
constabulary force in Ireland, and was soon to originate in the metropolis one of the same nature.
The strictures, however, could not have been
meant for the manufacturers, upon whom no special
obligation lay to provide for the public safety.
This displeasure, if it prevailed for a time, was

certainly not of long duration. In 1824 no trace of it remained.

Mr. Peel was saved by his private station at this time, from any participation in those counsels which led to the introduction of a Bill of Pains and Penalties against Caroline of Brunswick, the Queen Consort of George IV. The object of this bill was to degrade the Queen Consort from her royal state and dignity, on a charge of an adulterous intercourse abroad, between her, when Princess of Wales, and a foreigner. After the merited failure of this measure, the Marquis of Tavistock moved, in the House of Commons, for a vote of censure upon the ministers. Their conduct was commonly condemned in private, even amongst their own supporters. They stood in a manner, self-condemned; for it was known that they had originally been adverse to proceedings against the Queen, and had yielded to a mind which they should rather have directed to wiser conduct. As a vote of censure would have occasioned a transfer of the government to their opponents, and as neither the House of Commons nor the supporters of Government, amongst the holders of borough patronage, nor a majority of the constituencies, as then constituted, desired so entire a change, the motion was defeated by a large majority. Mr. Peel spoke against

the motion.   He was at that time in a private
station.   His past connection, however, with the
Government, and the general expectation that he
would soon be in office again, deprived his voice of
the additional weight, which the opinion of an able
and unbiassed supporter carries with it.   On three
minor points he censured, but on the general question he acquitted the Government,—the exclusion of
the Queen's name from the liturgy, the refusal of a
ship to conduct, and of a palace to receive her, were
the grounds on which he condemned the Government.
The grave constitutional objection to the punishment
of a subject by an *ex post facto* law did not strike
his mind with the force which it carries to mine.
The Queen Consort, though in a pecular relation to
the King, is still a subject.   There is small security
in troubled times, even in a free state, if a subject
can be struck down by a *coup d'état.*   An *ex post
facto* penal law is a *coup d'état* in a more gentle, and
therefore more insidious form of tyranny.   It violates
the first principles upon which a penal law should
stand.   Such an exceptional law, if it can ever be
supported at all, must stand on a real necessity.
The safety of the state must be endangered by the
impunity of the person aimed at.   A fanciful ag-
grandisement of a peril cannot raise even a grave

K

political inconvenience to the dimensions of a danger menacing the Government. The King, as Prince Regent, had for many years enjoyed the exercise of sovereignty. During this time the alleged acts had been committed. The character of his wife had not really impaired the efficiency of his government, nor sunk the dignity of the regal office. The insults of low ribaldry may be vented against an unhappy husband, but such a sufferer has general sympathy, unless his own errors have led to the calamity, but a cross of that latter kind should be borne patiently, in every station alike. The morals of the country, and the purity of its women were, happily, too soundly rooted to be disturbed by one more evil example, though in an exalted station. The return of the Queen therefore to England, at the highest but a grave inconvenience, was not an act fraught with real peril to the state, nor with real diminution of the sovereign's dignity. Its effect upon the King himself as a man could not be a justifying cause. Posterity will, therefore, perhaps think of this act as the calm reader of history now thinks of the cases of Fenwick and of Atterbury.

After twelve years of parliamentary life, of which more than eight had been passed in office, Mr. Peel became a cabinet minister,—no very rapid elevation.

Lord Liverpool had strengthened his administration in 1818, by the accession to the cabinet of the Duke of Wellington, and in 1820 by an union with the Grenville party. In 1821, Mr. Peel entered the cabinet. His elevation was well received by the public. The union of Lord Liverpool with the Grenvilles was very distasteful to Lord Eldon. He asks Lord Stowell in a private letter, in which he comments upon some recent preferments in the Church, and on the appointment of Mr. Grant, " can this man (Lord Liverpool) be in earnest?":—a splenetic effusion of the same character with several which we read in a series of private letters written by Lord Eldon in old age to near members of his family, and apparently not destined for publication. He would not, I think, on calm reflection have doubted the earnestnéss of a colleague with whom he had acted for many years, a man whose character stands as high for truth and integrity as that of the questioner himself. It was a principle of that cabinet to consider the Catholic question as an open one, and on all other material points there was no disagreement between Lord Liverpool and Mr. Charles Grant.

The death of Lord Londonderry, which soon followed, brought back Mr. Canning to his old office of Secretary of State for the Foreign Department.

This appointment was popular. From this time
until the breaking up of this administration, the
state vessel moved smoothly along with the stream,
propelled, though not very strongly, by the popular
breath. Mr. Canning's genius, his great and brilliant
talents, and his oratory, won their way naturally in a
popular assembly. He gave the ministry an ascendancy in debate, of which previously they had stood in
need. He did it another service,— in preventing the
further spread, at that time, of the schism which had
commenced between the Tory chiefs and the supporters of the ministry in the middle ranks of the
people, including the manufacturing and commercial
classes. Mr. Canning did not initiate any new foreign
policy, to that the cabinet would not have consented;
but he worked the old policy with a new mind
and in a new spirit. George IV., alarmed at the
prospect of a severance from the "great powers,"
asked for explanations on some point of the seeming
new policy, and was referred by the united cabinet to
a former letter written by Lord Londonderry to the
same effect, and approved of by the King himself.
There was no discernible difference judging by the
letter, yet the despatches and the general tone of
Mr. Canning with foreign powers gave rise abroad to
a belief that the foreign policy of England had

changed. The same opinion prevailed also at home. In these matters opinion is everything, and the way of saying a thing gives it half its significancy. The tone of Mr. Canning, though he wrote always with a polished instrument, had something of jealousy and disputation. His speeches also were in the same vein, the British statesman spoke in him in the national spirit of insularity. England should not be yoked in a team,—her march should be independent and alone. He was in spirit a true minister of a free people, a man of noble aims; he did not, I think, stoop to conquer, though he benefited by questionable influences. It is said that he courted them; it would be more true, I think, to say that they offered themselves to him, and that he did not reject them. He chained them through their interest to his own, and his own he considered the cause of the country. He had genius, eloquence, even poetry; a mind, not light, as some conceived, but capable of close and successful attention to subjects the most abstruse; thoughts deep as well as bright; and a soul liable to be deeply stirred. He was something of a *tête montée*, he had a kind of effervescence of the brain, and a love of scenic effects. Burke, the elder Pitt, Lord Carteret, Napoleon, Richelieu, Cæsar, Alexander, many more that could be named amongst great men, whether

orators, statesmen, generals or commanders, have had,
mingled with the highest qualities of mind, and the
loftiest genius, a love of exhibiting themselves, which
in lower natures degenerates into affectation, and a
vulgar desire of astonishing. He has been charged
with intrigue at this time, as at a former time; but of
this imputed habit, which admitted of easy proof, if
it had existed, no proof was ever produced. Two
parties at the least are needed to an intrigue. Intrigues within a cabinet implicate more than one
member of it, and who was there his accomplice?
Intrigues with his opponents must have implicated
other parties also; for though such intrigues are conducted by intermediate agents, they take place with
the sanction of the heads. It seems to me no more
than a party accusation generated by suspicion.
Parties are attracted to each other without intrigues.
It is a common and generally a false accusation. It
has been said of Peel, and even one of his colleagues,
Mr. C. W. Wynne, appears to have suspected such a
design, that he aimed at being prime minister, by a
vault into the seat, over the heads of elder and competent colleagues. What would this have been but
an intrigue, and a very base one? Mr. Wynne writes
in 1822 to the Duke of Buckingham: " Peel means
to run for the lead." " It seems to me that his object

is to break up the government." To Lord Liverpool
Mr. Peel was bound by every tie which can unite one
statesman to another. Whatever Mr. Wynne, in
the confidence of a private letter, and the hurry of
epistolary communication may have said, a little
serious consideration would have sufficed to show him
the injustice of this supposition. It would have been
an act, at once, of folly and treachery. To put in the
Whigs that he might put them out and take their
places, for such was the supposition of Mr. Wynne,
would surely have been an act of signal folly, since it
is not an easy task to unseat a ministry in possession;
and the Tory party would never have pardoned the
manœuvre. In no way could Mr. Peel have super-
seded Lord Liverpool without intrigue and disloyalty.
The act, its motives, and intended consequences
would have been no secret to any one; and an indig-
nant and scoffing public, who detest treachery and
underhand dealing, would have said: " If to come in,
Sir, only you go out—the way you take is *vilely*
roundabout." A wilder conceit never entered the
head of any correspondent of a Sir Politick-would-be,
the bored master of a dull house in the country,
fidgety about the post, and gaping for news. Mr.
Wynne writes: " Peel is cold and reserved." Then
he reports an unfriendly speech imputed to Peel,

about the Grenvilles. " Not that I believe it," says
Mr. Wynne, " he is much too cautious to have said it,
but he probably thinks so."   Soon after, Peel is out
of temper, he has been in a minority, and about the
same time he is described as having evinced more
spirit and good judgment than any man in the
cabinet.   Who, on the authority of such fleeting
thoughts, would venture either to praise or blame any
statesman ?

The services of Mr. Peel in the Home Office shall
be narrated in his own words : "I have the satisfaction of reflecting that every institution, civil and
military, connected with my office during the last
four years has been subjected to close inspection and
strict review ; and that I have been able to make
such temperate and gradual reforms as I thought
were consistent with the general and permanent good.
I have also the gratification of knowing, that every
law found on the statute book when I entered office,
which imposed any temporary or extraordinary
restraint on the liberty of the subject, has been either
repealed or suffered to expire.   I may be a Tory.   I
may be an illiberal, but the fact is undeniable, that
when I first entered upon the duties of the Home
Department there were laws in existence which imposed upon the subjects of this realm unusual and

extraordinary restrictions. The fact is undeniable that those laws have been effaced. Tory as I am, I have the further satisfaction of knowing that there is not a single law connected with my name, which has not had for its object some mitigation of the severity of the criminal law, some prevention of abuse in the exercise of it, or some security for its impartial administration. I may also recollect with pleasure, that during the several trials to which the manufacturing interests have been exposed, during the winter of the last two years, I have preserved internal tranquillity, without applying to the House for measures of extraordinary severity." The speech from which the above quotation is extracted was made in the House of Commons shortly after the formation of Mr. Canning's ministry in 1827. It has been thought to abound over much in self-praise. Mr. Peel, at that time, had been much, and unjustly, assailed. Lord Bacon has said that a man may sometimes wisely assert himself, and the time seems to be best chosen when others are attempting unjustly to run him down. The Jury Bill and the bills for the improvement and consolidation of the criminal law, are the most important of the domestic reforms to which this speech alludes. Since the Jury Bill, the charge of "packing juries" has ceased ; we hear this objection no more. The

Government has gained by the absence of an objection, which a convicted assailant was sure to raise, and to which the abuses of former times lent, even in modern days, some air of credibility. All these acts were carefully prepared and skilfully framed. Mr. Peel found a valuable assistant in Mr. Gregson, a learned lawyer, and an excellent man, whose skill and accuracy distinguished all the acts which he drew. The acts for the improvement of the criminal law occasioned fewer difficulties of construction and in their application, than any acts of equal importance, bulk, and variety with which I am acquainted. These measures have not been altered, except by the extension, in some instances, of the principles on which they were founded. They were meant to be advances, and not the consummation of the reform of the criminal law. It has been said that Mr. Peel should have assigned the merit of these acts to Romilly and to Mackintosh. He might well have thought that his praise would exalt neither, and that their labours and their fame needed no efforts of his to raise them. Their labours were recent and in the memory of all. These very acts resulted from the labours of a committee appointed upon a motion of Sir J. Mackintosh, upon which occasion Lord Castlereagh had paid a handsome tribute to the exertions of these great men.

Mr. Peel could not mean to filch the reputations of other men, or hope to succeed in the attempt. The merit of neither could be sunk. Although a part only of these measures was connected with the earlier efforts of Romilly and of Mackintosh, this speech might certainly have been graced by some such acknowledgment, as that which, a few years before, he had made of his debt to Mr. Horner, or as that which, at a later day, he made of the obligations of the country to Mr. Cobden. I leave the omission to the candid construction of my readers. Charity forbids a harsh interpretation of the conduct of any man, and reason condemns an accusation at variance with antecedent and subsequent conduct, with character, as with probability, and unsupported by evidence. It would be foolish to ascribe to Mr. Peel the merit of having been a great law reformer. He did not lay claim to that distinction. He was not in this nor in other reforms an inventor, an original discoverer of a first happy thought. It is a sufficient and no inconsiderable merit in a minister if he work up, at a proper time, in a proper manner, in a fit web, the threads which other hands have spun. They were, however, considerable reforms, judicious and safe steps in the right direction, pointing to further progress. In the preparation of the measures for the improvement of the criminal law, the late Lord Tenterden was much consulted, whose willing and careful hand contributed to the improvement of the work. This branch of the law was previously in a state of great confusion, and retained some objectionable remnants of semi-barbarous times. The common law of the land as to crimes, and the observation may be extended, overladen by a mass of confused statutes, had become a mess from which the legal appetite turned away disgusted; the mind laden with and fatigued by such ingestion became inert, and could scarcely grapple with principles. One specimen will suffice. At common law, felonies, with two or three exceptions, were punishable with death, but legal fictions, always introduced for a good end, were too hard for Moloch. The Church claimed its clerks. "Literatura," said the Church, "non facit clericum; tonsura facit." The law was so sharp-sighted that it saw a tonsure on the crown of every layman. A reader of a verse was a clerk, then a repeater of a verse, then the law presumed, violently, all men now read. But when a woman was arraigned, then the modest law declined. to feign for woman. But the statute law stept in to her rescue. The fair impenitents were burned in the hand, and imprisoned. Statutes were heaped upon statutes on this one subject alone. Sometimes questions arose whether the benefit of clergy was taken away from one only, or from all of several joint offenders. Was it taken away from accessories? if so, from accessories after the fact?—Did an act shut out principals, and let in accessories?—Was a convict to be burned in the hand?—Could a peeress be punished? The ruthless statute swept away benefit of clergy, with the whole mass of its antiquarian unedifying learning. About this time began also the bold invasion by justice of the territory of grammar, words in the masculine gender shall be hermaphroditically interpretable, one shall mean many, as many one. In short by one cunning device or another, the expert defender of prisoners, who used to be all points, piercing the very soles of the lazy feet of justice, could no longer revel in objections nor drive a coach and six through an indictment.

Mr. Peel, whilst he filled the office of Secretary of State, was called upon to perform the ungallant act of unmasking a lady against her will. She had assumed the dignity of a princess, and the royal title of Cumberland. She loved to exhibit herself. Seated in an open landaulet, drawn by labouring steeds, her servants dressed in the royal livery; right royally she rode. She might, to use the cautious potential mood, which our writers have adopted from diplomacy,

she might have been seen daily taking the air, and
ventilating her grievances.   Descending from her
high estate, in the language of elegant lady novelists,
she fell like some heroines, and like Theodore of
Corsica, into the hands of the myrmidons of the law.
She was immured — tell it not to Poland,—in a
spunging-house in Ludgate Hill!   Communica-
ting this outrage to the public press, she awaited a
popular convulsion.   Rheumatic, cased in flannels,
on a raw and gusty day in November, the muddy
Ludgate splashing to the waist, in the sight of the
sleepy British Lion, she sat at the window one cold
afternoon, so pensive was Olive, leaning on her elbow, a
patient sufferer, with looks commercing with the skies,
as if impatient to fly away, putting off the weight of
her humanity, to visit purer realms.

> "For only generous souls designed,
> And not a writ to find us there."

She forwarded a petition to the House of Commons,
setting forth her parentage, her claims, and her
wrongs.   Mr. Peel rose to answer the petition: he said
this lady was either an impostor or a dupe; she was
the daughter of one Mr. Robert Wilmot; there had
been two brothers, Dr. Wilmot and Mr. Robert
Wilmot, she was the daughter of the latter; but not

contented with this humbler rank, she aspired to royal lineage. She stated herself at first, to be the illegitimate daughter of the Duke of Cumberland, a brother of George III. Then discovering that to be a mistake, she asserted herself to be a legitimate daughter of his late Royal Highness. She offered some documents as proofs of this, but they were evidently fabricated. One, purporting to emanate from the King, was witnessed by Lord Chatham, when Lord Chatham was not in favour with nor in the habit of seeing the King. Another was attested by James Wilmot, who was at Oxford, in residence at the time, and could not have attested the document; another signature was wrong, being signed Brooke, a signature which was not then used by the noble Lord to whom it was attributed; the last name Adder, was also mistaken, and proved the fabrication, as it was, in this instance, a mere vulgar mispronunciation of the name Haddow, which was that of the person meant. After this crushing exposure of the case, Mr. Peel, with his old quiet relish of absurdity concluded that there was one title claimed by the lady, which he had no desire to dispute, that of a Polish princess. To the enjoyment of that dignity he left her, he only presumed to question her title to rank as an English princess. He then read to the House the following exquisite conclusion of her manifesto to the Polish nation. "Alas! beloved nation of our ancestors, your Olive lives to anticipate the emancipation of Poland. Invite us, beloved people, to the kingdom of our ancestors, and the generous humanity and wise policy of the Emperor Alexander will aid in the restoration of our ancient house!"

The administration of Lord Liverpool, which under the lead of Mr. Canning, in the House of Commons, was more and more drawing to itself the calm approval of the middle ranks of the people, bent on progress, but averse from organic change, was brought by the illness of that nobleman, a paralytic seizure, suddenly and unexpectedly to a conclusion. This administration, which, when it was formed, was expected to fall within six months, lasted sixteen years, and was then broken up by an accident. Various causes operated to prevent the union of the parts, either under Mr. Canning or any other chief. As the members of cabinets are mortal men, we may reasonably suppose that a mixture of motives prevented an union, which, in the opinion of their supporters, at least, the general interest required. Sir Walter Scott so supposed, and so wrote, sowing his censure broadcast, with an unstinting and impartial hand: —

"To John B. S. Morritt Esq., Portland Place,
London.

"How are you, as a moderate pro-Catholic, satisfied with this strange alliance in the Cabinet? I own I look upon it with doubt at best, and with apprehensions. At the same time I cannot approve of the late ministers leaving the King's councils in such a hurry. They could hardly suppose that Canning's fame, talent, and firm disposition, would be satisfied with less than the condition of premier; and such being the case,

> " 'To fly the boar, before the boar pursued,
> Was to incense the boar to follow them.'

On the other hand his allying himself so closely and so hastily with the party against whom he had maintained war from youth to age, seems to me, at this distance, to argue one of two things, either that the minister has been hoodwinked by ambition and anger, or that he looks upon the attachment of those to the opinions which he has always opposed, as so slight, unsubstantial and unreal, that they will not insist on them or any of them, provided they are gratified personally with a certain portion of the benefits of place and revenue. Now, not being disposed to think over much of the Whigs, I cannot suppose that a large class of British statesmen, not deficient certainly, in talents, can be willing to renounce all the political maxims and measures which they have been insisting on for thirty years, merely to become place-holders under Canning. The supposition is too profligate. But then, if they come in, the same Whigs we have known them, where, how, and when are they to execute their favourite notions of reform in Parliament? And what sort of amendments will they be, which are to be brought forward, when the proper time comes? Or, how is Canning to conduct himself, when the Saxons, whom he has called in for his assistance, draw out to fight for a share of the power which they have assisted him to obtain? When such strange and unwonted bed-fellows are packed up together, will they not kick and struggle for the better share of the coverlids and blankets? Perhaps you will say that I look gloomily on all this, and have forgotten the way of the world, which sooner or later shows that the principles of statesmen are regulated by their advance towards or retreat from power; and that from men who are always acting upon the emergencies of the moment it is vain to expect consistency. Perfect consistency, I agree, we cannot look for, it is inconsistent with humanity. But that gross inconsistency which induces men to clasp to their bosom the men whom they most hated, and to hold up to admiration the principles which they have most forcibly opposed, may gain a temporary triumph, but will never found a strong ministry or a settled government. My old friend Canning, with his talents and oratory, ought not, I think, to have leagued himself with any party, but might have awaited, well assured that the general voice would have carried him into full possession of power. I am sorry he has acted otherwise, and augur no good from it, though when or how the evil is to come, I cannot pretend to say."

In another letter, one addressed to Mr. Lockhart, Sir Walter Scott writes thus:—

"I understand that Peel had from the King *carte blanche* for an anti-Catholic administration, and that he could not accept it, because there was not strength enough to form such. What is this but saying in plain words that the Catholics have the country and the question; and because they are defeated on a single question—and one which, were it to entail no further consequence, is of wonderfully little import,—they have abandoned the King's service, given up the citadel because an exterior work was carried, and marched out into opposition. I can't think this was right; they ought either to have made a stand with-

out Canning, or a stand with him; for, to abdicate
as they have done was the way to subject the
country to all the future experiments which this
Catholic emancipation may lead those that now carry
it to attempt, and which may prove worse for worse
than anything connected with the question itself."

Thus says the old Scotch Tory. But I for one do
not believe it was the question of emancipation, or
any public question, which carried them out. I
believe the predominant motive in the breast of every
one of them, was personal hostility to Canning; and
with more prudence, less arbitrary manners, and more
attention to the feelings of his colleagues, he would
have stepped *nem. con.* into the situation of prime
minister, for which his eloquence and talent naturally
pointed him out. They objected to the man, more
than the statesman, and the Duke of Wellington,
more frank than the rest, almost owns that the
quarrel was personal.

Between Mr. Canning and Mr. Peel no personal
dislike existed on either side. There is no ground
for distrusting the statements which both of these
gentlemen made to that effect. Mr. Peel did not
undervalue, on the contrary, he fully appreciated
the services of Mr. Canning, as well as his genius
and his talents. He had long been of opinion that

no cabinet could be formed with any prospect of stability or advantage out of the ultra-Tory party, or
exclusively from men unfavourable to the Catholic
claims. He was too reasonable to expect that Mr.
Canning would serve under himself, and possessed
too moderate a mind to desire an exaltation of himself over an older, and in the common estimation, an
abler man. That the ministerial explanations which
ensued, do not fully satisfy myself, is owing, I trust,
in a great degree, to the nature of all such disclo-
sures. This practice of demanding from public men,
explanations why they unite not with, or why they
recede from, a particular ministry, may, in the long
run, be productive of public advantage. An in-
quisitorial proceeding cannot, however, be expected
to produce a full disclosure. However much men
may choose to pour themselves out, they do not like
to be pumped. Whether such an explanation be
volunteered, or extorted by question, it is still but a
submission to necessity. A variety of mixed motives, some of which are often hidden from ourselves,
operate simultaneously and promptly to give birth to
some act, the motives of which our own conscience,
even in the secret chambers of the breast, cannot
always fully unfold. A ministerial explanation therefore, however candid in itself, can rarely satisfy his-

tory.   The historian will probe for himself.   If I
am unable to ascribe the act of Mr. Peel, in declining to unite himself with Mr. Canning in that
statesman's adminstration, to the one sole motive to
which Mr. Peel attributed it, it is because I distrust
not his truth, but, in this instance, his self-examina-
tion and self-knowledge.   I think he may have
unconsciously ascribed to one, an effect which was
probably the result of several causes.   In order to
explain my meaning fully, I must take up the
matter at an earlier period of Mr. Peel's political
life.   At the beginning of his public life, he was introduced into office by Lord Liverpool, with whom,
and not with Mr. Percival, was his more immediate
connection.   Between that nobleman and himself a
mutual confidence, as well as a general and full concurrence in political opinions, always existed.   At the
earliest stage of Mr. Peel's official life, Lord Eldon was,
of all the ministers in a not very distinguished cabinet,
the one who enjoyed the highest individual reputation.
This had been acquired by his great legal knowledge
and high judicial qualities.   He was not then unpopular as a statesman, and, as a judge, he stood, at
that time, pre-eminent in fame, for the public had
not then begun to attribute, unjustly, the delays and
abuses of his court to his own habit of mind.   Lord

Eldon had not then developed that strong hostility to progress which sunk his reputation as a statesman, or if he had, it clashed then less with the public sentiment.   Mr. Peel looked up to him as to a man who had raised himself by industry and made himself all that he was.   At this time of his life, Lord Eldon was the object of his respectful admiration. This reverential habit no wise man will ever deride. It is never found in a bad soil, and never wholly wanting in a good one.   But as time went on, Mr. Peel's own stature grew, whilst Lord Eldon's declined, the faults of whose character increased with age. His adherence to things as they are grew more obstinate and intolerant of opposite convictions, his mind more and more impenetrable by any new light. No estrangement took place between Lord Eldon and Mr. Peel, but still there was a growing divergence, and consequently some abatement of that reciprocal confidence which a general agreement inspires.   Lord Liverpool was, upon principle, a supporter of free trade, Mr. Peel adhered also to that side.   It was substantially his father's side.   Lord Eldon was generally opposed to these and other changes.   A sort of schism was growing up and widening between Lord Liverpool and Lord Eldon. Mr. Peel agreed far more with the former than with

the latter.   His respect for Lord Eldon remained un-
abated, in respect of those personal qualities which
had won it, but, save on the question of the Catholic
claims, their agreement in politics was becoming continually less.   In truth, Mr. Peel may be described
as in a transition state, tending gradually and constantly towards the new order of things.   In this state
of things, Mr. Canning entered again the cabinet of
Lord Liverpool.   A man of Mr. Peel's discernment
could not but contrast the tranquillity and popularity
of the new era, with the turbulence and troubles of
the past, nor was he at any loss in ascribing the
effects to their proper cause.   Between Mr. Canning
and Mr. Peel, therefore, except on the Catholic question, a general, and a continually increasing agreement prevailed.   Some short time before that illness
of Lord Liverpool, which put an end to his administration, Mr. Peel, speaking of Mr. Canning to one
nearly connected with himself, said that when he
went down to a cabinet council on any matter of
importance, he generally found himself anticipated
by Canning, in the very view of the subject which he
himself had taken, Canning advancing the very
reasons on which he himself had proceeded, "clothed," he said, "in better language than any into which
I could have put them."   Writing to Lord Eldon,

at the time when the administration was breaking up, and referring to Mr. Canning, he expresses his own regret at being severed from a colleague, with whom he had cordially acted, and with whom, on all but one subject, he commonly agreed.   Mr. Canning stated, in the House, at this time, that there was, between Peel and himself as great a community of sentiment as could well exist amongst public men.   In the speech from which I have already made a copious extract, Mr. Peel fully renounces all claim to that sort of toryism which consists in hostility to administrative changes.   He even parades his reforms, and relies on the changes which he had introduced, the things which he had created, restored, or improved, as his chief claims to the approbation of his countrymen.   It was a sort of prelude to the celebrated Tamworth Address.   This is sufficient to prove, that between Canning and Peel, neither private dislike nor jealousy, nor general disagreement in political views, existed to cause their severance.   Why, then, did it take place?   He felt, probably, that he was doing right in not joining Mr. Canning.   One cause existed, and it was enough.   It was one pleadable to the country and to his own conscience; and he went no deeper.   But there were other objections, and weighty ones.

Had Mr. Peel possessed over the minds of his colleagues, Lord Eldon and the Duke of Wellington, over the heads of the Tory party out of the cabinet, over the great owners of borough patronage, and over the great men generally who gave their support to, and acted with the party, influence great enough to induce them to keep that party connected, I doubt much whether a difference between Mr. Canning and himself on this one question alone, grave as it was, would have sufficed to separate them. Mr. Peel, in that state of things, would have had to look at the question in a new light, to have weighed in new scales the danger to the Protestant ascendancy, against the danger of a schism in the Tory party. It was obviously his interest, as it was his desire, to keep the whole phalanx united. But as the schism existed, as it could not be prevented, as the Tory party would not accept Canning as their leader, the sole question for Mr. Peel to decide was whether he would leave his party, or leave Mr. Canning. His duty under the circumstances was clear. In joining Mr. Canning he would have had to enter upon a line of conduct far more at variance with his feelings and principles than that which he reluctantly adopted. To enter upon a road without seeing clearly where it was to lead him, to unite himself virtually with a new party, to leave old for new associates, with no certainty what changes or compromises that union would involve, would have been a course wholly distasteful to one of his cautious mind, a wary traveller on a new road.   Mr. Canning was of a different nature and temperament.   A genius, with the daring and some of the waywardness of genius, impulsive and trusting to his power of moving the public mind, he hoped to mould coming events at his pleasure, and to work out in his own way, and at his own time, the perplexing problem which disturbed thinking minds, — how best to fit old institutions to new things.   Although Peel agreed more generally with Mr. Canning than with Lord Eldon, still he agreed throughout his life, taken as a whole, more with the Tory party than with the Whigs.   An union with Mr. Canning, under the circumstances, would seem virtually an union with the Whigs.   He therefore did right to remain in the ranks of that party with which he had the most general agreement.

The union of Mr. Canning with the Whigs, in which nothing discreditable to either party can be found, except by an imputation of motives founded on an insight into a futurity which never arrived, necessarily threw the Tory party into opposition.

Towards the close of the session Mr. Peel appeared for the first time as an opposition leader. He was accused of indirect dealing, and Mr. Canning is supposed to have made a pass at him, with a pointed observation, which, expressing his preference of an open foe, is thought to have accused the other of fighting unfairly under cover. Mr. Dawson, the brother-in-law of Mr. Peel, had assailed Mr. Canning in no measured terms. Mr. Peel in the mean time had spoken words of amity, and held out something like a flag of truce. In the heat of party spirit, he was charged, therefore, with having prompted attacks which he feared to make in person. There was not the slightest foundation for this degrading suspicion. It was not in the least in the character of either opponent to act the part which the charge assigns to them. Each took his own line.

On the death of Mr. Canning, Lord Goderich was placed at the head of the ministry; which, in a few months, however, fell to pieces through its own dissensions. George IV. then sent for the Duke of Wellington, and directed him to form an administration of which his Grace should be the head. Between Mr. Huskisson and the Duke of Wellington something of the same feeling seems to have existed which unfortunately separated Mr. Canning and his

Grace, between whom a feeling existed, not exactly of hostility — and jealousy would be an equally inappropriate term to describe it,— but of separation. They were not well suited to, and repelled each other. It was an old feeling dating from the past times of the Spanish contest. The duke did not think highly of Mr. Canning's administrative talents, and attributed to mismanagement on his part that a large Portuguese force had not been sent to reinforce the British army before the battle of Waterloo.

The most important measure which came under the consideration of Parliament in the first year of the duration of this ministry, was a motion for the repeal of the Corporation and Test Acts. It was a memorable day, the first triumph for many years of the cause of Religious Liberty. The House was crowded, the gallery and its approaches full. Many dissenters were present calmly enjoying the scent of their coming victory. Slight as the grievance was in practice, it was still real; and to the feelings of the dissenters, acute. It must certainly be esteemed a heavy grievance to be placed by reason of the profession of a faith which we revere, in a position of inferiority, and to be driven to obtain the full rights of citizenship, as it were, by permission and connivance. Yet it was difficult out of the materials to draw the full picture of a sufferer for conscience. It would have taxed the imagination of a Sterne to paint a harrowing picture of a captive, if captives walked in and out of their prisons at pleasure. Lord John Russell had to contend with this difficulty. He spoke from a full mind.   He was earnest but not impassioned.   His speech, eloquent in parts, and in parts keen with epigrammatic point, rich in historical lore and constitutional doctrine, still wanted warmth. The fault, however, was not in the speaker. Mr. Secretary Huskisson spoke of his fears concerning the Catholic question from the success of this measure; but he made little impression.   Mr. Secretary Peel spoke fluently and elegantly, with some animation of manner; but it was not one of his best days.   His language was better than his argument.   The exhortation " *quieta non movere*," on which his speech in some degree turned, a wise maxim in its proper application, comes too late when the row has begun.   It is a sort of appeal which the man in possession likes best.   Here again the fault was in the subject. Who can be much alarmed at the removal of a wooden sentinel? or tremble at the entrance of one who is never shut out? A different line of argument from that which he adopted had been urged upon Mr. Peel by his friend Dr. Lloyd, the then Bishop of Oxford. Their correspondence on this subject is curious. It is contained in the posthumous memoirs of the late minister. It confirms, by the observations which Mr. Peel makes concerning the arguments fit to be addressed to a popular assembly, and the danger of advancing refutable doctrines, those observations which I have previously made upon the habit of his mind, and the formation of his opinions. The bishop observes that Mr. Peel had pitched his argument too low for his Oxford friends; they were dissatisfied that the claims of the Church to ascendancy were not placed higher. Might you not say when you next have an opportunity, that an established Church with equality of civil privilege, could not subsist? Mr. Peel, *more antiquo*, looking round the whole question, and viewing it from the station of the opponent also, replies, "Would they not cast up to me Scotland, or Ireland, even as between Protestants, — or France?" The bishop, though an able and acute man, had reasoned generally from the pulpit, and had not been exposed, like his pupil, to the fore-and-aft raking, and to the cross fire of debate. The thought, therefore, was not so constantly before him, "quæstio, quæ veniant diversâ parte sagittæ?"

When the Duke of Wellington was desired by the

King to form a strong administration, of which his
Grace should be the head, that commission was accompanied by a declaration that the King objected to no
person except Earl Grey, and a desire was expressed
at the same time by the King to retain in his service
certain named members of the Whig party. It was
plain, therefore, that no reactionary policy was intended. It was not to be expected that Earl Grey
would sit in a Tory cabinet, still less that he would
sit in any cabinet unless as its chief. This pointed
exception, therefore, whilst it disclosed that the King
could act upon an old resentment, displayed also that
he wanted that wisdom in a sovereign, of which a
prudent and becoming reserve is the sign. The
union of the whole Tory party with the Whigs, or
with any considerable section of them, was at that
time neither to be looked for nor approved. The
differences between them were then too great to render it probable that the government of the country
could be harmoniously conducted by such a coalition.
A like coalition was desired and suggested by William
IV. at a later day, for which also no justification
could have been found. But no objection could justly
be raised to the union which took place between the
friends of Mr. Canning and the Tory party under the
lead of the Duke of Wellington. Notwithstanding a

temporary division, all were still component parts of one great party. Mr. Canning had not abandoned the Tory party, nor had he abjured their principles. On the contrary, he had proclaimed his continued adherence to the principles which he had always maintained. No act of any kind had been done by him, or by his ministry, to place any gulph between the friends of Mr. Canning and the Tories. Personal resentment or jealousies ought not to divide those who can unite for the public service, and whose union, in a time of trouble, is desired by their sovereign. Oblivion of private feelings, which is the highest duty of a constitutional sovereign, a duty performed beyond all precedent by her present Majesty, should inspire corresponding sacrifices. Yet so apt is party spirit, in its appreciation of public character, to forget the obligations of a higher allegiance, that the personal friends of Mr. Canning were taunted with indifference to his memory, because they had not made his resentments posthumous, nor declined from the strained indulgence of feeling an union which was judged for the advantage of the public service by those, at least, who preferred the union of the Tory party to its dismemberment.

The future policy of the cabinet was to be presumed from the circumstances under which it was formed,

M

from the King's own expressed desire for a strong administration, formed upon a wide basis, from the members whom it included, as well as from the non-inclusion of one principal member of the former Tory cabinet, who had not been invited to aid its counsels.   It furnished, therefore, in itself, a sufficient assurance, not only that no retrograde policy was to be adopted, but that a policy of steady and gradual amelioration was to mark its course.   In this sense Mr. Huskisson said, when addressing his constituents at Liverpool, that he had received guarantees that the policy of the ministry which he had joined, would be such as he could consistently support.   The phrase "guarantees" was unfortunate, for it was ambiguous; and party spirit never receives an ambiguous phrase in the mildest sense.   Lord Eldon caught at the word, and interrogated the Duke of Wellington thereupon.   He, with the nice sense of honour of a soldier, fired at the very notion of any pledge being deemed requisite from him; and whilst he correctly expressed the meaning which, he said, Mr. Huskisson probably intended his words to bear, he spoke with lofty contempt of any other species of warranty.   Yet a little reflection would have sufficed to show, that even an express warranty of future policy, whilst it may be an imprudent and unstatesmanlike course, is, apart from motive, dishonourable in itself to neither party in a coalition.   There can be no dishonour in giving in words, or in asking to receive in words, that very assurance which conduct, under certain circumstances, conveys; unless, indeed, it were taken from distrust. Such an assurance would be ordinarily required, for the satisfaction of others, and might be required in order to dissipate public distrust, not of the giver, but of the receiver of the pledge.   It might also be required in order to avoid future misconception as to the regulating principles of an union.   With this view the late Sir Robert Peel, when he first made overtures to Lord Stanley and to Sir James Graham, did not forbear from offering to communicate the proposed policy of the cabinet, which he was inviting them to join.   A monarch who is asked for explanation by a friendly power, does not deem himself thereby dishonoured, and the honour of kings is as sacred a thing as that of soldiers.

This speech of the Duke of Wellington led to an explanation from Mr. Huskisson.   He expressed his meaning to have been that to which the very nature of the connection pointed.   He was confirmed in that statement by a bystander who had heard his speech, and understood it in the sense in which Mr. Huskisson explained his language.   This gentleman, the Rev. Mr. Shepherd, an Unitarian minister, a staunch

Whig, and a political opponent of Mr. Canning, had
those reasons for silence which would be likely to
operate on a low mind; but, being a man of high
honour and character, notorious for his piety, truth,
and virtue, he spoke as an honest man, in the cause
of charity and justice, and received his reward from
men in cold looks, suppressed resentment, or luke-
warm acknowledgments.   Calumny was loth to drop
its prey.   It was insinuated in some quarters, and
charged in others, that the explanation was a retrac-
tation.   From this sad beginning little was to be
augured but evil.   Another and a more fatal difference soon arose.   It was confined to two members
of the cabinet, the Duke of Wellington and Mr.
Huskisson.   The cause of the quarrel was slight;
the matter admitted of easy accommodation, but
neither would make concession, and from these
private feelings a rupture ensued, which severed
from the Tory party for ever, not merely the
seceding members of the cabinet, men, however,
whom no one, in the hour of calm reflection, would
lightly give up, but a considerable and influential section also of supporters out of doors.   Thus the desire
of the King for a strong ministry was thwarted and
unfulfilled.

A bill was before the House of Commons for extending the limits of a corrupt borough, East Retford, so as to include the adjoining hundreds. A bill was also before the House of Lords for disfranchising another corrupt borough, Penrhyn. Although the corruption of this latter place was notorious, the proof of it was slight, and the House of Lords was not satisfied with the proof. Their reluctance to disfranchise on suspicion, or slight proof, suited their judicial habits; and I desire not to be understood as arraigning their conduct. A strange sort of compromise had been entered into, to this effect, that if there were two boroughs to be disfranchised, the forfeited franchises should be so re-arranged that one should fall to the manufacturing or commercial, and the other to the agricultural interest. Yet the disproportion of representatives was then considerable in favour of the agricultural interest; and the non-representation of large towns was the blot on our representative system which most needed removal. Of old the constitution would have supplied, in the simple working of its true principles, the means of correcting such scandalous anomalies; but corrupt practice had made men so oblivious of first principles, that an ancient and salutary practice was treated in debate as a revolutionary innovation. Some pledge seems to have been given by Mr. Huskisson, that if one borough only was to be disfranchised, the forfeited franchise should be given to some large and unrepresented town. When it became probable that one borough only would be disfranchised, Mr. Huskisson was called upon in the House of Commons for the redemption of his pledge. He considered himself bound in honour, therefore, to vote against the ministerial measure. He had, however, previously agreed, in the cabinet, to the measure which was then under consideration, and it appears that he had supported and carried that measure in the cabinet, against the opinions of the Duke of Wellington and Mr. Peel, who were disposed to transfer that franchise to Birmingham. This, however, was done by Mr. Huskisson in the belief that both boroughs would be disfranchised; and to fulfil his promise, which rested on that contingency. In the debate which ensued in the House of Commons, on the East Retford Disfranchisement Bill, Mr. Huskisson was pointedly addressed, and required to redeem his pledge. He voted, in consequence, against the ministerial measure. The grave fault of his proceeding lay in his want of openness. It was due to his colleagues in that House, especially to Mr. Peel, the leader of it, to make his intention known. There was time for such communication, and it might have led to further consideration, and to some change of plan.   Still it was but a hasty, unadvised proceeding, indicating no treachery, a single act, the act of a goaded man, and as such entitled to indulgent consideration.   Mr. Peel viewed it in that light, and though, with his accustomed truthfulness, he admitted that he should have met Mr. Huskisson with some changed feeling in consequence, with " feelings slightly changed," yet still he admitted that he regarded it as an act of no important character or consequence, neither requiring nor justifying resignation.   Mr. Huskisson wrote that night, on reaching home, a letter to the Duke of Wellington, which, though capable of being understood in a different sense, was so expressed that any reader, unacquainted with its latent meaning, would have read it as a letter of resignation.   The Duke of Wellington so understood it, and was prepared to act upon it, in that sense.   He communicated, in his reply to Mr. Huskisson, his regret at the step, and at the cause which had led to it.   Upon this, Mr. Huskisson explained the sense which he intended his letter to bear, viz., that it was not an actual resignation, but a letter of offered resignation and acquiescence, should his Grace consider that step desirable.   The Duke refused to receive that explanation.

It was not fairly imputable to Mr. Huskisson that he had meant one thing, and then had falsely denied that meaning; it was simply a dispute between the writer and the receiver of a letter, as to the writer's real meaning. In courtesy, and according to common understanding in an ordinary case, the writer's explanation is admitted. He is commonly the best exponent of his own meaning. Had that course been adopted, the matter might have been allowed to drop. The Duke of Wellington, however, would not receive the writer's own explanation; he required, though not in express terms, that the letter should be withdrawn. He would have been entitled so to insist had the literal been the intended sense; but Mr. Huskisson could scarcely have consented to that step, without adopting the interpretation which he had already denied. A withdrawal under protest would have served no purpose of amity. The quarrel, therefore, ended, as quarrels commonly do, by involving all the parties to it in some fault. There was a precedent exasperation, and the minds of both these eminent men were in a state unfavourable to a peaceful accommodation of even a trifling matter. This great shock to the strength of the Tory party, though the matter seemed to turn on a mere punctilio, had a deeper foundation.   The old wound broke open at the slightest touch.

Mr. Huskisson, smarting under the consciousness of defeat, provoked by the Duke's sternness, and made unwise by anger, brought this painful subject under the consideration of the House of Commons, in the shape of a ministerial explanation. He charged the Duke with arbitrary conduct, and the cabinet by implication, and the Duke in express terms, with having sacrificed him to the resentments of the ultra Tories. This last charge would not have been preferred in a calmer hour. The Duke of Wellington was certainly the last man to whom any one would have presumed to dictate. To a charge that such a man had submitted to a disgraceful dictation, Mr. Peel had no difficulty in replying. He said, diminishing himself before his chief, that he himself would not consent to sit one hour in any cabinet capable of entertaining such a proposition; to the other part of the charge he made a less successful answer. The accusation was true in one sense, but it was true in one sense only. If it meant that in this instance the Duke had put an arbitrary construction on the terms of a letter, and had refused to the writer the ordinary courtesy of explaining his own meaning, it would have been

a charge difficult to refute.   If it meant to insinuate
also that his Grace sought to relieve himself from
the presence in the cabinet of an obnoxious colleague, it would have borne an air of probability,
though unfounded in fact.   If more were meant, if
it meant to impute to the Duke principles, and
general conduct, either in that cabinet, or in his
preceding ministerial life, inconsistent with the
relations of cabinet ministers to each other, to the
public, and to the Crown, it was untrue, and one
which Mr. Huskisson's own conduct refuted.   Mr.
Peel's answer, as to the treatment of the letter,
justified the Duke upon its literal construction;
but this was not the point in issue, since the
contest was whether the Duke was justified in
refusing to receive the writer's explanation of his
own meaning.   The same words admit of different
meanings according to the point of view from which
they are regarded.   Many disputes, which have dis-
tracted mankind, turn upon this, whether the letter
is to control the sense, or the sense the letter; the
sense itself being the subject of dispute.   The legal
maxim quaintly says, " Qui hæret in literâ, bæret in
cortice," and a defence which stuck to the letter
alone, answered this part of the case imperfectly.
The victory remained with the cabinet, but it was a

damaging victory. Many of the public thought that the party had been either too lightly admitted into, or too lightly suffered to depart from, the cabinet. Those who wished the Tory party to rest on its true and broader foundations grieved at a separation which threw it back too much upon the support of a powerful minority, whilst party spirit exulted in a manifestation of an unbending will, which, though displayed but in a single instance, and then under the influence of irritation, was assumed to be constant in its operations. It was now more easy than before to persuade the unthinking that the Duke presided dictatorially over the deliberations of his cabinet, treating the able, upright, and honourable men of whom it consisted as his mere lieutenants.

The speech of Mr. Peel, in this debate, is remarkable for one declaration which foreshadowed his future policy, and marked him as no longer the follower in the wake of other men. He declared that he was determined to follow neither Lord Liverpool's policy, nor the policy of Mr. Canning, nor that of any other man, but to give to each subject, as it arose, his best attention; and to his sovereign the best advice in his power. This is the true exposition of the duty of a minister to his sove-

reign. The interests of a whole people are not to
be sacrificed to a minister's character for consistency. Let these selfish counsels be clothed in
words, and what minister would dare to utter them?
"Sire, this course is for your interest, but I cannot
advise it, for it is against my own!" Resignation
of his office may be the duty of a minister who sees
the necessity of a change which he has resisted, but
this will be a merit or a fault according to motive
and to circumstances. The above declaration, that
he would be a follower of no man's policy, does not
support an opinion which a modern historian, Sir
Archibald Alison, has advanced, who, adopting as
"undoubted truth" a "felicitous expression" of Mr.
Disraeli, calls the mind of the deceased statesman
"a huge appropriation clause." No one can dispute
the claims of Mr. Disraeli, himself, to originality or
to genius, nor will any man who can appreciate wit
and humour, deny that he possesses both. The
clever epigrammatic point of the saying above
quoted, and its approximation to a truth, ensured its
success as a witticism. These light missiles are
allowed in party warfare. They serve their purpose
if they raise a laugh. No one thinks, therefore, of
putting such light coins to the test of a severe assay.
They are counters which pass for the true coin, an

inconvertible currency, not payable at the bank of wit, whose standard is truth. They serve the end, nevertheless, for which they issue, and no one stops to try if the bright surface is a wash. But when these counters are stamped as genuine coin, at the mint of the historic muse, when these false brilliants are stitched into Clios' dark robe, we are driven, in the interests of truth, to analyse a *bon môt*, and to ask if it can pass as history. What then was meant by the taunt, that the mind of the statesman was a " huge appropriation clause ? " The term was applied in an ill sense, as one of disparagement. By the appropriation clause, which is here referred to, it was proposed to apply a part of the property of the Irish Church to secular purposes, that is, to work a transfer of property, with an alteration of its uses. Call this as you will, spoliation, or wise application, it implies a loss to one and a gain to another, of the same property. In the evil sense, it means spoliation, or wrongful deprival, appropriation, or " conveyance " in the sense of a filch. In either sense, what analogy does it bear to the work of a mind which elaborates its own and foreign materials into new and useful products? Had the mind of Mr. Peel been compared to a huge elaboratory, the analogy would have been more correct, and the Alchemist might have furnished a witty mind with some apt quotations.

He produced, says Sir Archibald Alison, no *idée mère*. The phrase, in whatever sense we understand it, whether of fecundity or originality, absolute or relative, or of both combined, is not happily applied to any statesman. Such terms as *langue mère*, an underived language, as mother tongue or native tongue, such expressions as mother wit, mother church, or mother earth, are common metaphors, the sense of which is well defined. But the thoughts of the mind may be neither underived, nor native, may be exotics, not indigenes, and yet be original. They are not powers, but products, and may be the signs of original adaptive power. They may have no priority, they may even, through unfortunate incidence, prove barren, and still be original. On the other hand, though original, they may be but the first starved weeds of the first black soil. In the nineteenth century, when a parallel passage may be found for almost every fine or true thought, an *idée mère*, in the sense of a native, underived, unprecedented thought, raises a presumption against itself, that it is one of the vapours of the mind, an impregnation by the winds, a fume of vanity.

If we understand the phrase in the sense of a

fruitful thought, a thought-bearing fruit, every debate on a budget refutes it.   Originality cannot always be denied, even to a quoter.   To deny originality to every adapter, to every translator, and to every transmuter, would be a sign of a bad critic.   We judge men by their works, not by their occupations.   What true critic would deny to an adapter, like Le Sage, the merit of originality?   I take, for the purpose of my argument, the Spanish side of the controversy as to the origin of Gil Blas; an opinion with which I should not have dared to cite the concurrence of my own, had it not had the confirmation of the authority of Lord Macaulay, to whose attention I had the honour, long ago, of bringing this interesting dispute, and whose inimitable hand, I once hoped, would treat a subject which he was, beyond most men, competent to discuss, adorn, and adjudge.   The Fox and the Silent Woman, show an author almost as original and great in his applications and transmutations as in his pure inventions.

> " For what originally others writ,
>   May be so well disguised and so improved
>   That with some justice it may pass for yours."

The power of thus elaborating new and great products from old materials, call it what you will, is original: the spider's thread in the air, and the lobster's shell in the dish have suggested great works to great men.   Conjoin the habit of observation with the power of imitation and adaptation, and call it what you will, call it but industry, still there is an original, mighty, motive power.   By originality then, when it is wholly denied to a mind like that of the late minister, must be meant originality in some too restrictive sense of the word.   The poet has said, that the bee and the spider feed on the same nectaries. The way then to judge the claims to originality of such men as Peel, is to judge them by that which they extract; by their exports, not by their imports. What effect has a man produced as a statesman and an orator ?   If he have produced a great and a lasting impression, be sure that he was original.   No mere copyist ever made any lasting impression. One who though not an orator of the first class, is yet skilled and successful in debate, quick and apt in retort, ready in defence, persuasive, swaying long the minds of men, must necessarily have within him original power.   No study, no imitation, no warehousing of other men's thoughts, can make a great advocate, and such the great member of parliament is. The controversy whether men of this second class of orators are original and orators at all, is one of the same nature as that which has so long raged " whether

Pope was a poet?" The excluding line must be arbitrarily and too sharply drawn which shuts out original but inferior power. If a dispute be kept up for a century even amongst poets themselves whether a man were a poet or not, the very continuance of the controversy proves that he was a poet, in some sense, at least. Peel was in the senate, an orator of that order of which Scarlett was one at the bar. First in the second class of orators; but amongst winning advocates, inferior to none.

Sir Edward Lytton Bulwer, in his "England and the English," has made a more lifelike picture, and when it is remembered that this last and favourable picture of the powers of the late minister is from the hand of a man of genius, a close observer and powerful delineator of character, an eye-witness of that which he described, and a political adversary to boot, it must be conceded that it has no common claim to our attention. He finishes his description with an observation, which, whilst it denies to Peel the character of a great man, concedes to him the original power of becoming one, since the failure is declared to spring from the choice of a wrong side. Sir E. L. Bulwer has also asserted in this work, that Sir Robert Peel was in principle a democrat, and that he had undergone a life of suppression. I venture,

N

nevertheless, to think my own description the true one. It is fact against theory, and is founded on the evidence of my own ears. The opposite conclusion supposes that a man cannot be both Tory and democrat, Tory in principle and democrat in inclination; but surely this is possible, and not more uncommon than the converse union of patrician in feeling and democrat in opinion, of which some remarkable men of our own times have afforded pregnant proofs. Sir Edward L. Bulwer writes thus: —

"And in truth Sir Robert Peel is a remarkable man, confessedly a puissance in himself, confessedly the leading member of the representatives, yes, even of your reformed assembly; he is worth our stopping in our progress for a moment, in order to criticise his merits.

"It is a current mistake in the provinces to suppose that Sir Robert Peel is rather sensible than eloquent. If to persuade, to bias, to soothe, to command the feelings, the taste, the opinions of an audience often diametrically opposed to his views, if this be eloquence, which I, a plain man, take it to be, then Sir Robert Peel is among the most eloquent of men."

The whole passage is too long for quotation here. The author, in language which I am sorry that I can neither lay before my readers nor imitate, proceeds to describe the manner of the orator whom he terms a great actor, the effect of manner and of action, the material powers of oratory, not passing by unnoticed the more solid qualities of the statesman and speaker, he contrasts the opinions and arguments of the man with his votes, and concludes that chance had cast him into one party, whilst nature had moulded him for another; a conclusion from which I have already expressed my dissent.

The secession of Mr. Canning's friends certainly weakened the administration of the Duke of Wellington. The people, jealous at all times of military power, beheld with undisguised repugnance a soldier at the head of the civil government. It is vain to argue with feelings. They had their root in a repugnance which was based on an attachment to ancient usages; and although there is no ground for this jealousy, or fear of a soldier statesman in modern times, yet its existence had no alliance with illiberal feelings. The presence of the friends of Mr. Canning in the cabinet tended to calm this feeling. This jealous feeling was carefully exasperated by all the irritants which party spirit at its height is dextrous in applying. The modern warfare of parties, although it prohibits the use of many disgraceful

modes of annoyance, which formerly prevailed, still
affords too great a licence for the indulgence of evil
passions.   To hint a fault and hesitate dislike, to
impute motives by disclaiming the imputation of
them, to foment prejudices, to draw the eyes from
the merits to the faulty side of an opponent, to
attribute to wanton choice that which is often but a
sad necessity, of a selection amongst evils alone, to
forebode evil and disparage men or institutions;
these and similar arts of lowering a political opponent, each party, in turn, is apt to practise and
impute.   Arts, nevertheless, which, though immoral
in themselves and apparently dangerous, like the
grosser corruptions of popular institutions, are still
proved, as these latter have been proved, by experience, to detract but little from the practical
advantages of a mode of government which, growing
up by slow degrees, and submitting to the changes
of time, has produced more real freedom and sub-
stantial prosperity than the world has yet witnessed
under any other form of government.   A party which
has been long in the ascendant, gets encrusted with
the conceit and false wisdom which official life is apt
to cause.   It is too apt to undervalue all public
opinion that is not declared in its own favour, and to
regard discontent with its measures as ignorance or

malignity.   The Tory party at this time had been in
the ascendant for sixty years or upwards.   It had
acquired a large share of the bad habit of office, of
looking much to practice and precedent, and little to
principles.   In short it had ruled too long.

The last years of its ascendancy had now arrived,
and its end was not peaceful.   It was an uneasy,
unprosperous time.   Much distress and much discontent prevailed, notwithstanding that the condition
of the people was, on the whole, improving.   But
though this was an unprosperous, it was, nevertheless,
not a bad administration.   Its administrative reforms
were generally and cordially approved.   Peace, economy, and retrenchment, with fiscal, commercial and
other administrative reforms, were merits, which in
calmer times would have made the fortune of a
ministry.   The courage and public spirit which it
displayed in dealing, however tardily, with the
Catholic question, won the admiration of many; and
though it was highly unpopular at its close, it suffered
then rather the penalty of past errors of the party,
than a punishment which any faults of its own commission had deserved.   It is not necessary that I
should mention in detail the measures of this administration, upon one of which I have already observed.
During its existence, Mr. Peel conducted the business

of the government in the House of Commons with
merit and success.   He had little assistance in debate,
and the superiority in oratory was, at that time,
greatly on the side of the opposition.   In his conduct,
however, of the Catholic Relief Bill through the
House of Commons, he displayed, as an orator and
statesman, qualities of the highest order.   Scarcely
before had a minister stood in so painful a position.
A frank acknowledgment of error always wins favour,
but he had not even that support, for he adhered to
his old opinions, and had to urge merely that the
storm had overtaken the vessel of the state, and that
they must put about the storm which had been long
menacing in the horizon.   And yet amidst all these
grounds for discomfiture, all these self-disparaging
admissions, he prevailed, and gained by that fall, for
it was finally a fall, even a higher reputation.   He
won the calm and lasting approval of all conscientious
and wise men, who, expecting no infallibility, and
indeed rarely any superior intelligence in public men,
delight to find in them an absence of all self-seeking,
and a patriotic superiority to mere party obligations.
The moral qualities which he displayed in this painful struggle were of the highest order.   It is curious
and instructive to trace his internal struggles, the
conflict between a false and a true allegiance, and

the slow final triumph of the higher duty. He maintained throughout, midst many provocations, taunts
the most bitter, and invective the most fierce, a full
and perfect command over a temper naturally quick
and impatient of opposition; he showed an astonishing dexterity in meeting and answering objections, and
an eloquence suited to the high occasion on which it
was exercised. Yet here, as in other passages of his
life, when his feelings were most roused, at a time
when it might have been expected that he would
pour forth his whole soul in the original language of
passionate feeling, he still clothed his own thoughts
in the language of other men. He described the
agony of his mind in a fine passage from Dryden, as,
at a later time, in his scornful defiance of Mr. Cobbett, he concluded with a grand and animated passage
from Cowley. How was this? Was it poverty of
thought, was it the expression of an unreal feeling?
Those who knew the man slightly and superficially
might have said so. But it was not so. We find a
religious man, one who is imbued with the truths,
and familiar with the language of scripture, thinking and speaking in the words of Holy Writ. How
finely has Scott manifested this habit of the old
covenanters. Peel was gifted with a memory rarely
equalled, powerful in itself, and exercised with all the

skill of training from his earliest infancy. He was a great reader, and familiar with our finest writers. His thoughts ran in the grooves of the minds of the authors whom he loved, and he fell naturally into quotation, not from poverty of thought, not from an inability to express the same thought, but from the humility derived from a correct estimate and a fine taste. He had not a spring of poetry in his own mind. He was not the poet orator. He wanted the inventive power, the exquisite feeling, the imagery, and the diction of the poet, but he wanted not the· feeling of intense relish of high thoughts, and living words, without which no poetry can be enjoyed, and that very feeling led him to this habit of quotation. His quotations were generally most happy. He was not a stoic, far from it, his feelings were ever most acute. He had no sevenfold fence of overlaying pride to save him from the smart of the sharp arrows; he lived on the sifted praise of men, with a pardon-able vanity, probably unthought of by himself, "omnium quæ dixerat, fecerat que, arte quâdam osten-tator;" he varnished his deeds as men, says Lord Bacon, varnish ceilings to make them shine as well as last. No man was more abstinent from cause of offence, and yet he entered consciously and deliber-ately upon a course which, as he well knew, would by many be deemed one of unpardonable error, exposing him to those imputations from which he most shrank, and causing in the mind of a beloved and revered parent a sorrow which he the more dreaded to inflict, as he knew that it would be, as it was, gentle and uncomplaining. Yet he wished in some manner to avoid this cup of bitterness. Was there no way left of escaping from this pillory? Could he not resign? Might he not support the bill as a private member of the House? Might he not thus do the cause more service? These were not palterings with duty; they were the wary approaches to its highest duty, of a cautious and circumspect mind. Not plunging with the spirit of a self-immolating votary, afraid to think, impelled, and rushing with a mad delight upon ruin; his was the calm, steady, and deliberate advance to self-sacrifice of the trained soldier of duty.

The principal measures of this ministry during its short tenure of office were three,— the repeal of the Corporation and Test Acts, the Catholic Relief Bill, and the bill for the establishment of the metropolitan police. The conduct of the first was unskilful. The ministers might have foreseen the result, and have gained earlier that support which they obtained after undergoing defeat. They confirmed by their oppo-

sition to this measure the distrust or hostility of the
dissenters, and they gained for themselves, by their
concession, the distrust or hostility of many of their
own party. Their yielding was a proper and constitutional submission to the sense of the people,
expressed by their representatives in the House of
Commons, and was an atonement for the first error
of judgment. In the conduct of the Catholic Relief
Bill, the ministry evinced more confidence in themselves and in their cause, and a higher wisdom.
Their conduct has been stigmatised as a concession
to violence. In the same sense many supporters of
the Reform Bill might be stigmatised. Amongst the
supporters of the latter measure must be reckoned
many who, in their inner mind, would have desired
no reform at all, or would have desired a measure
proportioned to the existing defects in the representative system. Concessions of this nature to the
demands of an excited people, whether of a whole
empire or of a part, will be judged from the nature
of the demand, and the motives of those who yield to
it. The subject is finely treated by Macaulay, in his
speech on the first Reform Bill. The attempt to
protect a religious establishment by a fence of restrictive laws has been abandoned, and I trust for
ever, in these lands. But let not persons delude

themselves with the notion that we have as yet advanced far in a course of religious freedom.

One servitude will succeed to another, so long as men assume the power to tolerate, and so long as opinion is deemed a crime. The old tyranny is always reviving. A narrow spirit shying at every variety of teaching and observance; rigid observances imposed by statutes, as though a statutory religious deportment were worth a straw; restraints which are not even equal in their pressure, are melancholy proofs that men with the name of liberty ever in their mouths are daily violating its spirit in the most tender points of conscience.

Ere I dismiss this subject, it may be important to trace the course of the late statesman in this direction. He fell into the beaten track from his earliest childhood. The laws which made church membership a condition of civil office, had become, as it is the nature of such laws to become, so incorporated as it were in the minds of men with the things which they were but meant to guard, that it seemed almost a sin against religion, and a schismatic severance from the Church, to attempt to remove them. As the huge parasites of an eastern jungle, insinuating themselves, in their spiral involution, into the very body of the tree, so these prejudices grow into the

mind. In process of time doubts arose; it was the
dawn of a higher wisdom. In this, as in all other
things, he advanced gradually; but it is a course on
which, if a man once enters, the path opens as he
advances. He began by opposing the admission into
the House of Commons of all dissenters from the
Church, and he ended by voting for the admission of
the Jews. Let us hear his own explanation. He
insisted still that it was the duty of a Christian legislature to promote Christian truth. That the spirit of
Christian truth ought to preside over their deliberations. That differences in religion were vital things,
and that they could not, with due regard to the welfare
of a state, be viewed as things indifferent in themselves to the state's wellbeing: that the difference
between the Jew and the Christian was vital. But
here the old mind halted: the new spirit then
spoke. They had no mission, no authority, to punish
religious error. It was not by persecution that
religious truth could or ought to be inculcated: inequality of civil privilege was inferiority, a brand
upon opinions; that it was not the duty nor within
the province of man to fix those badges. God will
visit for Himself the offences against His truth,
"Vengeance is mine, says the Lord:" and thus at
length he came round to the light, under a pro-

founder sense of religious duty. Yet the difference is less than it seems, at first sight, to be, between his opposition to the Catholic Relief Bill and his support of the bill for the relief of the Jews; for in the former instance, he had not grounded himself on any obligation to repress religious error by penal laws. He had treated the question as one simply of civil expediency.

That he ended thus, was a certain consequence of his first advance, for, as I have said, he was an habitual searcher into the grounds of his opinions; and though a slow convert to a new opinion, yet when he was convinced he was won.

The last measure of the three, which I have named as the principal measure of this ministry, was for a time highly unpopular. It was costly, and it was new. The friends of order grumbled at it for these reasons only. The friends of disorder feared and hated it for reasons which cause it to be regarded still as one of the most salutary of many unpretending administrative reforms which we owe to the same hand.

In the June of 1830 died George IV. Sir Robert Peel moved in the House of Commons an address of condolence and congratulation to the new monarch. These complimentary harangues are scarcely the subject of criticism. I find, however, nothing stated of George IV. that is untrue, or much exaggerated; but the bright side of his character is alone presented. In epitaphs, or similar characters of the dead, the " primal sympathy," the soothing thoughts that spring out of human suffering, move us to embalm their memories, as bodies are embalmed, by burying their offal, and by the application of sweet odours. So that the cynical remark of one who, reading the tombstones in a churchyard, asked where our bad men lay buried, spoke but a slight acquaintance with the sweetness of charity.

The new king, having something of the frankness and generosity of the English sailor, with much good nature, became popular for a while, but as he had not talents to qualify him for rule, he was ill fitted for the times in which he reigned,—times which required a wise, moderate, and firm mind. The elections which ensued after he came to the throne, gave the Tory party, though with numbers much reduced, still a majority. If the ultra-Tory party could have conquered their resentments, the administration might have lasted somewhat longer. On consultation amongst themselves, this party, by a large proportional majority, determined on giving their help to the overthrow of the Duke's administra-

tion; a step which, though it may be arraigned for
want of political foresight, seems to me not fairly
censurable on any other ground; for, to further
progress they were conscientiously opposed, and had
lost confidence in the ministers as the resisters of
further changes in the constitution. They might
reasonably think that if a policy which they deemed
essentially a Whig policy was henceforth to prevail,
it should in fairness be entrusted to Whig ministers.

On the meeting of the new parliament, the
ministers being outvoted on the civil list, resigned,
and thus ended the long ascendancy of the old Tory
party. It is, of course, a matter of mere speculation
whether any line of policy, at this period, could
have averted their fall. The party had taken no
measures to increase its strength. After the death
of Mr. Pitt, for full fifteen years, it had been more
and more narrowing its basis. It not only made no
attempts to win the people to its side, but it seemed
bent upon abjuring their alliance. It took no
thought of the power, save when it winced under
the hostility, of the press. It had never attempted
properly to balance that power. There was the
same neglect in other ways. Young men naturally
incline to new things, and if no other impulse led
them to the side of change, they would be led there

by vanity. No matter how mere a parrot-repeater
of the thoughts of other men a young man be, if he
repeat on the popular side, he obtains, at once, a
certificate of merit; whilst old opinions in a young
mouth are received as the signs of a low or of an
inert intellect. The Whigs, with the activity of a
minority, looked out for and courted the young
mind, which ranged itself generally on their side.
The Tories, in short, had all the inertness and lazy
ease of an overgrown establishment, and their opponents all the spirit and energy of a rising sect.
The natural appetites for equality and for distinction
were often foolishly, if not rudely, balked. The
manufacturing and commercial leaders were suffered
long to remain in a position inferior to that of their
landed neighbours, — a folly which wounded their
feelings, and drove some reluctantly from the ranks
of a party to which they inclined. They were
rarely appointed justices of the peace, and seldom
served upon grand juries. The reasons assigned for
the exclusion were so futile that they exposed their
authors to the imputation either of folly or of in-
sincerity. After 1822, a better spirit began to
animate the counsels of the cabinet. New men and
new ideas were beginning to prevail; but it was too
late to set right much that had been done amiss.

An entire reversal of the faulty part of their policy was impossible, and, by its partial alteration, they seemed daily to be refuting themselves. The party, especially in the person of Mr. Canning, had declared war against every sort of amendment in the representation of the people, and could not, therefore, enter upon any course of gradual adaptation of the representation to the altered state of the country, without exposing themselves to damaging charges of inconsistency and sordid compliance. They stood, therefore, in a false position, from which they could only be extricated by that downfall which their own want of political sagacity, and the partial abandonment of the principles of their greatest leader had done much to precipitate. Still, to this great party much praise is due. The country advanced more during the sixty years of their power, than it had done during any century before. It is not just to say that the material prosperity and improved civilisation of the country was in no respect due to its government: that it had flourished in spite of a bad government. This was said in the depreciatory spirit of party. It is a saying that may be turned against every government; and which if it were true, would go a long way to prove that good or bad government is a matter of slight concern. The first

o

Sir Robert Peel, a sagacious and practical man, observed that no man understood, so well as Mr. Pitt, the commercial interests of the country; and that he knew that its greatness depended on its productive industry.   This rising power was certainly fostered by every exertion of that great minister, who showed a boldness and originality in his application of the principles of free trade, which even yet excite our astonishment and command our admiration.   The party exhibited throughout the long protracted struggle with Napoleon a noble courage and a truly English spirit.   It stood firm by the altar and the throne; and midst the horrors of the French Revolution, when license, rapine, and impiety, disguising themselves under specious names and forms, sought an entrance here, they did their best to expose the counterfeits and to protect this island from the contagion of false principles and evil example.

CHAP. V.

GENERAL POLICY AFTER REFORM ACT.

" The old order changeth, yielding place to new,
  And God fulfils himself in many ways,
  Lest one good custom should corrupt the world."

THE Whigs were in power again, after a long proscription.   The two preceding monarchs, unwisely,
with some forgetfulness of their dignity, as well as
of their duty, had identified their interests with
those of a party.   The differences between each
monarch and the Whigs assumed, on both sides, at
times, the nature, with the asperities of a personal
quarrel.   Their long banishment from office had
rendered the Whigs almost hopeless of entering in at
the gate.   When an unjust proscription, like that
under which they laboured, prevails long in a
country enjoying representative institutions, it be-

comes more and more difficult to work a compli-
cated state machine.   However much a party may
be bent upon embarrassing its opponents, it is naturally shy of embarrassing itself.   The prospect of
a return to office makes an opposition more provident, and more just.   The prospect of a return into
the ranks of an opposition, and to a sole dependancy
on the popular voice, makes a ministry more temperate in the use of its authority.   Strong lines
of demarcation, and the conversion of parties into
castes, give to a change of ministry something
óf the aspect of a state convulsion.   By many of
the Tories, the return of the Whigs to office, of
that party the name of which is associated with
the establishment of true constitutional government
in this country, was regarded as the first stage
of a revolution.   They had no better foundation
for their fears than faults which might, in prior
reigns, have been imputed to their own party, viz.
— that the party had been occasionally violent,
and factious, and included some members whose
loyalty was suspected by the government.   A minister
may be driven to rely on the turbulent, but he does
not prefer their alliance.   A constitution of a country,
like the laws of a people, cannot be understood

properly by a study of the text alone. All language is, in time, modified by the interpretations of custom to which it becomes subject. The prerogative of the crown, to choose its own ministers, still existed in terms, but two modern readings of the constitution, viz., that the king reigns and does not govern, and that a government must be conducted *by*, instead of through, a majority, in the sense of being supported by one, had brought this branch of the prerogative practically into abeyance. When an independent party existed in the House of Commons, this prerogative was a real thing, when it grew to be considered that the government must be conducted *by* parties, it fell into disuse. The Tories now adopted the new reading, and there was not found amongst them any who was willing to give a Whig ministry in a minority a fair trial.

Some colour appears to be given to the modern doctrine, in a passage of a private letter from Sir Robert Peel to Lord Hardinge, in which he says that he would not have continued minister one week by sufferance. This, it must be remembered, was a private letter, and we must not look for any calm and well-considered exposition of constitutional doctrine in such a document. It may have been a very proper sentiment, according to the sense in which he used the term "sufferance : "— if it were meant, for instance, in the sense of unworthy compliance. In any other sense, the sentiment would indicate pride rather than wisdom. When a country is broken into many parties, none may be able to maintain an absolute majority, and a government then must exist, if it exists at all, by sufferance.

Three years before this time Lord Grey seemed to stand separate and alone —

> "Like a Druid rock,
> Or like a spur of land that stands apart
> Cleft from the main and clang'd about with mews."

But now the old union was restored, and to him it fitly belonged to carry into effect the policy of a consistent life.

The reform question had latterly become a test of Whig orthodoxy. The long continuance of the Tories in office, and the large accumulation of borough influence, in the hands of some few great supporters of that party, had seemed so to weld office and it together, that many Whigs became Reformers from that cause alone. When the close boroughs were more equally divided, the popular voice had more of a casting vote. Many of the Tories were in favour of the representation of large towns. Others of that party, who had no private interest in its maintenance, looked with strong dislike on the influence which the nomination boroughs gave to a few large proprietors. When nine great men nominated sixty-three members to the House, the fate of the system was sealed; greediness bursts the bag: the Duke of Wellington spoke, in private, with a strong disapprobation of the selfishness and lust for influence in which this accumulation had originated. Sir Robert Peel hints his dislike of the same influence, in a letter to Lord Aberdeen, dated August 19th, 1847. "Times are changed," writes he, "since a prime minister, after ascertaining the sentiments of the Marquis of Hertford, and the Duke of Rutland, and the Earl of Lonsdale, could form a pretty good guess of the inclinations and public conduct of a whole party. I will venture to say that an exclusive confidential communication to the fourteen or fifteen to whom Lord —— refers, would have received very general dissent." "If, continues he, in another part of this remarkable letter, "I had tried to gain acquiescence, either by belabouring individuals, or by summoning the party generally, I should have received scarcely one promise of support. I should have had, on the part of the most moderate, a formal protest against the course I intended to pursue; to the most violent I should have given facilities for organised opposition. I should have appeared to be flying in the face of a whole party, and contumaciously disregarding their opinion and advice after I had professed to consult them, but (what is of infinitely more importance), *I should have failed in carrying the repeal of the Corn Laws.* Now, I was resolved not to fail; and if I had to fight the battle over again, I would fight it in the same way. Lord ——'s way was certain of defeat." Times were changed, indeed, and changed for the better. The time ought never to have been, when it was necessary for the minister of the Crown to make auricular confessions of his intentions to a few great proprietors of boroughs. However this influence may have smoothed over difficulties for a time, its fate shows that there is no safe walking out of the paths of the constitution.

Lord John Russell, a member of the ministry, though not of the cabinet, proposed on behalf of the cabinet, the first Reform Bill for the deliberation of the House of Commons. In a calm speech, the tone of which varied considerably from the nature of some of the arguments by which the measure was supported both in and out of the House, he exposed anew all the defects and startling anomalies in the composition of the Commons House of Parliament, declared that the House no longer possessed, nor could be restored to the possession of the confidence of the people, and contrasted its present state with its theory, and with his own views of the ancient practice of election. He then proceeded to explain the process of the proposed restoration or regeneration of the Commons House of Parliament. As views, so alarming to the minds of many, opened upon the vision of the doomed party, as they heard themselves devoted to what they deemed destruction, in a tone of calm exhortation to embrace reform, they might have been tempted to exclaim with Romeo:—

> "Thou cutt'st my head off with a golden axe,
> And smil'st upon the stroke that murders me."

I pass over the crimination and recrimination that ensued between the debaters militant as to the causes of the then prevailing excitement, for I have no desire to rake up the embers of old feuds. It was a struggle, the examination of which must be a subject of lasting interest to all thoughtful minds.

The Conservative aspect may be studied in the speeches which were delivered on that side, many of which, especially those in the House of Lords, were of the highest order of merit. The reformers' view may be studied also in many undying efforts of oratory and genius, which the great occasion brought forth. Never did the old parliament display higher powers, whether of eloquence, philosophy, or matured wisdom and experience, than those which it put forth in its dying song, and it is fair to observe that nothing so little resembling mere obedience to the dictates of an unbridled power was ever heard in a senate, as the thoughtful and highly-wrought arguments in favour of reform, which many speeches of the illustrious dead, as well as of the illustriöus living, unfold.

It is given to statesmen to see the present, and to review the past, but the future is hidden from them; their guesses at the future more often display the limits than the powers of the human mind. These glimpses through the dark curtain have nevertheless their value. The failure of prophecy abates our pride of intellect.

In his first speech on the first reform bill, Sir Robert Peel, roused by an allusion to some supposed change in the mind of Canning on the subject of reform, thus invoked the name, and sighed for the presence of Canning, " Oh! would to God that he were here."

"Tu que tuis armis, nos te poteremur Achille."

"Would to God that he were here to confound the sophisms and fallacies of reformers, and bring back the people by the charms of truth and eloquence."

After this tribute to the fame and memory of Canning, he quoted a fine passage from a speech of that great orator, which passage again is an expansion, though not an imitation of a thought of an old dramatist, so hard is it to hit on an *idée mère.*

> " Like one who has a watch of curious making,
> Thinking to be more cunning than the workman,
> Never gives over tampering with the wheels,
> 'Til either spring be weakened, balance bow'd,
> Or some wrong pin put in and so spoils all."

The Conservative view of all such questions. The hopeful mind of the sanguine improver, who is not content to let even well alone, wisely deeming change and progress the natural and appointed order of the world, may be read in another extract which follows from a mind of a rarer order. One who viewing some cankered boughs, and some cracked or discoloured fruit, thinks that he can improve on the apprentice hand of culture, and cuts boldly

amongst the ancient mossy boughs to bud afresh a
bearing tree; such is the type of the wise reformer.
Each habit, in its proper limits, is the sign of a wise
mind. Each presentation that of a truth, but neither
that of the whole truth. "We are challenged,"
said Macaulay, "to show that the constitution was
ever better than it is. Sir, we are legislators, not
antiquarians. The question with us is, not whether
the constitution was better formerly, but whether
we can make it better now. We talk of the wisdom
of our ancestors, and in one respect at least they
were wiser than we. They legislated for their own
times. They looked to the England which was
before them.". . . . "Unhappily while the natural
growth of society went on, the artificial polity continued unchanged. The ancient form of the representation remained, and precisely because the form
remained, the spirit departed. Then came that
pressure almost to bursting—the new wine in the
old bottles—the new people under the old institutions. It is now time for us to pay a decent,
a prudent, a manly reverence to our ancestors, not
by superstitiously adhering to what they did under
different circumstances, but by doing what they in
our own circumstances would have done." Fine,
but not pure truths, beautifully expressed, but also

needing to be wisely applied, and therein, alas, lies the difficulty.

The antiquarian part of the debate is not wanting in interest. The speech of Sir Robert Inglis on this subject should be read in conjunction with that of Macaulay, and with Lord John Russell's speeches on the introduction of the first and second reform bills respectively. The truth as to the original constitution of the electoral bodies and practice of election in boroughs seems to me to lie somewhere between these opposite opinions. The old borough franchise, when not otherwise defined or limited by express grant, was declared, in the free spirit of the common law of England, to be founded on a popular basis, and has been repeatedly declared by the House of Commons to be in inhabitant householders paying scot and lot. The modern plan of distributing the franchise in boroughs by reference to occupation and value has some disadvantages, of which not the least is its exclusion of a class which some of the old franchises admitted, the inmate or lodger, a class often more provident and better qualified for the franchise than many an householder.

Some limit undoubtedly must be drawn somewhere in every plan of representation, but whether a reformation of the old plan of incorporation might not have provided in many boroughs at once a popular and a more equal representation of the people, was a point which the public mind was then too impatient to consider. There is no sense in incapacitating a man because he is provident and defers his marriage and status of head of a family, or because he occupies but part of a house with its owner. Indeed the state of the law of elections produced distinctions between one occupation and another which turned on very technical grounds. The inclusion of large numbers destroys equality of representation, and affords no security for better legislation or for freedom. The exclusion of all below a certain line works also an unequal representation. The old system of incorporation produced, or at least was capable of producing, a more mixed and a more equal representation. The newly-created bodies have not been found free from that species of corruption which disgraced many of the old. Something is gained to the cause of progress and order when a valuable right, like the elective franchise, is to be gained by some merit of exertion and self-denial, and mere occupation alone furnishes an inferior test to that which some of the older franchises supplied.

Too much regard appears to have been paid in

the allotment of the franchise to the middle ranks of the people, an indefinite body, which may be contracted or widened at the pleasure of the thinker. No reason, in the abstract, can be given for the preference of one arbitrarily-chosen section of the people, over the sections below it, it rests on an unproved assumption of superior virtue or intelligence. The common law proceded on a different plan, and when there was a large population in boroughs, one too large for the convenient or safe exercise of the franchise, an incorporation of the borough obtained a reduction of numbers, founded on conditions as admission to freedom, birth, servitude, or the like, which drew no arbitrary distinctions between classes, and which even the humblest, as well as the more provident, might fulfil.

In course of time, corruption, from which the new body of electors is not free, grew into these institutions, and some were narrowed by corrupt or mistaken construction of their charters. In other places, population and trade decreased; so far the arguments of the reformers, as to the decay or corruption of boroughs, were well founded, and a restoring as well as a renovating hand was needed here. On the other hand, many boroughs never had had a popular basis, and the electors in them were always few,

Even in these, however, until it became of importance to obtain a separate interest in them, it is probable that representation, though limited as to the number of electors, was not simply virtual, but also, in some sense, actual, by reason of community of feeling, and that the electors commonly represented, in former times, the feelings of the people amongst whom they resided. Nothing, therefore, in the old order of things contradicted the argument of the reformers, that elections were once free and popular in spirit, even when not popular in form. But still this argument went but a small way towards a solution of the difficulty. The remark of Macaulay on this branch of the argument, that the House were legislators, not antiquarians, was rather sophistical than convincing, for the past might be one of the best instructors, and had been so appealed to. The measure had been recommended as a restoration, and had been by many so accepted. It is obvious that changes in things so uncertain in their workings, as constitutions, are then best made when they are modelled after something of which we have already had experience. This was so modelled; and that is its vindication. It was, in fact, only a partial change. Two parts of the actual constitution of the House were but slightly modified by the change.   Lord John Russell's exhortation to reform the representation by a comparison with things in the remote past, was a recommendation difficult to obey, unless their concomitants could accompany the change.

Assuming it to be true that the old representation of the people was, in most instances, more popular in its basis or spirit than the modern form, it should also be remembered that our parliamentary government, in any correct sense of the words, cannot be carried back later than the reign of William III., and that the comparison between parliaments in that age, or succeeding times, and the parliaments of the half century immediately preceding the Reform Bill, either as respects the election of them, or their conduct when elected, would not have been to the disadvantage of the latter.   In the remoter times of our history, a parliament elected even on a more popular basis than that which is called the common law right of election, might have stood in perfect security to both, with a Crown and a House of Lords, when these latter were at least co-ordinate in power as well as authority with the Commons of the realm, and when the spirit of the times accepted that equality as a reasonable condition.   Restorations can never be restorations, unless, with the outward

P

form we can restore the inward mind, and every surrounding circumstance which modified the things of the past. It was said by Macaulay, in another part of his admirable speech, that forms of government are but means to an end; in a certain sense this is true. Yet there must be some fundamentals in forms of government, there must be some things sacred from subversion. What government could endure constant discussions as to the fitness of its very foundations? Changes in fundamentals are revolutions, necessary, but rare exceptions,—a frequent recurrence of which liberty cannot survive. A monarchy and a House of Lords might become distasteful to the " respectable middle classes," without being injurious or distasteful to the people; for it might happen that republican opinions, as the preference of any other simple creed, might grow up and prevail for a time amongst a numerous, intelligent, and virtuous class, from an abstract preference of the simple to the complex, of the less to the more costly form, or from a notion that modern civilisation should wear a dress of its own: ~~opinions,~~ innocent at least whilst they are opinions merely, but the enforcement of which might endanger public tranquillity in every state.

A government which does not substantially answer

the purposes for which civil government is ordained, has, of course, no title to the allegiance of its subjects. But when it is argued that a government should not only merit but obtain the confidence of the people, the argument subjects governments to very dangerous probations. It must strike at once at the root of many acquisitions by conquest, plantation or colonisation, where feelings of race or religion exist to foment discontent; and yet these are, humanly speaking, the means ordained in many cases for the eventual civilisation and progress of mankind. The proposition was undoubtedly not meant to have an universal application, but even in a free country, possessing popular institutions, and an educated people, the right of an unhappy and discontented people, or of a large section of it, to subvert a government, if it be referred to the feelings of the former, instead of the existing demerits of the latter, must place the foundations of civil government on the shifting sands of transient feelings, or ill-regulated desires.

We may well understand with what mind the practical man, Conservative statesman, and experienced minister, would regard the promulgation of these opinions, not duly guarded in expression, true only when so guarded, dangerous in their naked expression, and doubly dangerous when so exhibited in times of excitement. We may well understand also with what disdain a high-spirited man would receive menaces in the form of exhortations; with what a wounded spirit an earnest, laborious, and good work-man would receive his discharge, his services unre-quited, his works made light of, his labours regarded as little better than a mischievous activity in doing wrong; with what depression of spirit and sickness of the heart a man who trusted in the people would perceive their estrangement from him, how he would chafe to hear that House of Commons whose applause was as the breath of his nostrils; that house where he had been planted more than twenty years, de-scribed as though things rank and gross in nature possessed it merely.

A mind so constituted, so finely wrought, so just and truthful, would see in these exaggerated and unjust expressions, additional reasons for dreading a transfer of power to those to whom they seemed truth, and it is not to be wondered at that he looked to his own side of the shield the more stedfastly, perhaps with some obstinacy, for such is the natural product of arrogant advocacy.

The first Reform Bill was abandoned by its authors in consequence of a defeat which they experienced on a motion of General Gascoigne's, embodying a resolution that the number of members for England and Wales ought not to be reduced. This part of the ministerial plan, good abstractedly, so far as it proposed a less numerous senate, but unpopular and perhaps unattainable under the necessities of our union, was abandoned in the second Reform Bill. The ministers were, at this time, in a minority in the House of Commons. Those of the Tory party who had joined in the hostile vote which was followed by the resignation of the Duke of Wellington and his colleagues, now, instructed by the consequences of that resignation, united themselves to the main body, and acted with the other Tories under the lead of Sir Robert Peel.

They were able to outvote the ministerial party. Sir Robert Peel, at this time, declared in private to a relation, that his party was the most numerous, and that he had some difficulty, in consequence, in restraining the ardour of his troops. Neither on this nor on subsequent occasions were his Fabian tactics altogether approved. It was not uncommon subsequently to hear him reproached with want of sympathy with those whose slender means rendered the loss of the emoluments of office a serious inconvenience. " It was all very well for Peel with his large fortune,

to be indifferent about his own return to power, but
he should think of others;"—natural bursts of impatience, certainly, under suffering with which he did
sympathise, though his policy could not be varied by
a knowledge of its existence. Others there were who
condemned this policy on other grounds. It was
said, that the Reform Bill should not have been
debated at all, that the party should have proceeded
to vote against it, under a sort of protest against any
discussion of a revolutionary measure. Prince Tal-
leyrand was cited as an authority against any parley
with revolution. The defenders of all establishments,
even of the best, if they undertake to prove their
case by argument against the Syren voice of change,
find that they have fought a drawn battle. Faith is
the mainstay of institutions. As the best human
institution falls far short, in its working, of those
expectations which its more perfect theory excites,
every defensive argument carries with it something
of an apologetic tone. If the audience sympathise
with the defenders, and retain their faith in the
things assailed, then their feelings will give the
triumph to a balanced argument. But if the audience be hostile or indifferent, the ablest advocacy
ever fails to make out a triumphant case, the very
advocate quarrels with himself, though the fault is

not in him, and retires disheartened as he finds how weak a weapon after all human reason is, and how much can be urged with apparent truth against our most cherished convictions. In certain cases therefore it may be politic to decline argument, even when we feel that we have a good cause : but this was not a case for the adoption of such a course. A measure introduced into the House of Commons by the ministers of the Crown, with the sanction and approbation of the Crown itself, which in terms at least professed to be no more than a repair, a measure supported by a large majority of the people out of doors, including many who were unlikely to aim at disorder; and which, at the lowest estimate of its value, included a large mixture of good, could not be repelled as an insidious and dangerous plague by one who felt a deep respect for authority, and a still deeper respect for, if not a secret awe, of the voice of the people when their hearts were strongly stirred. It did not follow however that the people were right, because the majority of voices was on their side; but they were entitled at all events to receive a respectful and serious attention. The opposite policy would have had about it a theatrical aspect of acted terror, and would have savoured more of finesse than of wisdom. Deserving no favour, it would have been in the temper of the times a disastrous failure. Independently however of any question of policy, there was a plain course before him, the duty of deliberation, the duty prescribed to a member of Parliament by the very writ under which a Parliament is summoned, a duty on the performance of which he had always earnestly insisted, and which he was as little disposed to violate out of a spirit of opposition to the Government, as from obedience to the mere behest of the many out of doors.

When it became apparent that the ministers could not carry their measure in that House of Commons, their obvious course was to advise the King to dissolve Parliament, in order to take the sense of the people on this measure. The King had consented to the reform policy, he had allowed Lord Grey to stipulate for a measure of parliamentary reform as a condition of his acceptance of the office of prime minister. The state of the House of Commons, and the strength of parties in it must have been tolerably well known to the King when he gave this consent. He could not therefore with any consistency have declined to give the minister the ordinary power of submitting the fate of his measure to the decision of the constituencies, when the existing Parliament proved hostile. The King could not have refused his assent to that step, without increased danger of public disorder. He would thereby have excited a strong feeling in the minds of the people that he had been from the first insincere, or that he was cruelly light and capricious in his actions.

To dissolve a Parliament when the nation was in such a temper, was undoubtedly a dangerous proceeding; but what course was then not a course of danger? The Conservative party have regarded this dissolution as the source from which all the bitter waters flowed; but the spring, whether of sweet or bitter waters, was in the breasts of the people, not in that of the King.

He had gone too far to recede. The motive power throughout these changes, which have been agitated with more or less success for the last thirty-five years, has resided neither in cabinets nor in the Houses of Commons, but without, it has been a power constant in action and prevailing in influence, which has gained its strength from causes neither temporary nor likely to retrograde. The power of resisting it effectually no longer existed; the unreformed House must have yielded further, as it had for some time been yielding to the changing spirit of the times, and very few, if any of the changes which have followed on the reform of the representation of

the people, could have been resisted, if demanded by
the same voices to which they have been yielded: —
a view of the subject, which, if statesmen would
receive it, would, by making inevitable changes
gradual, render them less shocking, and less dangerous.

This condemnation of the policy of dissolution is
one of the judgments on the things which we see;
there were things which those who condemned it did
not see. The propriety of the measure will be
differently judged, accordingly as we regard it from
the side of the reformers or from that of the
Conservative party. The former thought the measure unavoidable, but they regarded it also as good
and conservative. Obedience then to the public
voice was in them simply the performance of a duty.
The condemnation of the policy of dissolution
assumes the very questions in dispute, whether the
Reform Bill was a bad bill, and if it were, whether
any means of resisting it remained less fraught with
mischief than the measure itself.

On the other hand we must judge the conduct of
the Conservative party from their point of view.
They had been long in possession of office, and the
country had risen in intelligence, power, material
wealth, and dignity, to a degree unsurpassed till then,

if not unexampled, in the annals of our history. It
had suffered much, but it had also done much, and
this party was associated with the direction of its
affairs in the time of its greatest triumph. They
could not be expected to view the result, as the
Whigs, who had been in the minority, viewed it.
Each party looked on a part; each on one side only
of the shield. The Tories, who had ruled, could not
be expected to attribute the disasters of the country
to unwise rule, its glories to accident, or to a power
superior to their imputed misrule. They had had
the people with them for a time at least. They
would naturally attribute the hostility of the present
hour, to one of those fits of passion which sometimes
invade the public mind, therefore they would look
to see this enmity expend itself, and subside into a
spirit with which there might be some accommodation.
They could not deal with any state of the constitution except its actual working state. It was very
well to theorise about it, and to set down students to
the perusal of works of solemn imagination, written
to prove the harmonious working of discordant and
co-ordinate bodies; a triune junction, a neutralising
mixture, converting the separate evils of each of the
parts into a conjoint good. But when, in fact, had
this action been? The balance of the constitution,

if it had ever existed, except as a theory, was already
entirely gone. Nearly a century ago, Speaker Onslow
had declared our government to be a disguised re-
public. All real power resided in the House of
Commons; and unless a balance were found there,
in influence, where was it to be found? The constitution never had been in practice what it was in
theory in any part of the complex machine. As it
was working then, it had worked in practice, from
the time of the establishment of our parliamentary
system, in the reign of William III., with these exceptions, however, that the controlling power over
the abuses of government, which an enlightened
public opinion embodies and applies, had increased
constantly in augmentation of the force of the democratic power in the constitution, whilst the veto
of the Crown had become a merely nominal power,
and the influence of the House of Lords had been
constantly declining.

Though the influence of a few great men had
increased by the possession in a few hands of that
parliamentary interest which had formerly been
more scattered and divided, that influence was more
than balanced by that salutary deference to public
opinion, which made even the suspicion of a job, or
of an unbecoming veiling of the royal ensign to a

subject's flag, far more dangerous to a ministry than any resistance to those influences could be. It was conceded that there were anomalies in the Commons House of Parliament; but into what political institution did not anomalies of some kind enter? In theory an elective was better than an hereditary monarchy; in practice it was far otherwise. What could be more anomalous than the trial by jury, to which Englishmen were so fondly and so justly attached, twelve men more or less arbitrarily selected, probably unused to weigh evidence, and often but ill-informed on the subjects which they were called upon to decide, placed suddenly in a box, subjected to the seductive influences of interested advocacy, and starved into unanimity. The voice of the people was at all times entitled to a respectful attention, but they—the members of the House of Commons—were representatives, not attorneys or delegates, they were called together to consult and deliberate, and though they might listen to the counsels of the people out of doors, they could not obey its menaces. The voice of wisdom was not a threatening but a persuasive voice, and they were willing to listen to argument. But what arguments had been as yet addressed to them? They were told that they must obey the will of the people, but the constitution, and the mandate under which they sate told them otherwise, —that they must deliberate and consult for the safety of the kingdom. No proof was offered that the Government had been bad, that it had failed in performing the functions of a government, or had violated its duties. No attempt had been made to connect the sufferings of the people with any errors of the House of Commons.

Under every form of government some misery has existed, and must exist, much of which no government can alleviate or prevent. The passions which had been so artfully excited and called into play against the present constitution of the House of Commons, might be raised equally hereafter against any system which might succeed the present. This measure was in its very nature necessarily the precursor of further changes in the same direction. It had no character of finality about it: for as the majority would still be non-electors, every argument which was now raised to decry virtual, unequal, or partial representation might and would be raised hereafter by those who were shut out. If distress, discontent, desire of change, or desire of power, justified a change now, then since these causes have constantly their revivals, a change originating in them and fruitful in the like mutations, would create, both here and abroad, a distrust in the permanency of our institutions, and weaken the reverence, power, and influence belonging to the state.   Without reverence a government loses half its power; and where is the reverence for new things, in favour of which the voice of " hoary Time's appeal," cannot be raised?   What, said Sir Robert Peel, would my new peerage weigh in comparison with the old titles of our nobility, the Howards, the Cavendishes, or the Russells?   Such were in substance the arguments addressed by Sir Robert Peel to the unreformed House of Commons at various stages of this high debate, to urge them to let well alone.   The reformers denied that things had gone well; they denied also that they could not go better; they urged, and with much force and reason, that self-government must necessarily be progressive, that the ameliorations which a good government effects are the best of arguments in favour of the extension of those influences which produce them, under the limitations, however, which reason and experience supply.   They insisted that our popular institutions had not kept pace with the progress of the people, that they had rather retrograded, that the danger lay more in exclusion than in admission, and that the anti-reformers were the true revolutionaries.   To do justice to their

arguments, it would be necessary to quote largely from
the undying speeches which contain them.   The
extract which I have given from a speech of Lord
Macaulay's, sparkling with his diamonds, gives a
condensed view of the principal arguments for the
measure.

The House of Commons showed, by its concurrence
with the views of its constituents, as these latter
showed by their agreement with the non-electors,
that sympathy and community of feeling which had
always in truth prevailed when the mind of the
people was greatly moved.   In those moods the
people never spoke without being obeyed.   When
the people were divided, or indifferent, an anti-
popular policy might prevail, and between one
movement and another, there had been times of
lull; but even then the motive power, though less
active and constant, was still abiding in the people,
lately more recognised, more feared, and more commonly obeyed.   This measure, then, did not give to
the people a power unenjoyed before, but only a
power more constant, instant, and direct in its action.

We are yet too near the time to pass a final
judgment on this great measure; if dangerous, dangerous only in the mode of its advocacy, and in that
of its success, for it was carried according to the form

only of the constitution. The failure in a great degree of almost every political prophecy that has been uttered in my time, would deter me, if nothing better deterred me, from presuming to pronounce dogmatically on the consequences of a measure, which, even now, is showing that another and another still succeeds. We must consign it to the impartial award of history, which will pass on it a just judgment as upon its authors and its opposers, who, amidst the storm of conflicting feelings, interests, passions, and virtues, transported almost beyond themselves, failed to render to each other that justice which posterity will render to both, of having aimed mainly at their country's good. Though I dare not venture upon prophecy, I may be pardoned the expression of an humble hope that by "the universal culture of the crowd," under the blessing and hand of God, the people may be rendered fit to wield that power wisely which is about to be confided to them.

The elections went altogether in favour of the reformers. It is needless to repeat the arguments by which the re-introduced measure was again advocated and opposed. It passed the House of Commons by a large superiority of numbers, but in the House of Peers it was rejected by a considerable majority. A time of violence and danger ensued, in which the

Q

people seemed possessed by a sort of fury. No one could look on the state of things without the most serious apprehensions for the future. The conflicting parties could not agree who had raised this spirit; each accused the other, but both looked on harrowed with fear and wonder. It was soothed by promises that the bill should be passed unmutilated. After a short prorogation Parliament again assembled. The measure was again introduced, and passed the Commons. It passed the stage of a second reading in the House of Lords by a small majority. The ministers, being defeated in committee on a motion which they considered virtually to involve the mutilation of their measure, resigned, on the refusal of the King to create new peers, so as to ensure the safety of the bill. The Duke of Wellington was appealed to by the King in his distress. His Grace, actuated by his chivalrous loyalty, attempted to rescue the monarch, by forming an administration which should pledge itself to introduce a large measure of reform; the King considering himself pledged to such a measure. The wisdom of resistance was not made apparent by this stipulation and this concession. Sir Robert Peel declined to aid a desperate undertaking. The duke was unable to form an administration; and the Whig ministers resumed their offices. The creation of peers was, however, averted, for most of the opposing peers, in compliance with a suggestion from the Crown, absented themselves during the further progress of the measure, which was carried therefore according to the forms of the constitution.

The conduct of the Duke of Wellington on this occasion was fiercely assailed. The motives as well as the wisdom of his conduct were severely censured. The motives are now no longer questioned. The chivalrous sense of loyalty under which he acted, cannot, any more than an exalted religious sentiment which will earn for an enthusiast, even in a false faith, the crown of martyrdom, be brought to the bar of reason. He was under the dominion at the time of one virtue in excess; a rare instance in a mind in which the virtues were usually in good discipline, and marched well together under the command of duty.

The result, then, of the opposition which this measure experienced was a considerable augmentation of its danger. It is hard, certainly, to accept a fate, and it is not easy to foresee it; but what was gained by this long protracted struggle? perhaps wisdom for the future, and a finer sense to discern between a settled purpose and a passing whim. The concession in 1846 may have been one fruit of this vain resistance.

The Parliament was soon dissolved, and the first reformed Parliament was summoned to meet.

The Tory party was now stranded, at the lowest ebb of its fortunes. Some of its enemies said, rejoicingly, but without much reflection, that it was destroyed. If the power of those who had hitherto supported this party had been wholly destroyed in the House of Commons, by an unequal representation, excluding in that House the expression of their opinions, a new party, even there, of Conservative principles, must necessarily have arisen out of the dissensions of the dominant party. No legislative measure can really destroy a party in the country, though such a party may die out in time of itself. The Tory party, however, though not destroyed, was weakened and dispirited. It could not be restored with any vital power upon its old narrow basis. It must be reconstructed with reference to the future, rather than to the past, and give its support upon its old principles to the new things which were now substituted for the old. It must have a wider basis and a larger popular support. Upon this work Sir Robert Peel now entered. A person who loves to trace resemblances, and who delights to find a brave spirit moving in all ranks of life, and in all circumstances alike, will forgive me for pointing out here the resemblance in spirit which his conduct in the reconstruction of the Tory party bears to that of his grandfather, old Robert Peel, as the latter doggedly set to work anew when the hand-loom weavers destroyed his works, and sent him southwards, upon a new quest, on new enterprises of industry. There was the same resolute will with the same patient mind industriously working at greater things.

At that time the Tories were much disheartened, many dispaired of the future, and thought a revolution impending. Some took a gloomy pleasure in viewing things in their worst aspect; and picked their samples of a reformed House from a few men who were not amongst its temperate members. They chose to shut their eyes to the fact, that the great bulk of the members were inferior in no respect to the average of English gentlemen. Nothing like a fair sample could have been presented to the mind of Lord Eldon, who, generalising from a few instances, described the House of Commons as consisting of republicans. They were, undoubtedly, for the most part, men of strong liberal opinions, and in the excited state of men's minds at that time, it was to be expected that such would be the composition of the first reformed House of Commons. But all violence calms down in time. The conduct of Sir Robert Peel at this time was alluded to, in terms of praise, by Lord John Russell, on that sad occasion when he rendered to the memory of the deceased statesman, to use the language of Guizot: "Un hommage presque aussi beau pour celui qui en était l'objet que pour celui qui le rendait." Then, almost in presence of the dead, solemnly, thoughtful, and earnest not to go beyond his own view of the truth, in praise of a truthful man, Lord John Russell praised not the policy, but the truth, disinterestedness, and patriotism of his great opponent; one part of whose conduct, he said, had not been enough noted and praised. There was a danger, his lordship said, after the passing of the Reform Bill, that the passions which it had excited would lead some to absent themselves from Parliament, or to abandon public life altogether; giving rise thereby to class animosities of a dangerous nature, and that it was mainly owing to Sir Robert Peel that this evil had been averted. A sentence significant enough as to the dangers which even remedies may occasion. The conduct thus justly praised, with nice discernment, was that of a man labouring to prove himself mistaken, a false prophet of evil ; and no man worked harder, for this end, than he did, though necessarily at a loathsome work. He discouraged, to the best of his power, all peevish resentments, gloomy fears, and reactionary policy. The merit of loyalty in a dominant class is small ; but his loyalty proved true ; it was loyalty to his country, and to the Crown, as the state impersonated, but without the coldness of respect with which the worship of a mere abstraction is ever accompanied. He was as loyal in opposition as when in office, and was as true to the changed as he had been to the old order. He was doing his best to calm and quiet, without suppressing the appetite for change, by diverting it to the safe and wholesome aliment of old institutions, that so they might grow the more fruitful for the browsing. Far be it from my thoughts to hint any resemblances.

When the Parliament met, the Tory party in the House of Commons did not equal one-fifth in number of that whole body. No minister has had at any time so large a majority as that which supported Lord Grey in the first reformed House of Commons; but the very strength in numbers of the party which supported it was the real weakness of that ministry. The ministry itself was strong in every sort of talent, and in every branch of adminis-

trative skill, save one important branch, finance. It
was presided over by one who will shine in the
pages of history, as one of the finest specimens which
a great party has afforded, of the pure Whig : a man
of a high and noble nature, nothing of a leveller,
aiming, by high precept and a great example, to
raise a lower to higher nature; to create in others,
as he showed in himself, a patrician spirit with a
popular mind.   It was a great advantage, at such a
juncture, that the party of the movement possessed
such a head.   Unfortunately, he was far advanced
in years, at a time of life when a struggle with
younger and more ardent spirits always forces the
older man into retreat.   Had the Tories been more
in number, had they borne anything like the same proportion to the Liberal party, as that which the first
dissolution of a reformed Parliament gave them, the
ministerial party would probably have remained com-
pact and united in the face of a more powerful enemy,
and the pressure from without, of which Lord Grey
complained, might have been a more gentle warning.
None really seemed to be needed, for there was then
no inaction ; there was much to do, it was done with
a good will, and generally with no want of administrative skill.   A reforming ministry must, more or
less, exhaust its energies in time, or rather must

want work on which to expend them, for most of
the questions with which it will have to deal are not
subject to revivals, and only renew themselves when
the work is badly or insufficiently done.   There cannot be a perpetual duration of cries for the hustings,
unless they are merely factious, or factitious.   A rest-
less activity in legislation, is like the industry of
some modern Penelopes, who, though they do not
undo by night what they have done by day, have,
at the end of their industrious career, merely
rivalled the samplers of their youth, in works of
equal beauty and utility, an industrious trifling away
of life.

The position of Sir Robert Peel in the new House
called for the exercise of temper and discretion in
no moderate degree.   In the then heated state of
men's minds, he, as a champion of a long dominant,
and though defeated, still a dreaded power, scotched
not killed, was looked upon by the majority with
distrust and fear.   There was, at this time, as in
the infant triumph of all opinions, a certain dog-
matic assumption of superiority amongst many,
especially amongst the younger men, of the Liberal party, as though the mere carriage of a new
policy, were of itself, without any reference to
the derivations of individual faith, a sign of an

original mind, improved intelligence, and higher
wisdom :

"Tanquam feceris ipse aliquid,"

as the self-complacent traveller in a railway-carriage
swells with the miracles of steam, and ratifies the
discovery with the nod of a principal.

The House of Commons, however, soon abates all
arrogant and false pretensions, and gives to innate
power, when cultivated, experienced, and wisely used,
its legitimate authority.   Sir Robert Peel spoke to
a prejudiced but not to a dishonest audience.   The
labours of his life were not thrown away when exhibited to men, who were many of them engaged
in life's hard struggles and in its industrious pur-
suits.   His great knowledge and his accumulated
experience, set off by his powers of voice and language, and perhaps the more winning for a moderate
oratory, soaking into their minds as the rain into
the wool, could not but gain on such an assembly.
Sir Robert Peel, therefore, soon won the attention of
the House, and ere long, their esteem.   Sir Edward
Lytton Bulwer has remarked on his persuasive
powers over a hostile House, and has, therefore,
awarded, with much reason, the character of an
orator to one who gained by speech the end of a
persuasive art.

The first speech of Sir Robert Peel in the reformed House of Commons was marked by his usual taste and judgment.   Although I did not myself hear it, yet I had the advantage of hearing a contemporaneous account of it from an intimate and valued friend of mine, a Whig member of the reformed House, and subsequently a member of the Whig government.   Sir Robert alluded with feeling to his altered position in that House, and the generous sympathies of many of his opponents responded to this appeal.   He did not, however, adopt a whining, plaintive tone, he did not feign contrition, or sue for a hearing, or a fair construction.   He spoke out like a man.   There was nothing mean or hollow in his submission to that necessity under which he bowed; he took things as he found them, and tried to make the best of them.   A railing or a querulous voice would have been useless there, a hollow acquiescence would have deceived nobody; for, as Jeremy Taylor hath it: "Certain it is that no man can long put on a person and act a part, but his evil manners will peep through the corners of his white robe, and God will bring a hypocrite to shame, even in the eyes of men;" but a loyal, manly, English, common-sense accommodation to actual things was sure to win, as it deserved to win, the respect of an English House of Commons, men accustomed to the ways of the world and to business, and who feel an instinctive, heaven-born horror of impracticable men. Sir Robert Peel thus alludes to this subject in his posthumous memoirs: "In 1833 I took my seat in a small minority, as a member of the first Parliament summoned under the Reform Act. In the debate on the address, I used the following expressions:—' The King's government had abstained from all unseemly triumph in the King's speech respecting the measure of reform. He would profit by their example, and say nothing upon that head, but consider that question as finally and irrevocably disposed of. He was now determined to look forward to the future alone, and, considering the constitution as it existed, to take his stand on main and essential matters, to join in resisting every attempt at new measures, which could not be stirred without unsettling the public mind and endangering public prosperity.'" He was for reforming every institution that really required reform, but he was for doing it gradually, dispassionately, and deliberately, in order that the reform might be lasting.

Another cause of the early ascendancy which Sir Robert Peel acquired in the reformed House of Commons, was an injudicious attack which the late

Mr. Cobbett, more I think from a desire of self-display, than from any real malignity, directed against the fallen minister. If Mr. Cobbett had studied to do the object of his attack a signal service, he could scarcely have hit upon a happier expedient. To put upon a deserving, even if a mistaken man, now in his adverse fortune, a brand of disgrace, by expunging his name from the list of privy councillors, for an act too, which if it had been an error of judgment, was a common error shared by large majorities, whom he had not led away; majorities composed of men of all parties in the House, supporting opinions to which he had become late a convert,—was a proposal which ranged almost every man of feeling and of virtue in the House on the side of the accused, knit them together with him, for the time, in a bond of human sympathy, and provided an inspiring audience for an admirable defence, in which knowledge, argument, happy retort, sarcasm, invective, passion, and scorn, displayed a man more various, than till then, he had been thought to be. It opened to his audience a sight of a higher range, and a more varied growth. Adversity had brought him on in her severe school to his final growth. About the same time a new vein was worked; a vein of rich quiet humour, which few had suspected there, showing itself less in pointed sayings and lively images than in allusive sketches and apt applications.

One instance may be found in a debate on Irish affairs, when an Irish member of that time afforded an opportunity of a humorous reference and application to the legendary lore of Irish history. I remember well the surprise which this appearance in a new line, in comedy, if not in broad farce, occasioned. It was in vain that I assured those who expressed this surprise to me, that he had much humour, and was naturally addicted to quizzing; and that I had seen recently a humorous specimen of grave banter, something in the style of Swift, which had proceeded from his pen. He had seldom however, before this, given the rein to this dangerous propensity. It is a talent, the indulgence of which is little relished in a minister.

It was during this period of his parliamentary life, that the late minister was described by Sir Edward Lytton Bulwer, in his "England and the English." About the same time the late Mr. Daniel Whittle Harvey, an excellent speaker and a man of great talent, who sat in the first reformed House of Commons, drew a similar portrait of Peel. It is not a little singular that he won in a hostile House a higher reputation as a debater than he had hitherto gained; since men, from identity of opinion, feeling, and interest, are commonly more prone to exalt the orator of their own side. Was it that being no longer a protected interest, he had been forced to more exertion; or that his peculiar powers told most in a House which drew a larger supply of its members from the great workshops of the land?

In an article on the life and character of Sir Robert Peel, which appeared a few years ago in the Westminister Review, containing as fair a description of the man himself as any that has fallen under my observation, his gradual development is not left unnoticed. The reviewer observes that after the close of the short administration in 1834–5, Peel had risen thirty per cent. in public estimation. The remark is true. In 1825, the world would not have supposed him capable of that high and sustained effort. In 1822 Lord Liverpool appears to have thought him unequal, then, to the conduct of the ministerial business in the House of Commons; yet at thirty-five years of age, with thirteen years' experience of Parliament, and ten years' experience of office, he must have possessed the power which he exhibited five years later in the conduct of the same duties. Circumstances, however, had not then called for their display. So far from it being true that he aimed at the highest post *per saltum,* he rather in his steps, as in his developments, followed nature, who is said to do nothing *per saltum.*

Sir Robert Peel was at this time unpractised as a leader of opposition. He was not qualified by his habits, or education, or by the nature of his mind and disposition, for any other opposition than that which he conducted. The functions and duties of a Conservative opposition were dwelt- on by him in a speech which he delivered, in 1839, to the Conservative members of the House of Commons who met at the Merchant Tailors' Hall to animate each other, by numbers, good-fellowship, good cheer, and good speaking, in the pursuit of their common object. Some impatience had been expressed, more had been felt,—the Fabian policy was not approved. It required all the powers of a great manager to induce the impatient troops to wait within the lines of their Torres Vedras, disciplining themselves, and looking for the approaching disorganisation of their enemy. On this occasion the speeches of Lord Stanley and of Sir Robert Peel were excellent, each in its own style a masterpiece, but in their styles how different! that of Lord Stanley was a higher display of oratory, more eloquent, more aggressive, more animating; that of Sir Robert Peel was a masterpiece of skill and persuasive art, most to be commended, as an effort of oratory, for the dexterity with which a general policy was avouched with an avoidance of embarrassing details : leaving a free course for future action, and things unsaid which it might not then be safe to promise or predict; in short, a prelude suited to the future performance, insisting on the wisdom of a Conservative policy, soothing, exhorting to patience, and whilst preparing for a future assault, guarding their own lines against attack; the two united served, one to animate and one to restrain the ardour of the troops, till the joyful day when they should stand no longer behind the lines, but advance to assault and victory.

An opposition conducted on Conservative principles can never be very galling to a minister. The severest critics of Whig ministers have always been found amongst their liberal supporters. Sir Robert Peel's temperate opposition proceeded partly from policy, but more from his principles, his sense of duty to the Crown, and from his own experience as a minister of the disastrous effects of violent political agitation. He forbore from appeals to the passions of the people, and was content to win his way by a slower method. Throughout the course of this work, I have rarely vouched any friend of Sir Robert Peel to

R

warrant my positions; I have taken my proofs in general from the mouths of his opponents. Not that their testimony is really more valuable in itself, but I prefer it because it is a testimony in its own nature less suspectable. At the time when Lord Stanley and Sir James Graham were invited by Sir Robert · Peel to unite themselves with him in his administration of 1834–5, Lord Stanley accompanied his refusal of that offer with the following acknowledgment of the fairness of the course which Sir Robert Peel had pursued in opposition: "It would be most uncandid in me not to admit that since the passing of the Reform Bill, no one placed in such a situation could have conducted his opposition with more of moderation and fairness than you have done, and I acknowledge with pleasure my conviction that on repeated occasions your influence was successfully exerted to mitigate asperities, and to check the intemperance of injudicious and over-zealous followers." In support of the same opinion may be adduced the testimony of Lord John Russell, who alluded, after the death of Sir Robert Peel, to the times which followed immediately the passing of the Reform Bill, and to the healing influence of his example and moderate counsels on the inflamed animosities of that fierce conflict.

I pass over the interval between the passing of
the Reform Bill and the death of Lord Spencer.

Lord Althorp, who had conducted the business of
the government in the House of Commons from
the time when Lord Grey's ministry was formed,
was now removed, by his succession to the earldom,
from the scene of his useful labours, and the triumphs
of temper, moderation, sense, and judgment.   Without any brilliant qualities to attract or dominate a
popular assembly, he had prevailed by methods alike
honourable to himself and to those who submitted
to the force of reason and the influence of character.
The ascendancy of such a character in the first
reformed House of Commons is a sign of the sobriety of the English character even in times of
excitement and turbulent commotion; and that the
members of the House itself were congenial.   The
removal of the ministerial leader from the House
of Commons created a necessity for some new ar-
rangement as to the conduct of the government
business in that house.   It was understood that
Earl Spencer desired to retire from office altogether.
The ministry had been previously weakened, and
the loss of Lord Spencer, had he resolved to leave
the ministry, would have left it diminished in character for efficiency, but still with numbers unim-

paired, and ability equal to the work which lay before it. The public mind was not then prepared for a change of ministers, nor was any union then practicable between members of opposite parties. The King had attempted in the month of July, when accepting the resignation of Earl Grey and Viscount Althorp, to form a government by "an union in the service of the state of those who stood at the head of the respective parties in the country." His Majesty had placed a memorandum in the hands of Lord Melbourne, expressing a wish to the above effect. That noble lord assured his Majesty that he had considered the memorandum with the attention which its importance demanded, and " with that solicitude which must be excited in every mind by the present very critical position of public affairs." Whilst acknowledging the "patriotic sentiments" of the King, and the enlarged views which his Majesty took of the state and condition of the country, Lord Melbourne, appreciating also the natural desire of his Majesty to avert from his government for the future the difficulties and danger from conflicting interests and opinions to which it had been continually exposed, proceeded in a well-written paper to point out why he was not able to perceive any ground upon which men so opposite in their opinions

could then be brought together, "nor any chance
of such an accommodation as should be consistent
with their own avowed principles and satisfactory
to the country." Lord Melbourne in this paper
expressed himself as " ready to admit that all general
rules must be subject to exceptions arising from
peculiar circumstances, and that there never was
a moment which more imperiously required that
men should not suffer themselves to be bound and
shackled by preconceived opinions, but should act
in that which appears to be the best mode of meeting
the exigency of the immediate crisis."

Lord Melbourne throughout his paper shows the
mind of a statesman, and of a high-minded gentleman; considerate and just towards his opponents,
respectful, grateful, and firm in his language to the
sovereign, acknowledging the patriotism, and superiority to prejudice of the King, but not disguising
his sense of the impracticable nature of a proposal,
which in less than three years after the passing of the
Reform Bill sought to unite in one cabinet the Duke
of Wellington, Sir Robert Peel, and Lord Stanley,
together with Lord Melbourne and his principal colleagues and supporters : " in order to bring them
together, and to establish a community of purpose."
A community of purpose they all had, but no com-

munity of opinion, and the differences between their followers could not be reconciled by the union of the heads of parties.

Lord Melbourne communicated the proposal, by the order of the King, to the persons for whose consideration it was designed. They returned answers corresponding in substance with the opinions which Lord Melbourne had expressed. Sir Robert Peel observed, "that such an union could not in the present state of parties, and the present position of public affairs, hold out the prospect of an efficient and ·vigorous administration." He remarked, in substance, that Earl Grey's government had been dissolved from within, and not from without, and that a selection in one cabinet, of men, from parties opposed to each other, offered a slighter prospect of agreement.

The King replied to this communication in a few lines expressive of his satisfaction to find his motives understood and appreciated " in so respectable a quarter ! "

What a stimulus to exertion in this spare allotment of praise ! A man would work hard to become a person in the royal blazonry. The metaphors of state papers have a mission to destroy metaphor.

Although this desire of the King in the month of July 1834 could not be gratified, and resulted in nothing, it is important to bear it in mind whilst considering the subsequent crisis in the ministry, to which the death of Lord Spencer gave rise. It does not appear that between the month of July and the month of November in that year, anything had occurred to create a variance between the King and his ministers. In July the return of Lord Althorp to the government had overcome the difficulty of the hour; but when his services were about to be lost to the King's government in the House of Commons, where his influence and power were the greatest, it is reasonable to suppose that the King, who five months before had been so sensible of the weakness of his government, as to desire to prop it by a coalition, now again felt a renewed desire for a stronger administration, and sought, as a coalition could not be, to strengthen his government by a change of men. No evidence is furnished of any personal quarrel, or of any proposal made to the King by Lord Melbourne, which was likely to abate the good opinion which his Majesty had entertained of, and expressed to his minister, in the preceding summer. It seems therefore to be probable that the change which the King now desired to effect, proceeded only from a wish to have a more efficient government, and it bears the aspect of an injudicious, rather than of a fitful exercise of the royal prerogative.

Lord Melbourne having waited upon his Majesty to communicate the proposed arrangements which Lord Spencer's removal from the House of Commons had rendered necessary, was informed by the King that he had decided upon a total change of administration, a communication which was received by Lord Melbourne with his accustomed good breeding. His good manners seem to have been interpreted very strangely. "Lord Melbourne," writes the Duke of Wellington, "is delighted;" the same . ecstasy was imputed by his Grace to all the retiring ministers: their subsequent conduct evinced either how short-lived is the joy which a sense of freedom inspires, or how falsely we estimate each other's enjoyments; or it may be that the zeal and interest of others forced them once more into bondage.

When the King took his unadvised resolution of forming an entirely new administration, Sir Robert Peel was in Italy. The Duke of Wellington wrote thus concerning the step: —

"(Private and confidential).

"MY DEAR PEEL,   "Brighton, Nov. 15. 1834.

"You will observe that the King's case is not quite one of his ministers quitting him. I think that it might have been such a one if his Majesty had not been so ready to seize upon the first notion of difficulties resulting from Lord Spencer's death.

. . . Lord——swears that they are turned out. However, it is quite clear that they could not go on, and they are all, particularly Lord Melbourne, delighted to be relieved; I am not astonished. If they had remained in office till a difficulty should occur in Parliament, the King could not have allowed them to quit him. This is the reason for which he is in such a hurry to get rid of them now, and to dissolve.

"I don't think that we are at all responsible for his quarrel with them; it was an affair quite settled when he sent for me,

"Believe me, &c.,

"WELLINGTON."

This letter proves that the dismissal of the late ministry was in fact the King's own proceeding; and it proves also that the King did not, in fact, consult the Duke of Wellington as to that precedent act, but merely consulted his Grace as to the filling up of offices which the King treated as vacant. It proves also that the duke regarded the vacancy as *un fait accompli*, "an affair quite settled:" matters which it will be important to bear in mind hereafter, in the consideration of a constitutional question which was subsequently stirred.

Notwithstanding the duke's imaginings of the state of bliss, with which the ministers after their purgatory of office were at length blessed, the King alone, amongst the principal actors in this drama, manifested any satisfaction. He was described by the Duke of Wellington as " in high spirits," and in a letter to Sir Robert Peel, the King spoke thus of his own feelings : —

" The King, having had a most satisfactory and confidential communication with the Duke of Wellington on the formation of a new government, calls on Sir Robert Peel to return without loss of time to England, to put himself at the head of the administration of the country." This royal mandate, together with the above letter from the Duke of Wellington, was conveyed to Sir Robert Peel by Mr. Hudson, who held the appointment of resident Gentleman Usher in the Queen's household. He was introduced to Sir Robert Peel by a letter from Sir Herbert Taylor. The letters from the King and the Duke of Wellington to Sir Robert Peel, reached him at Rome on the night of Tuesday the 25th of November. They were put into his hands on his return from a

ball at the Duchess of Torlonias'. He returned immediately to England, in obedience to the King's
command; and after a hurried and fatiguing journey,
arrived there on the 9th December following.

"The interval between my recall from Rome, and
arrival in London, afforded me," he observes, "ample
opportunity for considering various and important
matters coolly, and without interruption. In my
letters to the King and the Duke of Wellington from
Rome, I had merely given an assurance that I would
return without delay to England. As I should, by
my acceptance of the office of first minister, become
technically, if not morally, responsible for the dissolution of the preceding government, though I had
not the remotest concern in it, I did not at once,
upon the hurried statement which was sent to me of
the circumstances connected with it, pledge myself
to the acceptance of office. I greatly doubted, indeed,
the policy of breaking up the government of Lord
Melbourne at that time. I entertained little hope
that the ministry about to replace it would be a
stable one; would command such a majority in the
House of Commons as would enable it to transact the
public business. I was not altogether satisfied by
the accounts I first received, with the sufficiency of
the reason for the dissolution of the late ministry;

namely, the removal of Lord Althorp to the Lords, and the objections of the King to Lord John Russell as Lord Althorp's successor in the lead of the House of Commons. Very little consideration," he adds, " was necessary to convince me that I had no alternative but to undertake the office of prime minister instantly on my arrival. The King's course had been decided on. The former government was dismissed from office. Had it been possible that I should have been consulted previously, I might have dissuaded the act of dismissal as premature and impolitic; but I could not reconcile it to my feelings, or indeed to my sense of duty, to subject the King and the monarchy to the humiliation, through my refusal of office, of inviting his dismissed servants to resume their appointments. My refusal could only have been founded on avowed disapprobation of the course taken by the King; and the same reasons which must be assigned for the refusal of office by myself, ought to be conclusive against my cordially supporting others of similar political opinions in the attempt which I should have declined on my part to take.

" Little sanguine as I was of success, I was firmly resolved therefore to obey the King's commands, and to direct every energy to the arduous duties which awaited me on my arrival in England.

"I arrived in London very early on the morning of the 9th December, having travelled all night from Dover.

"I waited upon the King immediately before I saw any other person, and placed my services at his Majesty's disposal, informing his Majesty that I thought it of importance that I should not delay a moment in accepting the office of First Lord of the Treasury and Chancellor of the Exchequer. I mean, that I should not show that doubt and hesitation which consultation with others might imply, or make my acceptance of office contingent upon the answers which I might receive from others whom it might be my duty to invite to enter into the King's service."

The long unentered promised land, on which his old father did not live to see him plant his foot, was now entered: an estate entered upon not with the hopes of the brisk minor panting for twenty-one, but under a doubtful and disputed title, with the certainty of a hard struggle for its enjoyment, and the prospect of a speedy ejectment.

In the first interview which he had with the King, he had obtained his Majesty's ready assent to a proposal which he now hastened to make to Lord Stan-

ley and to Sir James Graham, for the benefit of their
co-operation as colleagues in the cabinet. He wrote
therefore to both. The letter which he wrote to
Lord Stanley is given at full length in the posthumous memoirs of the late statesman. The commencement of this letter, in which he addresses Lord
Stanley by the title of "Sir," an error so much at
variance with his accuracy, and attention even to
trifles, seems to me to mark the hurry of his mind:
an inadvertence which would not have been committed probably but at a time when both mind and
body were in an unhabitual state of commotion and
fatigue. I have myself observed, in former times,
traces of his minute attention, in erased, and but ill
erased pencil marks, suggesting but slight verbal
alterations, wherein the altered expression indicated
a mind intent on stripping official communications of
that tinge of discourtesy which they sometimes bear :
a trenchant style perhaps necessary sometimes to cut
off the communications of bores.

Lord Stanley and Sir James Graham declined then
to enter the Tory cabinet. The proposal followed
too closely upon differences which were yet scarcely
cold. Their union, then, might not have received
the public sanction. Sir Robert Peel, who knew

himself better than they, or the public then knew him, could with propriety make an offer which they were justified in declining; for time had not then been afforded him to show with what sincerity he spoke when he avowed his determination to look not to the past, but to the future, and to accept honestly the settlement which the Reform Bill had created as final and irrevocable.   It is to be observed that Sir Robert Peel in his letter to Lord Stanley offered "to give the most frank and unreserved explanation of his views on the several points on which it might be required by Lord Stanley," not considering that public affairs have any special rules at variance with the dictates of reason in the ordinary affairs of the world.

Some declaration of the future policy of the cabinet was necessary.   No pains had been spared to impress the public with false notions as to its origin and intended policy.   In order, therefore, to calm the public mind, and to satisfy those whom truth and reason would satisfy, that no reactionary policy was really meditated, he sent forth, with the consent of his colleagues, to whom it had been previously shown, his celebrated address to the electors of Tamworth, a skilful paper, written also with more attention to style, and less use of official language, than his state papers commonly received and exhibited. The faults of his style may have been the result of the habit of early fluency; a practice dangerous to the acquisition of a correct and nervous style, which cannot well be acquired until men weigh both their words and their conclusions, and adjust them under the guidance of thought.

As this Tamworth address is the prospectus of his future policy, the document with which all his subsequent measures ought to be compared, I shall quote it at some length, omitting merely its formal parts, and its references to some particular measures which were then engaging, or had lately engaged, the public attention.

He wrote thus: "The King, in a crisis of great difficulty, required my services. The question I had to decide was this: Shall I obey the call? or shall I shrink from the responsibility, alleging as the reason that I consider myself, in consequence of the Reform Bill, as labouring under a sort of moral disqualification which must preclude me, and all who think with me, both now and for ever, from entering into the official service of the Crown? Would it, I ask, be becoming in any public man to act upon such a principle? Was it fit that I should assume

that either the object or the effect of the Reform
Bill has been to preclude all hope of a successful
appeal to the good sense and calm judgment of the
people, and so to fetter the prerogative of the Crown
that the King has no free choice among his subjects
but must select his ministers from one section, and
one section only, of public men.

"I have taken another course, but I have not
taken it without deep and anxious consideration as
to the probability that my opinions are so far in
unison with those of the constituent body of the
United Kingdom, as to make me, and those with
whom I am about to act, and whose sentiments are
in entire concurrence with my own, to establish such
a claim upon public confidence as shall enable us to
conduct with vigour and success the government of
the country.

"I have the firmest conviction that confidence
cannot be secured by any other course than that of
a frank and explicit declaration of principle; that
vague and unmeaning professions of popular opinions
may quiet distrust for a time, may influence this or
that election, but that such professions must ultimately and signally fail, if, being made, they are not
adhered to, or if they are inconsistent with the honour
and character of those who make them.

S

" Now, I say at once that I will not accept power on the condition of declaring myself an apostate from the principles on which I have heretofore acted. At the same time I never will admit that I have been either before or after the Reform Bill, the defender of abuses, or the enemy of judicious reforms. I appeal with confidence, in denial of the charge, to the active part I took in the great question of the currency — in the consolidation and amendment of the criminal law — in the revisal of the whole system of trial by jury — to the opinions I have professed and uniformly acted on, with regard to other branches of the jurisprudence of the country,— I appeal to this as a proof that I have not been disposed to acquiesce in acknowledged evils, either from the mere superstitious reverence for ancient usages, or from the dread of labour and responsibility in the application of a remedy."

Of this address he wrote at a subsequent time : " I held no language and expressed no opinions in this address which I had not previously held while ·acting in opposition to the government. I did not attempt to mitigate hostility by any new professions, or to court popular favour by promises of more extensive reforms than those to the principle of which I had assented before I took office. It was said by my opponents that I held a new language as to the reform bill. I certainly tried to calm any anxiety on that head, among the advocates of the reform of Parliament, by an explicit declaration that I considered the measure final and irrevocable. But was the language I held, new? was it adopted for the first time, because it was convenient in my altered position, to disclaim hostility to the measure that had passed into a law." In disproof of this charge, Sir Robert then refers to his speech on the address, in 1833, which I have before quoted. I have compared its language with that of the Tamworth address. The sentiments in both accord.

The conduct of Sir Robert Peel from the moment of his return to England, until the resignation which ended the feverish existence of that short administration, is fully recorded in his own posthumous memoirs. The whole history of this part of his life is there disclosed; his motives as well as his acts are before the world. The parliamentary debates of that time record, on the whole, a spirit stirring and brave struggle with adverse fortune. The moral victory was with the vanquished. His labours and exertions in this contest were unexampled: amidst many mortifications he displayed a rare command of temper, and a mind which difficulties and defeat seemed only to nerve for fresh encounters. Not even in the heat of debate did a rash or unguarded expression escape him. He had not amongst his own party, and he did not seem to need, great support in debate. His quickness in seizing whatever was presented to him, his power of working it up instantly for use, his experience, his store of knowledge which he brought to bear on every subject readily, fitly, and fully, his knowledge of men, his excellent memory, acute intellect, powers of argument and of statement, sound judgment, and almost instinctive sense of consequences, all combined to form an amount of administrative and debating power, rarely united before in one minister; and in his time it was less easy to rule than it had been in the days of the second Pitt or of Walpole.

The struggle called forth all his powers. As he fought against great odds, fought well and bravely, though beaten, he won the sympathy of the bystanders.

The elections which took place on the formation of this ministry, had given the Conservative party a larger and a fairer share of the representation than that which they had possessed in the last Parliament; they were, however, still in the minority. Had the numbers which the first reformed Parliament showed remained unaltered, it would have been clear that one inequality had succeeded to another.

The measures which this ministry introduced were judicious and liberal. They were in entire conformity also with the principles which the Tamworth address put forth. There is no ground for the assertion which he has himself refuted,—that the Tory creed was veiled or changed in this address. I find, on the contrary, almost in its every line, the devotion of a mind to the old theories which it has been trained to love and revere: a tempered devotion to the Crown, a desire to uphold its authority, and to save it from humiliation, a clinging to the ancient faith, and an exposition upon its true principles of that "golden mean," which, though "subject to the misconstruction of the extremes," was still the old faith, shrinking from change, and standing by preference on the old ways. These feelings pervade every line of this address, and though they are coupled with the expression of a sincere desire to remove every proved abuse, and to introduce any amelioration which may be proposed, still that desire is made subject to the law that these new things must be simply reparations of the old. It is substantially, therefore, what it was meant to be, not a recan-

tation, but an exposition. There are bigots in politics as in theology, who will insist that articles of
faith can have but one interpreter, and him an
interpreter who interprets in their own sense; who
insist not only that all men should arrive at a
certain stage, but that they should all travel thither
by the same road; who will pester with their narrow
exposition a mind struggling for elbow room, and
stigmatise as dangerous neology every new face of
old truth; who would fain dress the mind in its
robes of infancy for ever. Viewed in a similar
spirit, Peel's versions of the Tory creed may be
stigmatised as neology, or as an heretical pravity;
but there is nothing in them abhorrent from the
true principles of that creed, or from his own previous and enlightened expositions of it. The following passages from his own letter to the Bishop
of Durham, which is given at length in his posthumous memoirs, may serve as an exposition of his
general principles with reference to change.

"It is a matter of extreme difficulty to determine
when it is the duty of a minister of the Crown to
undertake the interference with ancient usages and
venerable institutions. If he determine to do nothing,
he may incur the risk of insuring interference by
ruder and more hostile hands. If he advises and

undertakes interference, he appears to the unthinking to be needlessly departing from principle, to be unsettling what it may be very dangerous to disturb, and to be establishing a precedent which may be appealed to against himself by those dangerous innovators whose intervention he wishes to avert.

" I know no other guide that he can take to regulate his course amid such difficulties, but his deliberate and conscientious conviction of what may be ultimately the best for the security and permanent interests of the establishments he desires to protect and serve."

One of the first batteries which was opened upon him, was a charge that he was answerable for the dismissal of the late ministry, a hair-splitting construction of constitutional law, which the occult science of special pleading might have reckoned amongst its triumphs. The construction which prevailed, and to which Sir Robert Peel himself gave some sanction, rested for support on a mistaken application of a legal maxim, " omnis ratihabitio retrotrahitur, et mandato æquiparatur."

Lord John Russell, a high authority certainly, declared that Sir Robert Peel was responsible for the dismissal of the late ministers; though we have seen that he was not consulted concerning it, and if

consulted, would not have advised it. This opinion
his lordship supported by analogy to the legal
doctrine of relation. Sir Robert Peel, he said, by
accepting office, had ratified the former act of dismissal. This does not accord with a correct application of the legal doctrine of ratification by relation;
since the King himself was the principal, acted for
himself as principal, and not with reference to the
interest of any person whose authority was to be
procured and used to ratify a precedent act. The
subsequent connection between the King and his
minister was one not of mandate from the latter,
but of delegation or appointment by the former. It
was merely the choice and appointment of a new
servant, an act of sequence and not of relation.

Sir Robert Peel, in a passage which I have already
quoted, has adopted in a qualified manner, this subtle
reading of the constitution. He says that he was
responsible, at least, technically. But what is a
technical responsibility? The Duke of Wellington
conceived in his straightforward way, as a man of
common sense would conceive, that the new servant
is not responsible for the master's quarrel with a
predecessor whose place he fills. The word responsibility has long been vaguely used. In diplomacy
especially, men take refuge in phrases. By respon-

sibility in a minister, I understand that for grave
faults he is liable to be impeached; or for lesser
faults, dismissed, or censured.   I understand also
that he, like other men, only in a higher degree,
is subject to public opinion, the most powerful perhaps of checks, and from which no person is exempt;
in another sense again he is responsible to his own
conscience, and in all, to God.   In every sense of
the word however, I understand something real; and
a technical responsibility I do not understand.

The acceptance of office involves a real responsibility.   That responsibility Sir Robert Peel had incurred, and did not dispute; but it commenced on
the 9th December only, when he accepted office;
till then he had done nothing, he had simply obeyed
the King's direction to return to England.   There
was no need to resort to fictions for the time which
his acceptance and enjoyment of office covered.   A
minister by accepting office, if that step be a wrong
one, which, *primâ facie*, at least, must be supposed to be right, exposes himself to censure by
that acceptance alone.   In considering the propriety of that act of acceptance, the preceding act
of dismissal, its motives and probable consequences,
the comparative merits of the two ministries, the
state and feeling of the country and of Parlia-

ment may all, or any of them, together with
many other things, have an important bearing on
the quality and the act of acceptance.   But in thus
estimating the quality and character of that act itself,
we do not resort to fiction.   To give that act of acceptance a relation back to another which merely
preceded it in time, and with which the succeeding
minister had had, in fact, no connection whatever,
was straining a valuable maxim of the constitution;
such efforts may recoil to the injury of the constitution
itself. The act of dismissal is an act complete in
itself.   The good or the evil, in the joy or the
sorrow with which it may affect the public mind,
may be, and generally is, inchoate, if not complete,
before an appointment of a new minister can be made.
Some minister, there must be: if the King who has
dismissed his minister cannot form a new ministry,
and the dismissed minister is restored, who is then
responsible for the act of dismissal?   Or, let it be
supposed that he declines to return, who is then
responsible for the act of dismissal?   In either of
these supposed cases, the act of the Crown remains
unsheltered by any vicarious responsibility.   This
is its true character always; for the constitutional
quality of an act, complete in itself, cannot be af-
fected by subsequent accident. The King may change

his ministers for a bad reason, and the act of removal may be wrong in its motive and object; yet if he choose a better, would it not be at once ridiculous and mischievous to prejudice the interests of the country by insisting on a restoration? Even a bad minister might struggle against an evil suggestion, and be dismissed in consequence for an upright act. The dismissal might begin and end in wrong, and still the evil might end there, and the evil design terminate with the dismissal. If the change be for the better, of what has the country to complain? If it be for the worse, the House of Commons by address, or vote, by the exercise of any of its constitutional powers applicable to such a case, may get rid of a bad minister, or of one who does not enjoy its confidence, without any resort to fictions, which are either nonsensical in attempting to fix censure where it cannot rest, for vicarious blame is nonsense; or unjust and immoral, in setting up a whipping boy to bear the punishment of a royal fault in which the minister has not concurred. In those very few instances in which the King, if he act at all, acts alone, the constitution leaves him unsheltered by any vicarious responsibility, but even in those cases he does not avoid responsibility to public opinion. In those instances where he must act through a minister, the vicarious responsibility attaches to the compliance. The King's choice of and dismissal of a minister, are acts which the constitution entrusts to the King alone. It appears to me, that the plain reading of the Duke of Wellington is the true reading of the constitution. It would be a serious addition to the responsibilities of a minister, if his mere act of accepting office, involved him in the consequences of prior disputes and intrigues, to the correct history of which he might be unable to obtain a clue.

One unpopular appointment and some trifling errors of judgment may be imputed to this administration; but, on the whole, it raised the character of Sir Robert Peel as a statesman, and restored the party with which he was connected to an increased share of the public confidence.

People heeded little now that he came of a Tory stock, " qu'il naquit Tory," —

" Nobilis hic, quocumque venit de gramine, cujus
Clara fuga ante alios, et primus in æquore pulvis."

On the resignation of Sir Robert Peel and his colleagues, the ministry of Lord Melbourne was restored. The King desired to reward his retiring minister with high rank in the peerage, but the offer was declined, partly from policy, but more from dis-relish in a moderate mind. He was complimented by Lord John Russell for having fought the battle, walking strictly in the paths of the constitution.

In two instances only can I find any trace of his having swerved from the correct line, in his constitutional course. One, when he resigned his seat for the University of Oxford; the other that upon which I have just observed: in both instances the motives were pure and honourable; but if a constitutional maxim be surrendered or weakened, the evil of an inroad on the constitution is not the less real because the motives which have induced it are not evil. The first act was a virtual admission that a member of Parliament is a delegate; the second seemed to weaken the undoubted right of the Crown to dismiss its ministers of its own authority, by involving the succeeding minister in acts with which he had no connection.

The administration which followed was, like that of the Duke of Wellington, unprosperous, and from causes somewhat similar. When the Whigs came into office this second time, the tide was beginning to turn against them. They set out with a failing tide of popularity. The excitement which the Reform Bill had occasioned could not be kept up at its height, and a temporary lull was to be expected. The people were now satisfied that progress would

not be retarded if Sir Robert Peel were restored to
office, and his administrative talents were now more
clearly perceived and more justly appreciated.   The
people became therefore more indifferent about a
mere change of men ; and as a ministry can always
be outbid in merely popular concessions, that ground
of strength was sure ere long to fail.

The opposition was strengthened by the union
in one party of Lord Stanley and Sir James Graham
with Sir Robert Peel.   The Conservative party
during all this time of its growth was very prudently and ably led.   The Fabian policy, notwithstanding some loud murmurs, still prevailed.   The
new reign which it was thought would confirm the
Whigs in power, did not add really to their strength;
for a Whig ministry which is thought to stand too
well at court, declines in favour with the popular
party, their true support.   The Tory party had no
real cause to regret the failure of the attempt to
form an administration in 1839.   The particular
cause of the failure of that attempt has now lost
its interest.   It is now generally conceded that Sir
Robert Peel took the constitutional side on that
occasion.   It may however be doubted whether it
was worth while to raise the question.   Something
has been gained by the experience which succeeding

years have afforded; and fears of undue influence
from such sources have now happily subsided.

For the first time in his life Sir Robert Peel was
exposed to a charge of disloyalty, and the imputation pained him. His manner in the House of
Commons when repelling this accusation showed that
he felt the imputation acutely. He betrayed unusual emotion.

The subject led to discussion and debate, and in
the House of Lords it was treated by Lord Brougham
in a manner which excited universal admiration of
his great and varied powers. A member of the
then House of Commons, a Conservative, one on
whose judgment I could always depend, assured me
that though when he listened to Peel's speech in
the House of Commons he thought it excellent,
yet when he passed into the House of Lords and
listened to Lord Brougham speaking on the same
subject, he felt that he had come into the presence
of a higher power; so vain after all is it to hope
from any culture those products which cultivation
can extract from the few favoured spots only on
which genius has shed a benigner ray. We must
class the great orator with the great poet, beings
improvable, but not made by art.

The years that followed were marked by the slow

decline of the popularity and power of the Whig
ministry, which decline will be attributed to various
causes, according to the opinions of the authors who
treat of their policy. The position in which they
then were, and the position in which their opponents
also stood, viewed in relation to the public mind
in that its calmer mood, seem to me to account
very naturally for that "collapse" of the Whig party
which has been set down to their fault by those
writers who expected more from the Reform Bill than
it was intended to effect, or was capable of effecting.
Be this as it may, I have neither the vocation nor
the desire to censure a policy, with the true causes
of which I may not be acquainted; and it is not at
all necessary to the completion of my work that I
should enter upon subjects more proper for the pages
of history than for the work of a mere biographer.

Sir Robert Peel in his memoirs, as well as in a
letter to Lord Hardinge, which appears in the same
work, has blamed the Whigs for remaining in office
after they had lost power, and for dissolving Parliament when they could not reasonably expect to
obtain a majority by that step.

Upon the first of these charges I am not able to
express an opinion. Upon the second, as it puts
forth a questionable doctrine, I am tempted to make

a few observations. I cannot assent to the position that the prospect of obtaining larger numbers without a majority does not justify a dissolution. It is not well to lay down in such matters any general propositions, since they can rarely be applied without modifications so frequent and so great that they destroy the rule itself. If we suppose the means incorrupt, and the constituencies to be fairly constituted, the increase if it be obtained will simply be a truer representation in the House of the state of the minority in the country; and the more exact the proportion in the country is to that in the House, the more exactly will the end of representation be obtained. If, for instance, a House of Commons be elected in some hot fit of the public mind, it may in a few months be a very imperfect representation of the sober feeling of the country. It may be a disadvantage to be too strong. History teaches us by several examples, some in the present century, and not in our own country only, the dangers which may flow from being too numerously and too ardently supported. The desire, therefore, to obtain an increase of numbers by a dissolution, though without the hope of a majority, may indicate in a minister the purest patriotism, or it may be simply a factious move. In the last case the cen-

T

sure must be directed against the motives of the act.

After various defeats, or victories as damaging almost as defeats, the Whigs were left in a minority in the House of Commons on a resolution expressing that the ministry did not enjoy the confidence of the country. This vote was followed by a dissolution, and in the succeeding elections the Tory party obtained a large majority. The Whigs were out-voted again on a similar motion, in the new House, the Whig ministry resigned, and the last administra-tion of Sir Robert Peel was formed.

In the preceding year I left England. I did not return to England until the year 1855, five years after Sir Robert Peel's death. During my absence I heard occasionally from him, but our correspon-dence was not frequent, and it related entirely, I think, to private affairs. I heard occasionally some-thing, but not much, from persons well informed as to public affairs; but I heard little that I might not have gathered from the ordinary channels of public information.

I remember well my last interview with Sir Robert Peel. It was, in one respect, a melancholy visit to me. I was about to leave England for many years; and felt myself as most men, I suppose, feel who are leaving their country for the first time, with a remote and uncertain prospect of a return; more strongly held than ever by all old ties. He was very kind. I wish now that I had had courage to tell him all that was in my mind; but I never felt entirely at my ease in his presence. He used to come to my father's house when I was little more than a child, and I was accustomed to hear him spoken of with a respect which other young men of his age did not inspire. It is not easy to conquer a feeling of that nature, an early born respect allied to reverence. When he told me to remember that I owed nothing whatever to him, I felt, nevertheless, that I did owe him something. I owed something to his example; I owed, also, to one interview with him, my first determination to read more, to do things no longer by halves, and to follow my profession as the business of my life. I went home, from that interview, to my chambers in the Temple, and I began that very afternoon a course of hard study which for many years was uninterruptedly, though, in a money point of view, not very profitably pursued. This is the confession which I had not the courage to make to him, and I make it now, not for the sake of bringing myself upon the scene, but that it may be seen that I have some reason for insisting on the power of good example, and its influence over an evil habit.

He spoke to me principally upon the subject which then engrossed my thoughts, — my new life and prospects. He presented both to me in the most favourable light; he said that if I had remained in England, and he were restored to office, it was his intention to offer me a high appointment here, but that in his opinion the career that was before me, offered prospects quite as inviting, and even a more ample field for usefulness. He saw, probably, that I was out of spirits. He then asked me some questions about a great dinner at which I had been present the night before, and alluding to some speeches which appeared in the papers of that morning, he gave rather a glimpse than a full sight of some humorous thoughts which were passing through his mind : the old fight between his sense of the ridiculous, his humour, and the love of decorum.

About a year and a half after this time, his son William, then quite a boy, a young midshipman on board the frigate which brought out Lord Ellenborough as Governor-General to India, paid me a visit at Calcutta.

The late Bishop of Calcutta, a man who united

much simplicity of mind with great talents, piety, and virtue, invited the youth to breakfast with him, and when the boy came back to me, and related the conversation which had passed between the good old bishop and himself, the former telling that he had at length forgiven Sir Robert for his conduct on the Catholic question, but that it was long before he could forgive him; and then questioning his guest abruptly as to his father's designs with relation to the Church; " What does your father mean to do with us ? " I marked the same glance of the eye, the same lurking smile playing about the corners of the mouth, the same quiet relish of fun, the same sense of propriety, and the same reserve, and marvelled how these resemblances came about.

CHAP. VI.

REPEAL OF THE CORN LAWS.—HIS DEATH.

" Blest statesman he, whose mind's unselfish will
Leaves him at ease among grand thoughts; whose eye
Sees that apart from magnanimity
Wisdom exists not; nor the humbler skill
Of prudence, disentangling good and ill
With patient care."

" Oh! sir, the good die first,
And they, whose hearts are dry as summer dust,
Burn to the socket."

My absence from England during the last ten years
of the life of Sir Robert Peel, may appear to some to
disqualify me from being the historian of this period
of his life.

I am not conscious of being placed by that circumstance alone under any disqualification.   The history
which I have undertaken to write, is that of a mind
which, previously to this last period of the life of the
statesman, had manifested its full development. This
last is the harvest time.

Whether we regard the talents and characters of the statesmen who sat with Sir Robert Peel in his cabinet, or the numbers, property, and character of those who gave it their support in and out of Parliament, we must pronounce it a strong government. It bore nevertheless in itself from its commencement, the germs of its own dissolution. Questions were still unsettled, the settlement of which could not long be averted, and about the settlement of which, neither the cabinet nor their supporters were at all likely to be of one mind.

Sir Robert Peel's avowed policy was that of progress; the removal of every proved abuse. If things should hereafter be proved to his satisfaction to be abuses, which he did not yet hold to be such, he stood pledged to their removal, if the removal of them lay in his power; and as I have already observed, a process was constantly at work in his mind, which has been termed a process of "active doubt," by which his opinions were from time to time subjected to his own strict assay. Had he been a minister of the order of those who are content to be merely party leaders, and who think that their duty to the Crown and to the people is satisfied by being the eloquent and animated exponents of the opinions and policy of a party, his tenure of office

might have been accounted more secure. But
unless the party which supported him could march
as quickly as himself, their agreement could not
long be depended upon. The attention of the
country was then fixed on economics. The principles of free trade, which had now for several
years been under trial, were becoming year by
year more approved; and accumulated experience
was confirming theories which the practical men
had for some time scoffed at, and then regarded
askant. Now they were beginning to look them
full in the face and to like them. But, connected with these questions was one, which, even
then, was predicted to be the rock on which the
vessel would split. The success of free trade
measures would be sure to imperil the corn laws,
and, in the settlement of this question, the predicted
rupture happened.

It is scarcely to be expected that a great party will
readily conform to changes. It is a wise compliance
of which time and suffering are the best teachers.

In 1841 the party included more of the old school
than the same party now contains. The young men
grow up, taking more the colours of their own times,
and the older members of a party, as they profit by
experience, see things differently in the course of a

few years, but it was too early then to expect from this great party that entire accommodation to the times which they have wisely manifested since the death of Sir Robert Peel. Had that spirit then possessed them, their tenure of power might have been of longer duration. The fundamental principles of a party should indeed be kept inviolate; but administrative changes do not strike at the vitals of the constitution. Parties in their inconsistent criminations of each other, impute as sins to their opponents the very things on which they pique themselves, and that is termed in their opponents base compliance which in themselves is a wise and constitutional submission. It is possible indeed for the same person to be wrong both in his opposition and in his concession, in the mode or time, or motive, but the charges are not applied with these nice discriminations.

The contests between free trade and protection had now come to be understood as contests between the many and the few. Formerly they had not been so regarded. Protection to each of many interests had been regarded as protection to the whole community, and it was not a conscious preference of the few to the many.

In every contest that was now to be between the

many and the few, the power being now more constantly than formerly with the many, they were sure
in the end to obtain the victory. Sir Robert Peel's
policy was to proceed experimentally, to put the
principles of free trade still further to the test of
experience, and to proceed gradually in the course,
as success might point to further probations. He
was entering upon an experimental and a gradual
course, and where it was to lead him was not as yet
clear to his own understanding.   The final separation
of Sir Robert Peel and the party with which he had
uniformly acted was not occasioned by the adoption
of any new principles in the mind of the Conservative leader, it was not the result of the development
of any principles which had been suppressed before,
for he was an avowed free-trader, but it was the mere
consequence of the necessity of following up in office,
consistently and fully, those principles which he had
constantly avowed.   It was the mere result of causes
which existed from the first, and which were sure
sooner or later to break up his cabinet, unless the
party with which he acted could be induced to make
those concessions which have since been made.   The
very disfavour into which the Whigs had fallen, was
the best possible monitor that the policy of the new
government must be one of active movement in some

course of progress. Organic changes were out of the question; in what direction then could progress be made, except in the prosecution of social and economic reforms? The ministry could not have applied themselves to minor reforms exclusively, without losing character altogether. The suffering state of the people, the depressed condition of commerce, the decline and insufficiency of the revenue, were the subjects to which it was necessary to apply immediate and adequate remedies. These forced the mind of the minister on the discovery of new channels of irrigation, now that the old watercourses seemed clogged.

Sir Robert Peel had been, as I have said, always a free-trader. The questions to which he had declined to apply these principles had been viewed by him as exceptional. The corn law had been so treated by many able exponents of the principles of free trade. Lord Bacon, in his history of the reign of Henry VII., has a remark which shows that our navigation laws were not adopted from mistaken notions of political economy, but rather from considerations of policy to which those of wealth were made to bow.

As soon as the ministry was formed, speculation was rife as to its future policy. The country was in a state of great suffering. We were on the eve of a terrible disaster in the East, the result in part of mistaken policy, but more of military incapacity. We had a Chinese war, a costly and troublesome, though not a dangerous warfare, a recurring plague. The finances for a year or two had been, and were still, in an unsatisfactory condition, with a serious annual deficit, and the old troubles had begun to break out again in Ireland. Trade was in a depressed state. The Chartists, however, were then quiet; and there was no prospect of domestic disturbance. It was not a cheering prospect: but it was not a worse state of things than that which the Whigs under Lord Grey had applied themselves in 1830 to remedy. At that time every political disaster or evil was imputed by the opposition to the Tory government: and the late Whig government had now to endure the same crimination, with about equal reason.

Sir Robert Peel was urged to make some statement of the future policy of his government. He prudently and firmly resisted every attempt that was made to draw from him premature declarations of intention. His plans were not yet matured. He has given in his posthumous memoirs two minutes which were prepared by him and laid before the cabinet in 1841, and which indicate very clearly the course of experimental policy on which he was about to enter. They read to me like the pleading of a man who knows that he has some fixed opinions to combat, and who is slightly an apologist for the freedom of his own. They foreshow the consummation, though he did not see what was to come. Reading them now after the event, it is easy to see that his proposed modification of the corn laws was but the first step, which full concession must follow, in spite of the design of its framer. Population, he argued, had been outgrowing its supplies of food, especially the supply of wheat; we must give the people more food and at a cheaper rate. This had long been in his mind; but how to do it was not yet clear: for if their wages rose and fell exactly as prices, the question concerned them little. Old Sir Robert Peel said in his speech on the corn laws, that Mr. Pitt had always been anxious to keep the food of the people at a low price. This principle some of the original supporters of the corn laws did not attempt to gainsay, but contended that the effect of protection in its encouragement of agriculture would bring about ultimately a lower average price than the average price under a system of free importation of grain. Something which fell from Sir Robert Peel in the course of the debates on the corn laws, shows that his mind had been occupied, whilst perusing the works of some Italian economists, with a further problem concerning the distribution of wealth, " when wealth no more shall rest in mounded heaps; " and it is evident that the subject had been long engaging his earnest attention : that his mind was unsettled appears to me from the following quotations from the first of these minutes. "The consumers ought not to pay a penalty for the neglect or want of skill of bad farmers. If fair competition should compel improvement, it will be an advantage to agriculture and the public interests generally." The old spirit of self-reliance speaking. The concluding paragraph speaks a different mind, that of a peace-maker who is seeking to make up a difference. "As I have before observed, it is a proposal of a scale for consideration and discussion. It is that which appears to me to afford the groundwork of a fair adjustment of a question which it is of vital importance to adjust without delay upon principles which the intelligent and reasonable portion of the community, agricultural and commercial, shall consider equitable and safe." Here speaks the spirit of accommodation and compromise: the desire of some safe middle passage, if any such could be found. The proposal of an income-tax in time of peace was a bold measure : it showed that the Reform Bill had not relaxed the springs of Government. No

Tory minister in an unreformed House of Commons would have ventured upon this remedy. It was submitted to as a hard necessity of the times, and the reduction of protective duties with which it was accompanied, did not make the measure more acceptable to the country interest. But generally the measure was regarded with approbation, and the results of these experiments were looked to with something more than hope, with confidence.

By the imposition of the income-tax the finances were gradually restored to a sound condition, and in a year or two there was a surplus of income over expenditure. His measures of finance, and reduction of protective duties had been successful, and they led to still further reductions of such duties. But in the meantime the corn laws were subjected to fiercer assault, and more continued agitation. The modification of the sliding scale had been ill-received by the agriculturists, and had incurred the strong condemnation of the free-traders. It had not tended to quiet the agitation which was kept up, and the agriculturists could not look upon it as a settlement; it had cured some defects in the former law, and it had lowered the protective duties, but it had done no more. The Corn-Law League was carrying on the war of agitation against the protectionists, with an energy and power which their opponents either could not or did not equal, and it was clear enough how the contest would end. In Ireland an organised system was kept up, which bade defiance to all regular government. This had commenced before the formation of Sir Robert Peel's last government, but it was continued with great zeal and acrimony. The monster meetings showed, at last, so plainly the character of menace and attempt at intimidation, that they could no longer be endured, if any respect for order and an established government were to be maintained. A prosecution was consequently set on foot in Ireland, against Mr. O'Connell and others, which ended in a conviction. On an appeal to the House of Lords, the judgment was reversed, on technical grounds of error; but the good effects of this too long delayed vindication of the law were experienced subsequently.

The Maynooth Bill, a half approach to a great question, and another bill which merely quieted possession, and confirmed the actual state of some religious trusts, enjoyed by Unitarian Christians, had angered the more zealous Protestants and the orthodox party. Soon after this, the establishment in Ireland of what were termed, reproachfully, the

"Godless Colleges," added to the excitement and distrust; and all these causes were bringing about the final rupture.

The age has now bowed all in turn to its will. All have now conformed to the temper of the times: none can, with any consistency, impute inconsistency to others. As we cannot see the motives of a prudent conformity, we had better interpret in the spirit of charity all such conversions in a time of change. When old things are passing away, those who stand up for their maintenance must be content to be in the minority, and to remain in opposition. If they rule they must conform, at least in a free state.

The final separation was precipitated not caused by the failure of the potato crop. The evils then impending brought the question to an issue. The whole is so fully treated, the motives and the reasons so fully set forth, both in the posthumous memoirs, and in the parliamentary debates, that no further light can be thrown on the subject. "Were I to write a quire of paper," wrote he to Lord Hardinge, "I could not recount to you what has passed, with half so much detail and accuracy, as the public papers will recount it. There are no

U

secrets.   We have fallen in the face of day, and with our front to our enemies.

" There is nothing I would not have done to ensure the carrying of the measures I had proposed this session.

"I pique myself on never having proposed anything which I have not carried."

The old spirit again: and a self-congratulation which would not have been excusable unless it had come from a mind in which caution was carried almost to excess.

He sacrificed to his country's interests the guidance of a great party,   He had, undoubtedly, the martyr's consolation ; but we must strip the crown of martyrdom of all its glory, if we set off consoling hopes against present suffering, and strike the balance.

He was fully warned of the consequences.   Mr. Goulburn, a true friend of Sir Robert Peel, but in this instance misled by friendship into counsels too soft for duty, wrote thus to him :

" MY DEAR PEEL,

" I have such an habitual deference to the superiority of your judgment, and such an entire confidence in the purity of your motives, that I always feel great doubt as to my being right when I differ from you in opinion.   But the more I reflect upon the observations which you made to me a few days since, as to your difficulty in again defending a corn law in Parliament, the more do I feel alarmed at your taking a different course from that which you have previously adopted.   An abandonment of your former opinions now would, I think, prejudice your and our characters as public men, and would be fraught with fatal results to the country's best interests.

" Under these circumstances, it appears to me that the abandonment of the corn law would be taken by the public, generally, as decisive evidence that we never intended to maintain it further than as an instrument to vex and defeat our enemies.   They will, I fear, tax us with treachery and deception, and charge us, from our former language, with having always had it in contemplation."

Mr. Goulburn would not, I think, have acted as he counselled Sir Robert Peel to act.   His friendly zeal led him to offer advice, which, if it had been acted upon, would have substituted for the temporary reproach which Sir Robert Peel endured, the stings of his own mind, and the general condemnation of a future time.   Mr. Goulburn did not take into account the actual state of his friend's mind, and judged of the case of another from his own conscience,—a frequent source of false judgments.

"It appeared to me," writes Sir Robert Peel, "that all these considerations,—the betrayal of party attachments — the maintenance of the honour of public men—the real interests of the cause of constitutional Government, must all be determined by the answer which the heart and conscience of a responsible minister might give to the question — What is that course which the public interests really demand?

"I was not insensible to the evil of acting counter to the will of those majorities, of severing party connections, and of subjecting public men to suspicion and reproach, and the loss of public confidence; but I felt a strong conviction that such evils were light in comparison with those which must be incurred by the sacrifice of national interests to party attachments."

It is clear from the contents of Mr. Goulburn's letter as well as from the whole history of the transaction, the large majority in the cabinet against the opinion of Sir Robert Peel, and the reluctant acquiescence of the cabinet in the measure finally adopted, that the charges of treachery and simulation which Mr. Goulburn truly predicted, had in truth no foundation whatever. The characters of the men should have protected them from such charges.

Out of the whole cabinet four only agreed in opinion with Sir Robert Peel, that the corn laws could no longer be maintained; and Sir Robert Peel himself was a tardy convert to that opinion.

He says with reference to this subject. "It was from the combined influence of these various considerations — from diminished confidence in the necessity or advantage of protection — from the increasing difficulty of resisting the application to articles of food of those principles which had been gradually applied to so many other articles — from the result of the experiment made with regard to cattle and meat in 1842 — from the evidences of rapidly increasing consumption, — from the aggravation of every other difficulty in the maintenance of the corn laws, by the fact of their suspension in the first real pressure, it was from the combined influence of these considerations that I came to the conclusion that the attempt to maintain these laws inviolate, after their suspension, would be impolitic, that the struggle for their maintenance would assume a new character, and that no advantage to be gained by success would counterbalance the consequences of failure, or even the evils attending protracted conflict."

Amongst the causes assigned for this change of opinion, one is advanced, viz., "diminished confidence in the necessity or advantage of protection," which may reasonably be supposed to have been aided by the result of the experiment as to cattle and meat in 1842; and when it is considered how many converts were made from men of both parties, to the new opinions, by the results of similar experiments, it is strange that he alone should have been subjected to the accusation of a timid or interested submission.

In another part of the same memoirs he shows by a reference to dates, that the charge of his having changed his course in consequence of Lord John Russell's letter to the London electors is equally groundless; and the antecedent discussions in the cabinet, and their result, equally disprove the charge which is conveyed in the close of that letter, that the cabinet were seeking for some excuse to change their policy.

In writing to Lord Hardinge, in the same letter from which I have already given an extract, he observes : "Two hours after this intelligence was brought, we were ejected from power ; and by another coincidence as marvellous, on the day on which I had to announce in the House of Commons the dissolution of the Government, the news arrived that we had settled the Oregon question, and that our proposals had been accepted by the United States without the alteration of a word." In conclusion he says: "I have every disposition to forgive my enemies for having imposed on me the blessing of the loss of power."

These concluding words were sincerely written. He was firm in his resolve never again to accept office. The responsibilities of office preyed upon a sensitive mind. The difficulty of the task was not diminished in his mind by the experience which office had given him. He felt it to be a growing difficulty,—in every letter, in every minute that was written on any important question, may be traced one predominant thought, that the government of the country was growing daily a more difficult and a more onerous task. But this thought was accompanied with a resolve which generally carries men through difficulties, a determination not to be overcome. "I pique myself on never having proposed anything which I have not carried." Now came the mellow autumn. No repinings, no querulous railing bespoke a man ill at ease. Content with what had been, and looking with a tranquil mind, and with trust, to the future, he submitted to his fortune, not as a philosopher, but as a Christian. He had nothing of the stoic in him. His was not an indolent repose; he was always occupied, and though he had lost office, he had not declined in influence. To the colleagues who, from a sense of duty to the Queen and to their country, acted and suffered with him, perhaps even a larger meed of praise is due, than that which was awarded to him, for all were not sustained by his convictions, that the measure itself was sound. I have some reason for thinking that one or more of his colleagues would have been glad to receive from him an acknowledgment similar to that with which his memoirs conclude. Yet there is a difficulty, and he as a modest and a reserved man would have felt that difficulty, in offering personal thanks and acknowledgments as for a private favour, for conduct which it is at once more wise and more graceful to attribute to the higher motives of allegiance and duty: and an apparent discourtesy is often the highest courtesy which a delicate mind can render.

He thus concludes his memoir : —

" One word before I bring it to a final close.

" In the course of this memoir, I have acknowledged the deep obligation which I owe to the colleagues with whom I acted in the administration of public affairs—·to those in particular who were united with me in the service of the Crown after the failure of the attempt of Lord John Russell to form a government.

"But I should do injustice to one of those colleagues, with whom from the nature of our respective offices, my intercourse in regard to the transactions which form the subject-matter of this memoir, was the most frequent and the most intimate, and whose responsibility was equal to my own, if I did not express, in the strongest terms, my grateful acknowledgments for the zealous support and able assistance which I uniformly received from Sir James Graham.

"Sir James Graham has had his full share of the obloquy with which I have been assailed, and I close this memoir with the hope that the evidence incorporated with it may serve to rescue his name, as well as my own, from some degree of unjust accusation and unmerited reproach."

The retirement of Sir Robert Peel, and the return of the Whigs to office, produced no material change in the public policy. During the four remaining years of his life, he gave his support to the Whig ministry, whose measures, in his last speech in the

House of Commons, he described as liberal and
conservative. The fear subsided into which some
had worked themselves up of that deluge which
was to follow the expulsion of the Conservative
party from office. Even Mr. Goulburn and the
Duke of Wellington seemed to consider his administration as the sole breakwater against revolution.
Strange exaggerations of the importance of any
ministry. A revolution which is thirty years in
coming has at all events the pace of a tortoise,
and its momentum is not terrible. Equally groundless has proved the fear that the great Conservative party would be broken up by his means.
This party has its roots too deep in the soil to
be thrown down by any one man's efforts, whether
directed by treachery or by error. Such parties
may languish in quiet times, but they revive
in their strength when any real danger menaces
our institutions: the moderate men of all parties
then enlist themselves in the rifle brigade, and
unite to resist a common danger. In this country,
fortunately, the State rather takes than gives a
character: "The worth of a State in the long run,"
says a philosophical writer, "is the worth of the
individuals composing it:" and this is true of parties
also. Consequently, until the Conservative feeling

is spent in the country, the fault of a leader, cannot destroy it. It will reform itself under surer counsels.

I have now brought to a close this history, not of an extraordinary mind, but of a mind extraordinarily tempted and tried : tempted in the most dangerous and insidious way, by specious errors which look so like the truth, that more than half the world accept them as truth itself; the errors which in a conflict of feelings and of duties tie men down to the lower obligations. Let me now sum up and conclude the investigation. A mind well gifted, but not richly endowed with rare gifts : a sound mind in a sound body: a fair jewel in a fit setting. One or two such will be found in many a house, and for want of high culture they come to nothing. A mind of this order in a feebler body breaks down in the training, and from over culture comes to nothing. Here, then, was the fortunate, it may be the wise union, of high culture with a fitting nature. Next came the higher advantage of an early aim : culture steadily directed to one certain and not unreasonable end. But against these must be set the disadvantage of that divorce from childish nature which is inseparable from all early culture severely applied. The mind, treated as the hand of the artisan, and

forced overmuch on one application: the faculties
strained to one absorbing pursuit; a reason in its
infancy put upon man's work; a memory over cultivated; a fluency of speech too early acquired
brought their ordinary results, — an imagination
starved, a diction correct and flowing, but. without
stops or varied beauty — the level lawn of language.
A vigorous understanding, an inquiring mind, an
acute intellect, a feeling heart, an honest and truthful nature, reverential, and deferring to authority,
these united in a young man entering upon public
life, shortly before the dawn of eventful times of
change, what do they foreshow? They foreshow
necessarily a life of change.   Unless it had chanced,
as it now and then may chance, that by some
fortunate and rare accident, original opinions had
hit the golden mean between actual things and
struggling tendencies; but this was not his case.
" Il naquit Tory;" and though born in a moderate
house, yet the toryism of the times was in an
excited and extravagant form.   Change, then, was
inevitable, but in such a nature it was also sure to
be timid and reluctant; no new birth or sudden
conversion, but the gradual slow development of a
growing stature.   An honest conformity to a changing
world.

Mr. Disraeli has said of him that he was not a great orator, nor a great statesman, but that he was a great member of Parliament. On the first point I have already expressed my opinion, that he was first in the second rank only; on the second point, I think the judgment correct in certain senses of the word statesman; but in the public life which he led, if he were a great member of Parliament, he was also a great statesman. It is not easy, however, to define a man — such as he was England is proud of him, and will forgive even greater errors in another Robert Peel.

I have not concealed those political errors, which, in my judgment, he committed: errors resulting for the most part from early associations, education, and the temper of the times in which the first five and twenty years of his life were cast.

It fares with political more hardly than with private character. When a statesman is living, he is judged by samples unfairly picked. After death we deal more justly. We look on his whole life: and we compare the dead with his fellows. We can then allow for the necessary admixtures of evil with all earthly good; and can pass in a spirit of charity and of truth, taught by our own human hearts, a juster judgment on the dead than on the living.

Peel is now undergoing this test. The more he is
studied as a whole, the more strongly marked appear
his earnestness, his devotion to duty, his labour, his
zeal, his truthfulness and his unselfishness. United to
these we find an inquiring and a timidly doubting
mind, reluctantly admitting into itself the probe of
speculation. A sensitive mind also, not at ease unless
sure of its conclusions. Hence his mutations, for to
be convinced with him was to change.

A few minor specks appeared on the bright side
of his, as they may be seen in every shining character. These noted often with some severity during
life fade away entirely after death. The old motto,
" de mortuis nil nisi bonum," condemned only when
misconceived, recognises this truth. Every man
understands that, as there are shadows cast on the
brightest day of sunshine, so must we take into
account, in every estimate of human character, some
little outbreaks of temper, of vanity, of unseemly
triumph, some excesses of the spirit of advocacy,
some undue tenacity of opinion, or of sway, some
occasional lack of courtesy, spots and freckles which
will at times disfigure the fairest face which the
world can show. We think not of such things as
these when the dead lies in his vault, in the old
church-yard, " with his face up to heaven," we

feel then that a loving spirit stirs in us, and that in
our charitable thoughts God is visiting us; we judge
then as we would be judged, and can feel how
human errors may fade away before mild and pitying
though unerring eyes.

We may apply here, with a Christian mind, in
another sense, the words of the heathen poet:—

> " Ubi plura nitent . . . non ego paucis
> Offendar maculis."

It may be remarked that I have not described the
private life of the late minister. The little which I
could say on this subject, of my own knowledge, I
forbear from saying. I object altogether to the un-
roofing of men's dwellings; and have no desire to
make their chimney-tops, the very stones, as it were,
of men's houses prate of their whereabout: an
amusement of a merry one—but a devil. It is a
poor reward for the services of our statesmen if they
are to think that when they pass away, their inner
sanctuary is to be profaned, and their household
gods are to be paraded along the highways. How
wretched to put up the shutters of the heart in a
man's own house, or to fear a Boswell in every guest.
Suffice it to say that the English domestic life never
showed itself elsewhere in a calmer or a purer form;

and that Asmodeus might have visited his house in vain.

Monsieur Guizot has taken, with a master's fine touch, a pleasing sketch of the statesman in his home. It is the more interesting as it is a French version of the English domestic life, the sober livery of the joy of which must appear somewhat dun-coloured to our more gay-spirited neighbours. This picture recalls to my recollection a very similar description which many years ago I heard from Baron Cuvier, to whom I had the honour of being presented by the late Mr. Sutton Sharpe. Madame Cuvier also dwelt on the kindness and warmth of the reception which Sir Robert and Lady Peel had given them in England, and it was easy to perceive that this acknowledgment was more than a mere civility. They at least had not been chilled by any coldness. It happens however, frequently, that the English reserve melts away in the presence of foreigners; and especially under a foreign sky. It seems as if our insular qualities take up livelier colours under a continental sky. These pictures are, after all, mere sketches of a kind of life which will not bear a minute description. That the English domestic life may remain what it is, it is necessary that it should be private. *Le public n'entre pas ici.* His last speech in the House of

Commons was a fit and touching conclusion. In reading this speech it seems as though that most excellent gift of charity, the very bond of peace, had been that day poured into his heart from a two-fold measure, to inspire his mind with all wholesome thoughts, so that, not even in the very storm of debate, his tongue might be led to utter on that last day, one word that one would wish to blot. The nature of the question, and the turn of the debate drew from him a calm, well-reasoned, and dignified vindication of the foreign policy of the Government over which he had presided. But he spoke without asperity. With a generous and just appreciation of Lord Palmerston, the statesman whose policy had been contrasted with his own, he paid that last tribute to merit, which he was always eager to render. He satisfied also the claims of friendship and esteem in a just tribute to the solid and unpretending virtues and talents of Lord Aberdeen: he spoke earnestly as the advocate of peace and justice, the champion of the humble and weak, a fit conclusion to the public life of a Christian senator. Finally, he praised "the liberal and conservative policy" of those who had ejected himself from office.

When he left the House it was day. He felt for

x

the last time the freshness of the morning air, the
breeze from

" The river flowing at its own sweet will :
Oh, God ! the very houses seem'd asleep,
And all that mighty heart is lying still."

He passed for the last time in health and calm
under the threshold of his door to sleep for the last
time the sleep of health in that house which he had
built, the quiet retreat of the domestic virtues, where
he had lived usefully and happily a virtuous life.
After a few hours' rest he arose to his last day's work,
a day not of severe employment, but still a day of
work.   Then towards the close of day, the bolt, but
in mercy, fell : a swerving horse, a heavy fall, a
racking pain, a moaning voice, a fainting, a slow
transport home, a rally at his own door; again a
fainting fit, a suffering body, impatience of the pain,
a few hours of trouble, and then came the calm : the
solemn offices of religion, the inward prayer, the
gentle murmured blessing on wife and children ; and
all was over in that once happy home, from which
the shadow never afterwards quite passed away.   The
sorrow which long abode in that house is too sacred
and solemn a subject for my pen to trace.   But there
was a sorrow without of which I can bear to write.

How touching the patient waiting, and the subdued inquiries of the humble without the gate: their sympathy with one who had felt for them, and who had suffered in their cause: a self-reliant and a hard-working man, who showed in his own person a great example to them, in the power of those homely virtues. Their sorrow brings to my recollection the simple and feeling lines of Wordsworth on the death of Fox: —

> " And many thousands now are sad —
> Wait the fulfilment of their fear —
> For he must die who is their stay,
> Their glory disappear.
>
> " A power is passing from the earth
> To breathless Nature's dark abyss;
> But when the good and great depart,
> What is it more than this? —
>
> " That man, who is from God sent forth,
> Doth yet again to God return!
> Such ebb and flow must ever be,
> Then wherefore should we mourn? "

The House of Commons, hearing of his death, adjourned, after a few words of feeling from Mr. Hume.

In both Houses men forgot their party animosities, and spoke sincerely in praise of the deceased, in the good old English spirit. What I admire most in

these touching tributes of respect is their plainness.
They contain no exaggerated expressions. An exaggerated panegyric would have been singularly inappropriate to one justly described by Mr. Goulburn on
that solemn occasion as a man of very simple habits,
hating ostentation and parade, and above all detesta-
tion of parade, detesting a pomp in funeral. In the
best temper and in the best taste were these several
tributes rendered. A public funeral was offered, and
gratefully and modestly declined. He had fixed in his
lifetime the place where he desired his body to lie
after death—near his parents. A place was left next
his own for the body of his widow, where it is now
deposited in compliance with her earnest prayer that
their bodies might not in death be divided.

In the same grateful and humble spirit the offer of
a peerage was declined.

Perhaps, when, in future times, the interest shall
have subsided concerning some questions, which in
his time so rent the world, and men speak of Peel as
we now speak of Walpole, with calm approval of a
wise and moderate statesman, it may be recorded of
him as his highest honour, that whilst others spoke
of his talents, his works, and his virtues too, Wellington, a man truthful himself above most men, in
his old age, on the very brink of his own grave,

spoke of one virtue which was particularly prominent in Peel, and praised him as one of the most truthful men he had ever known; a golden key to unlock the " enigma " of his character.

It is from a mind accordant in this with his own spirit, that I forbear from describing the posthumous honours which were awarded him. There are pictures, busts, statues, buildings, walks, and parks, to commemorate his name, more than I can enumerate, but the heart of the people is his best monument.

CONCLUSION.

When I began this work, I began it in some fear. I knew the difficulty of imparting some truths which are engrained in a man's own mind, as to which, though he has a full conviction that they are truths, he yet fears that they may seem to others too unsubstantial for delineation.

I see resemblances too strong for words to paint them, and yet I may fail to make others see them. My theory may seem a fancy, or a fiction, but I feel, I may say I know, that I have written the truth. Compare him with his older line. He was simple and unostentatious, so were they. He was cautious and prudent, reserved and inexpansive to strangers, so were they. He was earnest, industrious, and self-relying, so were they. He rose superior to difficulties, and had a mind bent on not being beat, "piquing himself on carrying all his measures." They had the same order of mind. His grandfather, after the riots, repairing his fortunes, and he labouring at the reconstruction of the Tory party, are types of the same order of mind. Their faith in, and their inculcation of their faith in the power of self-reliance and of industry over fortune, that a man is *faber fortunæ suæ*, were observed also in him, in a more marked degree.

His refusal of a peerage, and of the garter, his desire to have a private funeral, his exhortation to his sons and family to accept no title for his services, to rely on themselves, and to earn honour for themselves; these have been quoted as signs that he was in his heart a democrat. I look upon them as the clear signs of a wise and moderate mind; I think I see therein, following a pleasing Eastern story, the Vizier sitting in the dress of his humble fortune; I note also the sign in this of a derived character, for they were feelings which pervaded the whole older race. My father never would permit his carriage to come to his house of business, but in all weathers walked to it.

Can all these resemblances, as the resemblance of his son William to himself, on which I have remarked, have been things of chance? I think not. I think they were derived. But how derived let men of genius or of science determine.

His character has been termed an "enigma." It is no enigma to me. His apparent inconsistencies, for I think them apparent only, cause me no surprise. He is an enigma only in the sense in which all true, high, and struggling nature is an enigma. The true life of thought is a life of struggle. His inconsistencies are the outward and visible signs of his struggles. Man has been termed a "bundle of habits;" he might be called also a bundle of inconsistencies.

His mind might have been in some instances more constant, but that constancy would have been gained at the cost of its truthfulness. The struggles of his political life resemble those of the religious life of many an earnest man. Examine the life of a Luther; see the reluctance to move, the tardy steps, the faltering, the halting steps, a backward step or two, the doubts whether the speaking spirit be of heaven or of hell, the final, full, and glorious close; let a man then look inward; let him insert in his own mind the "tent that reaches to the bottom of the worst;" let him ask himself in earnest if he has not felt these agonies, at various stages of his life, and of his opinions, and I think he will find within himself a solution of the question why this great man's character has appeared an enigma. My solution of it appears in the pages which I have written. A dishonest man, in the like case, would have been less of an enigma, as he would have suppressed his emotions, and concealed, perhaps stifled, his convictions. In a calmer time, these developments would probably never have been produced, for not only must we have the seed and the ground, but we must have, also, a fitting season.

Long after this fugitive work shall have perished, it may be that one anecdote which it records may live. It may be that a thoughtful provident father, desiring, like the father of the statesman, to lay a good foundation, may tell by his fireside, to his children, the tale of this great statesman, pointing out to his young companion, the poor man sweeping up the leaves, may point the moral, and adorn the tale; may point to a series in one family, including his glorious instance, of the triumphs of self-reliance and industry, and with the earnestness of a father, the family priest of his own homestead, may conclude, glancing in his prayer at this life, and at its

Y

derivation, with teaching akin to old Michael's lesson
to his loved prodigal.

> "Lay now the corner stone,
> As I requested, and hereafter, Luke,
> When thou art gone away, should evil men
> Be thy companions, think of me, my son,
> And of this moment; hither turn thy thoughts,
> And God will strengthen thee; amid all fear
> And all temptation, Luke, I pray that thou
> May'st bear in mind the life thy fathers lived,
> Who being innocent, did for that cause
> Bestir them in good deeds."

THE END.

LONDON
PRINTED BY SPOTTISWOODE AND CO.
NEW-STREET SQUARE

In Four Volumes, 8vo. with Maps, Plans, and Portraits, 54s.

HISTORY OF THE LIFE
OF
ARTHUR, DUKE OF WELLINGTON:

THE MILITARY MEMOIRS FROM THE FRENCH OF
Captain BRIALMONT,

WITH ADDITIONS AND EMENDATIONS:

THE POLITICAL AND SOCIAL LIFE BY THE
Rev. G. R. GLEIG, M.A.

CHAPLAIN-GENERAL TO THE FORCES, AND PREBENDARY OF ST. PAUL'S.

"MR. GLEIG'S narrative is rich in anecdote, and presents important explanations on many points still in dispute with reference to the Duke's actions and sentiments. Indeed, his home career is that which Mr. Gleig depicts most elaborately. These volumes contain a full review of the Duke's history as a civil administrator, a legislator, and the member of a great political party. We see him in Parliament, in the Cabinet, and in Cabal drawing-rooms; but we also visit him at Apsley House, at Strathfieldsaye, at Walmer, where he is dining, or sipping coffee, or sitting to a portrait painter, for Mr. Gleig is full of personal reminiscences: and though he all but worships his patron's memory, his comments are generally sober and subdued. He had ample materials to begin with. The present Duke of Wellington placed the whole of his father's papers at Mr. Gleig's disposal; Lord John Russell opened to him the despatches at the State Paper Office; then, his own recollections were extensive and minute; moreover, many friends were ready with their contributions. Thus, that which promised at first to be no more than an annotated translation of a French biography, turns out to be the best book that has been written about the Conqueror of Waterloo."
Athenæum.

"THE military part of the present History was first written by a soldier, who gives ample proof that he unites the requisite professional attainments with the large and just views and literary skill of a competent historian. He adds another unusual merit to these. He is a foreigner, and belongs to a nation whose prejudices would impel him neither to exalt nor to disparage the successful general of England. Accordingly we find in the Belgian Captain Brialmont neither the tendency to idolatry which English biographers exhibit, nor the ungenerous depreciation which distinguishes French writers when commenting on the actions and character of the greatest antagonist and only rival of Napoleon. Still there exists sources of information essential to a perfectly just estimate, which a foreigner might be apt to overlook, or might find not easy of access. The attempt to depict the political and private life of an English statesman must be especially difficult to any one who has not been bred amid our political and social institutions. Fortunately, therefore, the military portion has been translated, and the remainder entirely rewritten, by the Chaplain-General to the Forces, who possesses singular qualifications for the task..... He enjoyed the personal acquaintance and regard of him who is the hero of the work, and whose biography he has, he tells us, all his life anxiously desired to write. Finally, he has had an opportunity of consulting state papers and private documents as yet unpublished, and of quoting from them, so far as a due regard to the feelings of other actors of the time who yet survive would permit. His faithful translation of the military portion of the work is accompanied by valuable comments on dubious or disputed points, or where he conceives the Belgian writer to be in error; distinguished by brackets. The reader thus possesses, in the most convenient form, a very careful, impartial, and scientific account of the Duke's career, elucidated and completed by one who possesses peculiar qualifications for the office."
BLACKWOOD'S MAGAZINE.

London: LONGMAN, GREEN, and CO. Paternoster Row.

LIST OF WORKS BY LORD MACAULAY.

I.

MISCELLANEOUS WRITINGS of the Right Hon. Lord MACAULAY: Comprising his Contributions to *Knight's Quarterly Magazine;* Articles in the *Edinburgh Review,* not included in his *Critical and Historical Essays;* Biographies written for the *Encyclopædia Britannica;* Miscellaneous Poems, &c. 2 vols. 8vo. with Portrait, price 21s.

II.

THE HISTORY of ENGLAND from the Accession of James the Second. By the Right Hon. Lord MACAULAY. New Edition, revised and corrected. 7 vols. post 8vo. price 42s. cloth; or separately, 6s. each.

III.

LORD MACAULAY'S HISTORY of ENGLAND from the Accession of James the Second. New Edition. VOLS. I. and II. 8vo. price 32s.; VOLS. III. and IV. 8vo. price 36s.

IV.

CRITICAL and HISTORICAL ESSAYS contributed to the Edinburgh Review. By the Right Hon. Lord MACAULAY. Library Edition (the Ninth). 3 vols. 8vo. price 36s.

V.

LORD MACAULAY'S CRITICAL and HISTORICAL ESSAYS contributed to the Edinburgh Review. A New Edition, in Volumes for the Pocket. 3 vols. fcp. 8vo. price 21s.

VI.

LORD MACAULAY'S CRITICAL and HISTORICAL ESSAYS contributed to the Edinburgh Review. The Traveller's Edition, complete in One Volume, with Portrait and Vignette. Square crown 8vo. 21s. cloth; calf, by HAYDAY, 30s.

VII.

LORD MACAULAY'S CRITICAL and HISTORICAL ESSAYS contributed to the Edinburgh Review. The People's Edition, complete in 2 vols. crown 8vo. price 8s. cloth; or in 7 Parts, price One Shilling each.

VIII.

LIST of Fourteen of Lord MACAULAY'S ESSAYS which may be had separately, in 16mo. in the TRAVELLER'S LIBRARY:—

Warren Hastings ....1s.	Lord Bacon ....1s.
Lord Clive..1s.	Lord Byron; and the Comic Dramatists of
William Pitt; and the Earl of Chatham.....1s.	the Restoration ....1s.
Ranke's History of the Popes; and Gladstone	Frederick the Great ....1s.
on Church and State........................1s.	Hallam's Constitutional History of England 1s.
Life and Writings of Addison; and Horace	Croker's Edition of Boswell's Life of John-
Walpole ....1s.	son ....1s.

IX.

SPEECHES of the Right Hon. Lord MACAULAY, corrected by HIMSELF. 8vo. 12s.

X.

LORD MACAULAY'S SPEECHES on PARLIAMENTARY REFORM in 1831 and 1832. Reprinted in the TRAVELLER'S LIBRARY. 16mo. 1s.

XI.

LAYS of ANCIENT ROME. By the Right Hon. Lord MACAULAY. With Illustrations, original and from the Antique, by GEORGE SCHARF, jun., F.S.A., engraved on Wood by S. WILLIAMS. New Edition. Fcp. 4to. price 21s. boards: morocco, by HAYDAY, 42s.

XII.

LORD MACAULAY'S LAYS of ANCIENT ROME, with IVRY and the ARMADA. 16mo. 4s. 6d. cloth; morocco, by HAYDAY, 10s. 6d.

London: LONGMAN, GREEN, and CO. Paternoster Row.

www.ingramcontent.com/pod-product-compliance
Lightning Source LLC
Chambersburg PA
CBHW060521030726
47498CB00004B/1022